The Doctor Who Made House Calls

The Doctor Who

MILTON R. BASS

Made House Calls

G. P. Putnam's Sons, New York

For YUSSIE
my friend

The knowledge that death is not so far away, that my mind and emotions and vitality will soon disappear like a puff of smoke, has the effect of making earthly affairs seem unimportant and human beings more and more ignoble. It is harder to take human life seriously, including one's own efforts and achievements and passions.

—EDMUND WILSON

i

THE bronzed hand squeezed the rubber ball decisively, and the mercury spurted up the tube. Squeeze-spurt. Squeeze-spurt. Squeeze-spurt. One hundred . . . thirty . . . forty . . . sixty . . . eighty . . . STOP!

The long fingers deftly unscrewed the aluminum disk, and the air began to whoosh softly as the mercury dipped to . . . BUMP! . . . One hundred and sixty . . . MARK! Eighty-eight. Right on the nose. One hundred and sixty over eighty-eight.

Sir, according to your systolic reading, you have what is known in laymen's terms as high blood pressure. Essential hypertension. Cause unknown. Physician, heal thyself.

He unsnapped the air bag and removed the apparatus from his arm, dropping it on top of the clothes hamper. The mirror revealed no extraordinary symptoms. Cleanly shaved jowl and cheeks. Eyes clear. No edema. The hand came up and rubbed along the chin. Good strong chin. Good strong hand. Any problems?

No problems.

Work going all right?

Fine, just fine.

Everything all right at home?

Why do you ask that?

Why don't you answer that?

Why shouldn't everything be all right at home?

Is it?

Let me answer it this way; it had better be.

Sex life?

Really, Doctor.

No, seriously, what about your sex life?

There have been no complaints. Why wasn't the face grinning? This was funny stuff, really funny. The face wasn't laughing because it knew it was going to die. But everybody dies. The face knows that. But doctors are supposed to keep people from dying. The face grinned. That was funny, really funny.

He broke away from the mirror and carefully folded the apparatus into its black case, pulled loose the stethoscope, unlocked the door and returned to the bedroom. All of a sudden he felt loose and easy, so much so that he was tempted to check the pressure again, but he hesitated only a moment before dropping the case and scope on the bed and putting on his shirt, tie and jacket.

His foot was dipping for the first step when he remembered the machine, *the mothering machine,* and he returned quickly to the bedroom, where he scooped up the two objects and tucked them into his right buttock, *the old hidden ball trick,* and descended to the dining room where he had left his bag the night before. The box was halfway into the bag when she entered suddenly from the kitchen. *Oh, Jesus Christ!* He finished tucking it in and snapped the clasps. She was looking at him peculiarly, brow creased, hands wrapped in a dish towel.

"How come you brought your bag in?" she asked.

He could feel it rising in him, the pressure coming up from God knows (for sure, the doctor doesn't) where, and his hands tightened in readiness to . . . to what? . . . to strike out? . . . is that what? . . . easy . . . easy . . . easy

"Samples," he said evenly.

"What?"

"I had some samples I wanted to bring in."

"Oh." She turned. "Do you want eggs?"

"No breakfast," he said.

She stopped, still facing the kitchen but back twisted slightly to indicate there was an expression of pain on the face. He could feel the strain as his fingers tried to form into fists.

"But you are staying for breakfast," she said, the voice hoarsened somewhat by massive internal effort. Christ, he could program her a week ahead.

"No breakfast."

"But Jo has to eat and you might as well eat while you're waiting for her."

"Waiting for her for what?"

"The orthodontist. You said you would drop her off."

He remembered. She had told him about it on Thursday. Jo had to be at the orthodontist and the cleaning woman's car had suffered a massive hemorrhage and . . . he had said he would. He remembered saying he would.

Slipping into his topcoat, he carried the bag into the kitchen. The three of them were sitting there slopping up cold cereal. The bathroom diagnostics had slowed him longer than he thought. Heal thyself. "Just coffee," he said, and sat there sipping it while they shoveled in the empty calories as though he weren't there.

"No time for toast," he barked, as Jo reached out for a piece, and she paused, hand in midair, her face turned toward her mother. The others stopped, too, waiting to see how far the ripples might spread.

"Go brush your teeth carefully," the voice of peace said quietly, and the child moved off and the spoons went back into service.

Congratulations, he told himself. A big battle won. Against a woman and a small child. And a piece of toast. A good way to start the day.

The woman said nothing as he went out the door and got in the car, but the child began burbling at him the moment they started down the road, her constantly moving lips no more than an inch from his right ear as she stood in the narrow aperture, clutching the seat back with both hands. The sound of the light treble was pleasant, since everything was of equal importance to her and there was no attempt to emphasize anything through decibels.

He sorted out the day—what had to be done, what should be done, what could be done, what postponed, shoved aside, dismissed. It didn't look too bad. Maybe some handball could be worked in.

She broke through. At the moment his mind blanked preparatory to deciding on who might be available for a late-afternoon game, her sound became words, meaningful, provocative.

"I know the difference between boys and girls," she said.

"What? What was that?"

"I know the difference between boys and girls." Seven-year-olds didn't mind being asked to repeat what they had said. It happened often enough to be accepted as something that was expected of them.

"What's the difference?"

"Girls have a vulva," she said, somewhat righteously.

"That is correct," he agreed, clinically.

"And boys have cuticles."

"What?"

"Boys have cuticles. You know. Like Jeff has between his legs."

"Those aren't cuticles. Those are testicles."

"Testicles, cuticles, what's the difference?" she said, the gold-framed head moving side to side in semantic archness.

"Well, if you got kicked in them, you'd know the

difference," he yelled, and laughed, surprising the child, who couldn't remember ever seeing her father laugh out loud. Sensing the expression on her face, he turned to look, and the right front tire bounced on the soft shoulder, twisting the wheel in his hands, as he wrestled strongly to keep them from the steep bank. The moment lasted forever, and then he sensed the four wheels grasping solidity with even tension, the powerful motor dropping back to its regular purr.

His heart was racing wildly, and he could feel the adrenalin pumping through his system, tightening the muscles and clouding the eyes with mist. Two hundred. That column of mercury would go two hundred even right then, maybe more. The child babbled on again, aware only of a lurch, taking the silence for permission to continue, completely unaware of how close her thread had been to strain or even severance.

The drops of sweat were working down his sides, and he took several deep breaths, letting the air come out his open mouth. He patted the steering wheel as he would a girl to whom he had just made love, acknowledging the closeness of what they had been through and grateful for the effort. A real victory? Or just another piece of toast?

Traffic was light, and there were several open parking spaces in front of the building housing the dentist's offices. Orthodontists have everything going for them, he thought bitterly, and pulled up directly across from the entranceway, unlatching the car door and shoving it open. She unhooked the catch and pushed the seat down in front of her, edging out to the sidewalk before turning to look at him, waiting for the inevitable repeat of instructions.

He looked at her face. The hell with it. She'd been told once by her mother. He pulled the door shut without a word and took off, revving the motor just enough for a soft roar. The light stopped him at the first intersection and he glanced in the rear mirror. She was still standing there looking after him, tiny in the distance. Then she turned and went into the building. Another piece of toast.

"Cuticles," he said aloud. "Wait till I tell that one."

The light changed, and he shifted fast and hard, leaving the other cars behind him. The greens were with him the rest of the way, and he zoomed through the hospital gate with a double downshift that rolled him into the restricted parking zone with barely a murmur. He thought back on that moment when the car had gone off the road, and he grasped the wheel hard, squeezing with all his strength before unlatching the door and slipping out. His knees were uncertain about carrying the weight. The near accident? Blood pressure? It might be a good idea to eat some breakfast first thing in the morning. All the doctors recommended it. He looked at his watch. Ten minutes past eight. Time to get going.

ii

IT wasn't until the cleaning woman had been set well into her routine that Betsy Hewitt took the time to go up to her bedroom and shut the door, go into the bathroom and shut the door, hike up her skirt, pull down her panties, sit down on the john and cry.

The tears rolled down her cheeks in a steady stream, dropping on the insides of her thighs, and she reveled in the release, not concentrating on anything particular, just unhappy, unhappy, unhappy.

"Oh, God, I am unhappy," she muttered, wanting to hear it aloud, to let someone else know that all was not well in the Hewitt household, that Mrs. Hewitt was living with one of the world's great pricks—her back arched in sensual, subliminal remembrance—yes, one of the world's great pricks, and she could take no more, take no more.

If no more could be taken, then something had to be ended. Alex? Oh, you son of a bitch, she thought fiercely, squinting her eyes hard, oh, you son of a bitch. She couldn't end Alex. He'd kill her. There was no way. The man had no weaknesses. He'd kill her and walk off.

Walk off. Walk away. End the marriage. That she could do. Just walk away. Take the kids and walk away. There, you son of a bitch, it's ended. We're walking away. Just let us live in peace. Live in peace and leave in peace. Would he let them walk away? Just like that? "Alex, I can't take any more. I've been your slave for seventeen years." Seventeen years. Had it all been bad? All seventeen years? The first few months? When just touching him had been enough to make her shiver with anticipation. Had she been afraid of him then, too? Was the shiver due to fear as well as the thought of those bronzed hands with the finespun golden hairs on the back sliding around her body and slowly squeezing her breasts until they hurt—HURT!—and she moaned softly, sitting on the toilet seat, the tears dry on her cheeks, her arms clutched tightly around her.

Seventeen years. Where do you go after seventeen years? Could Mommy go home to Mommy? Remarry? Her mind started to search through the men she knew but was closed off before any face, any name, was able to shape into actual being. Thirty-eight. Young enough. But in two years, forty. Less than two years. A year and a half. Forty would be different. They'd say it; they'd all say it. *My God, she must be forty if she's a day.* But still time at thirty-eight. Still time at thirty-nine.

How soon hath time, the subtle thief of youth . . . Professor Oakes, his little tummy sticking out, his eyes closed as the words rolled off . . . and Denny brushing his leg against hers and then back to his room and two, three, once even four times with his roommate banging at the door . . . that dear, sweet, nice, nice boy; in California, I think . . . and the tears started rolling again for time lost, boy lost, unhappiness found.

The subdued roar of the vacuum cleaner slowly advancing *up* the stairs brought the other senses to bear on legs cramped and seat cutting as Betsy sagged against the cool enamel, muscles released from tension and urine spurting in the bowl. She wiped, stood, pulled, smoothed and flushed. She wet a handcloth and held it against her eyes for a long moment. The mirror revealed a woman of cool good looks and tranquil mien. Still time at thirty-eight. Chicken soup. She'd give her chicken soup and a tuna fish sandwich.

...
iii

STERN was standing at the elevator bank, stethoscope in his left hand, twisting the rubber with his fingers as though it were a string of Greek worry beads. "He wants to make sure everybody knows he's a doctor," one of his close enemies had once remarked.

"Good morning, Doctor," said Stern, flicking the stethoscope in acknowledgment.

"Hi, Irv," said Alex. "Time for the merry-go-rounds?"

"Ten dollars here," said Stern, "ten dollars there. It adds up."

"I had a good one this morning," said Alex. "I was driving my kid to the orthodontist and. . . ." The elevator door opened to reveal an orderly with a patient on a stretcher table. The two doctors aided him in bumping his carrier over the threshold, and as they accomplished this, two nurses, a man with a big brown paper bag and a young technician gathered to accompany them on their ascent. By the time all the floor buttons were punched correctly, the full attention of the nurses and the technician was on the two doctors.

"I'll tell you after rounds," said Alex, and debarked at three with the technician. The floor nurse was not at the station. Alex pulled Mrs. Markham's metal case from the slot and studied the chart. Dr. Stanley recommended that because of the advanced age of the patient, no radiation treatments be undertaken. That was that. He entered his initials, returned the slot and walked down to 312.

The new roommate was lying with her eyes closed, the face still ghostly pale from the operation. But Markham was propped up, her eyes focused out the window on whatever God was offering that day, ready for anything and grateful in advance for whatever it might be.

"Do you think it's nice enough out there for you to go home?" he asked.

Her head turned quickly, a smile brightening the thin, alert face.

"You're late, Doctor," she said, not accusingly, just to put things in their right place.

"I was drafted for emergency taxi service," he said. "My daughter's braces suddenly slipped a gear."

"I'd like to see those children of yours," she said. "They must be real beautiful."

"Just like me," he laughed.

"Just like you," she replied seriously.

"Well, do you want to go home today or not?" he asked.

"Might as well. I'm not doing anybody any good around here."

"You'll be at your daughter's for a while?"

"She's got enough to take care of. I'll be fine at my place."

He sat down on the edge of the bed and took her right hand in both of his.

"Absolutely not," he said. "I don't sign the discharge papers unless you promise you'll stay with her until the wobble goes out of your legs."

She studied his face for a moment, opened her mouth,

closed it again. He could feel the trembling through his fingers.

Or was it he who was trembling? Who's doing the trembling around here, he wondered, this old lady who's going to die soon or this here doctor who's going to die a little later? Or maybe sooner. Who needs the encouragement? The Polack's voice drummed in his ears, Czarnecki, the senior resident. *The trouble with you, Hewitt, is that you don't give one goddamn for the person you're treating, only the ailment. It's the chase that excites you, the hunting down. You don't give a shit one way or another about whether the person lives or dies as long as you do it correctly, win or lose. So you're going to have to learn to fake it. As long as you're working under me, you're going to act like the patient means something, like you care what happens to him and his family and even his dog. You're going to be Dr. Butter-Won't-Melt-in-His-Mouth around here. Because if you don't, if ever I see you performing like you're a mechanic rather than a human being, I'm going to run your ass out of this residency and this hospital and maybe even the profession. You can be a cold prick on your own time, or afterwards when I can't get my fangs into you, but right now you're Mr. Nice Guy.*

Where was he now, that son of a bitch? Was he being as nice to old ladies as old Hewitt was? Holding their trembling hands in. . . .

"Doctor," she said, "I don't know if you can understand this. You think that everybody is like you. My daughter is not like you. She says she wants me to stay with her, and she may even think she wants me to stay with her, but she really wants me to die and disappear. . . ."

"Mrs. . . ."

She squeezed one of his hands with hers to silence him.

"I am seventy-eight years old, and I am ready to die, but I am afraid to die. When I am alone in my apartment, at least I don't feel that I am in anybody's way. I don't want to be in anybody's way. I don't have the strength to fight that."

"You don't have the strength to fight anything right now," he said. "It's either stay here occupying a bed that's needed by someone else or going to a nursing home until you feel stronger or to your daughter's, who, I think, doesn't feel you are that much in the way."

She looked him in the eyes and brought her other hand around to cover his.

"I'll stay with them for two weeks," she said finally.

He pulled the stethoscope from his pocket and warmed the end in his palm for a moment, saying nothing. Then he placed it gently on the thin chest. She watched his eyes flatten out in concentration and wanted to reach out and touch his cheek, feeling within her a stirring that was reminiscently disturbing. Alex wasn't seeing, only hearing. The beat sounded good, but there was an edge of something, a catch that was just outside the comprehension, a feeling within him of more than his ears could hear. But to all purposes and appearances, the beat was sound. He pulled the apparatus from his head and replaced it in his pocket.

"I don't know why I waste my time with you," he said. "There are some really sick people who need my attention."

"Two weeks," she said softly.

"Two weeks," he echoed reassuringly.

As he turned to walk out on her grateful smile, he noticed the other woman had not stirred. She didn't look right to him, and he paused for a moment at the foot of her bed, cocking his head to give psychological perspective to his sight and hearing. He started to walk around the foot of the bed, stopped, turned and went out to the hallway.

The nurse was sitting in her corner and stood up as he approached.

"Mrs. Markham will be leaving this morning," he said. "Her daughter will be here about ten." The nurse handed him a clipboard with the form, and he signed it. She said nothing, and he walked out to the stairwell and climbed swiftly, two steps at a time, till he reached five.

He was pulling his stethoscope out of his pocket as he approached 516 but stopped at the doorway as he saw that the furniture was all moved around and a black cleaning woman was washing down the springs on the bed.

"Where's Mr. Bardwell?" he asked from the doorway. She looked at him uncertainly, fear showing in her eyes.

"The man who was in that bed," he said harshly. "Where is he?"

She mumbled something indistinctly and he started to go into the room closer to her when a wave of dizziness passed through his head and he thought he was going to vomit. His right hand found the wall, and he leaned hard against it, the bile bitter in his throat. The woman was staring at him, and he opened his mouth—to appeal for help? To repeat his question?—but he realized the futility and stood silently until the feeling passed, until he swallowed. He went back to the corridor and down to the central station, where two nurses were working over charts.

"Where's Mr. Bardwell?" he asked abruptly. The nurses' heads snapped up, their eyes as blank as the cleaning woman. The floor supervisor, a chunky blonde, stood up.

"What's that, Doctor?" she asked.

"Bardwell. The man in Five sixteen. Where is he?"

"There is no patient in Five sixteen," she said. "It was empty when we came on duty."

"He was there at nine o'clock last night," said Hewitt. "Mrs. Driscoll was on duty. What's going on here?"

The second nurse stood up, and the two of them turned into stone. He didn't know either of them. The goddamned nurses had everything their own way, working two hours every other rainy Thursday if that's how they wanted it, and it was impossible to keep track of who was who.

"I had a patient in that room last night," he said evenly. "Donald Bardwell. A kidney operation. I saw him at nine P.M. Now no one checked with me about moving him or sending him down for tests or X rays. Dr. Stanton would have informed me of anything like that. I want to know where he is." His voice had risen. He could feel his heart pounding as it had in the car, an irregularity of beat that was abnormal even under tension.

"Dr. Hewitt," said the blond nurse. "We have no record here of any Mr. Bardwell. Mrs. Driscoll didn't say anything about anyone in Five sixteen. Neither of us has been on this floor in two weeks."

"I don't give a good god. . . ." He saw the nurses' lips move into that thin line he knew so well. They wouldn't budge an inch from here on in. Well, somebody was going to budge. Somebody was going to budge all right.

He turned and headed for the stairs, his other patients forgotten, and started down the five flights so fast that his heel caught on one of the steps and almost pitched him headlong down a marble length. He stopped and grasped the rail with both hands, took two deep breaths and then continued evenly to the bottom. His heart was pounding so strongly that he could feel the flutter in his throat. Explode, you son of a bitch, he commanded. Blow me right out of this whole fucking mess.

A man was standing in front of the cashier's grille, painfully considering a sheaf of bills in his hand. Hewitt stuck his face past the papers and confronted the clerk.

"Do you have anything on a Bardwell checking out? Donald Bardwell?"

The girl disappeared for a moment behind the filing cabinets and returned with a card in her hand.

"Donald Bardwell," she read tonelessly. "Kidney operation. Dr. Stanton and Dr. Hewitt. Room Five sixteen."

"He's not there," said Hewitt.

"Yes, he is, Doctor. Room Five sixteen."

"I just came from there. Room Five sixteen is empty. Bardwell is not there."

She looked at the card again. "He is in Room Five sixteen," she said positively.

Hewitt looked at the girl holding the card, and the girl holding the card looked at Hewitt. He turned around quickly, shoving the man with all the bills out of his way, and headed for the administrator's office.

The secretary was seated at her desk with a little tray before her, containing a plastic cup of coffee, a plate with two fried eggs and toast on it and another plate with a prune danish. She was in the process of propping the morning tabloid from Boston on a couple of medical texts.

"Where's Mr. Adams?" he asked in response to her inquiring look.

"He doesn't get in until nine, Doctor," she said, and moved to adjust the newspaper once more.

"Well, who the Christ is in charge until he does get here?"

The girl, emboldened by the knowledge that her eggs were getting colder by the second, tossed her head and said, "I'm sure I don't know."

He wanted to pick up the plate of eggs and dump them on her fat head. His hand started to move in that direction. She sensed the fury in front of her and dropped her eyes. It didn't pay to make a doctor mad at you, especially this particular son of a bitch. Everyone knew about the time he'd thrown the bedpan at the student. They still called her "Tinkle" Haskins right to her face, even though she was a supervisor.

"He'll be in at nine," she said weakly, without really lifting her head.

He walked out to the main corridor. The clock showed it was forty-six minutes past eight. If Adams' usual practice was to come at nine, then he wouldn't get there till nine on the nose. He did everything by the book. His book.

"Hey, Alex, how about a coffee?"

A tent of rumpled whites was moving toward him from the gift shop area.

"Jesus Christ, Casey," said Alex, when the figure halted in front of him, "you look like one of those jellyfish things in a science-fiction movie. I'd like to see a slide of your tissue. In living color."

"We pathologists know how to feed the cells," said Casey. "Come on, let's get a coffee."

"I can't," said Alex. "I've got nine more patients to check, and I'm missing one somewhere."

"He get up and run home on you?"

"Not unless he stuck three tubes up his ass to keep the liquids flowing. I'm serious. I left him here at nine last night, and today he's not in the room."

"What did the nurses say?"

"It's a whole new shift, and they just gave me the blank look."

"Well, he's got to be somewhere. Finish your rounds, and I'll meet you in the cafeteria in half an hour."

Hewitt tried to move through his other patients quickly, but one of them was having trouble passing urine and the resident breezed in with three interns while he was installing the catheter, and the routine turned into an exact teaching session, and then Mrs. Perenick was having her postpartum crying jag and wouldn't let go of his hand, and it was ten minutes past ten before he wrapped it up.

Neither Adams nor his secretary was in the office, and Alex stood there ten minutes, unconsciously counting the crumbs on the desktop before the administrator strode in, a silver gray suit complementing the silver gray of his hair and the closely shaved pinkness of his face.

"Morning, Alex," he said, stopping quickly and turning his full attention on the doctor. "What's the problem?"

"I have a missing patient."

"Missing patient?"

"Donald Bardwell. Room Five sixteen. Checked him at nine last night and found him gone this morning."

"What did the floor nurse say?"

"She said the room was empty when she came on duty. I've asked all the usual places, and nobody knows anything."

Adams thought a moment, said, "Come on," and headed into his own office. Hewitt followed and stood there while Adams stared at the phone, then picked up the receiver and dialed three numbers.

"What can you tell me about a David . . ."

"Donald," said Hewitt.

". . . about a Donald Bardwell who was in Room Five sixteen with a . . . ?" He looked at Hewitt.

"Kidney," said Hewitt.

"Kidney condition."

Adams listened for a moment and then sank back a bit in his chair, waiting while somebody checked somewhere. His eyes went up to meet Hewitt's, but neither man said anything.

Adams leaned forward again and listened closely. "Thank you," he said. He stood up and came around the desk.

"Died at two fourteen this morning," he said. "Coronary arrest."

"Jesus Christ," exploded Hewitt, "why wasn't I called?"

"Of course you were called," said Adams. "That's regular procedure."

"I sure as shit was not called," said Hewitt. "What kind of barn is this?"

"Wait a minute, Alex," said Adams. "Don't go shooting off before we get all the facts."

"That man was in here for a kidney stone operation," said Alex. "He had no coronary problems whatsoever."

"Who did the operation?"

"Frank Stanton."

"Then that's who they called."

"Both of us should have been called."

"That's true. But maybe Frank told them not to bother waking you."

"See if Frank is working here today," said Hewitt.

Adams dialed zero and said, "This is Mr. Adams. Would you see if Dr. Frank Stanton is in the hospital and have him call me if he is available."

They looked at each other for a few moments, and then Adams, sensing the rage that was building before him, asked, "Golf game holding up?"

"I've packed it in for the season."

"Have you seen the new cobalt machine?"

"No. I've been meaning. . . ."

The phone rang, and Adams picked it up before the echo died. "Adams here," he said. "Yes, Doctor. I'm here with Dr. Hewitt. There seems to be some communications breakdown about the death of Mr. Bardwell." He listened. "Yes, at two fourteen this morning . . . I see . . . Well, I can't understand that. . . . Yes, he's right here." He handed the phone to Hewitt without saying anything and without really looking at him.

"Yes, Frank," said Hewitt.

"Alex, I've been operating since seven thirty. What's this about Bardwell?"

"They tell me he died of a coronary early this morning, but nobody called me about it. I went up and found the room empty."

"He seemed fine yesterday. No complications."

"Nobody called you then?"

"No. This is the first I've heard about it. Are you going to follow through on it?"

"You bet I am."

"Well, keep me informed. This is peculiar, to say the least."

Hewitt set the phone down carefully and turned to Adams.

"Jon," he said, "there'd better be some fast answers about this. Fast and good."

"I will investigate it personally as soon as I can."

"What do you mean as soon as you can?"

"Well, we've got a crisis situation here right now."

"Christ, how many other bodies are missing?"

"No, it's the nurses."

"What about the nurses?"

"They're demanding representation on the board."

Hewitt looked down at the pink face, the lips pushed out petulantly, marring the classic features under the smooth silver hair.

Who was this dizzy son of a bitch to rule over a house of healing, who was more upset about the possibility of a negative vote than about death in the night?

"Listen," said Hewitt, "you've got one big thing to worry about. You've got to find out what happened here last night and give me and Dr. Stanton a full report. A full report. Because if we're not satisfied, we'll blow this place apart. And maybe you with it."

"You can rest assured, Doctor," said Adams evenly, "that correct procedure was followed here. Right now I don't know why you and Dr. Stanton weren't called, but I will find out. And I will give you the full facts as soon as possible."

Hewitt leaned over to say more, to break through that shell, but space suddenly took on a new dimension, and his head seemed about to float away from his body. Not here. Not here and not now. He snapped himself erect and turned out of the room. The receptionist was coming through the doorway with two candy bars in her hand and was forced to give a little leap to get out of his way. She

stood staring after him, her mouth a circle of indignation, tore the wrapper off a Milky Way and took a large
bite. She hated doctors, all of them.

Hewitt went straight to the doctors' waiting room and
searched out Donald Bardwell in the phone book. He
dialed the number, which rang six times before the receiver
was picked up. "Hello," said a young voice.

"This is Dr. Hewitt. Is that you, Trish?"

"Yes."

"Is your mother there?"

"Yes."

"I'd like to speak to her."

"She's crying."

"Go tell her Dr. Hewitt wants to talk to her."

"My daddy's dead."

"Yes. I want to talk to your mother."

"Good-bye," said the young voice gently. And the receiver was placed carefully on the cradle.

Hewitt held the phone in his hand for a moment and
then lowered it slowly to the base.

"Doctor." He heard the voice, but it was as if from a distance.

"Doctor!" He turned and looked at the man.

"Doctor!" It was McCord. It was that fucking McCord.

"Yes," said Hewitt, almost a sigh.

"Are you going to the meeting tonight?"

"Meeting?"

"The society meeting. Tonight."

"Yes," said Alex. "Yes, I suppose I am." There had been
no trace of any coronary problem. Nothing. Nothing at all.

"Let me pick you up," said McCord. "There's something
I have to talk to you about."

"Pick me up?" said Alex.

"Yes, you're right on the way. And there's something important we have to discuss."

"You don't have to pick me up. I'll see you at the meeting."

"No, there's something we have to discuss before we get there. I'll pick you up at a quarter to eight."

He had to get away from this idiot. NOW! Tell him to shove it and get out. "All right," he said weakly, "a quarter to eight," and walked quickly out to the parking lot, where the attendant was leaning against the fender of his car.

"Get your fat ass off there," said Hewitt.

"Nice cars, these Porsches," said the attendant, taking his time about straightening up. "I wish I was a doctor."

"You've got the brains for it," said Hewitt, settling in and starting the motor with a roar.

"I hope you treat your patients better than you do this engine," said the attendant, moving just fast enough to avoid getting hit as Hewitt burned a touch of rubber on his stop turn.

"Just don't ever have your back to the gate," Hewitt said as he whirled by him and out the exit corridor.

"Up yours, you mean son of a bitch," the attendant muttered as he watched the machine zoom up the street. He hated doctors, all of them.

Hewitt had been to the Bardwell house only once, the Sunday before, when the wife's third call had indicated that aspirins and ice packs weren't going to handle the situation. It was a nice house with a nice lot, everything in its place with an electrical engineer's orderliness. He rang the bell, and the door was opened almost instantly by nine-year-old Trish.

"Hello, young lady," he said, "is your mother still in her room?"

She nodded and stepped aside. He headed right up the stairs, his bag banging against the post as he made the turn at the top. The door was closed, and he knocked softly. There was no answer, and he turned the knob and went in.

She was lying on the bed with her face toward the door, up on her elbows, staring straight ahead. The tears were gone, the face drained of all moisture. Just streaks, random streaks. But through it all the prettiness shone, the sweet curve of the cheeks, the fullness of the mouth, the clarity of the skin. Life had treated her well; death had not.

"What happened?" she said. "Why? What happened?"

He placed his bag on the floor and sat on the edge of the bed, his hands within reach of her. He opened his mouth and closed it again. Christ Almighty, what was her first name? Gloria? He didn't know any Glorias. Then why should it come to mind? He tried visualizing her folder at the office, but all he could see was Mrs. Bardwell. Mrs. Bardwell, Donald C. He couldn't call her Mrs. Bardwell at this moment.

"It's one of those things," he said. "Everything checks out perfectly, and then some natural outrage shocks the body. It was a coronary; his heart."

"But he never had any heart problems. You've been our doctor since we were transferred here last year; you know he didn't have any heart problems."

"It often doesn't show in examinations or tests. It didn't in this case."

"But he's so young. And Trish. . . ." Her elbows could no longer bear the weight, and she collapsed on the bed, burying her face in the spread.

He put his hand on her shoulder, the heat of her body gripping his palm like a suction pump. What the Christ was her first name?

"What about your family?" he asked.

She lifted her face off the cover. "Our folks are in California," she said. "I called them when I came back from the hospital and. . . ." She raised her head to look him directly in the eyes. "They told me you had already left when I asked where you were. One of the nurses said she had seen you go out. I was so mixed up I almost called you at home, but then I decided you would have stayed if there had been anything you wanted to tell me, so. . . ."

"They," he broke in, "they . . . I couldn't stay. Another patient," he mumbled, withdrawing his hand and reaching down for his bag for something to do.

"I'm going to give you . . ." he said.

"No!" she snapped, sitting up, "I don't want anything. We never believed in taking. . . ." She dropped her head to her chest, and he noticed the fullness of her breasts, how solid and unperturbed they seemed amid the disarray of the rest of her body. A pretty woman.

"All right," he said, standing up. "I'll be in touch."

She backed off the bed on the other side and stood looking at him, all need gone, all thought gone, all tears gone. Just numbness.

"Which funeral home is handling . . ." he said.

She looked at him without answering, seemingly not to have heard. Just as he was working out how to reword the same question, she said, "Harney's. The nurse said that was a good one."

He picked up his bag, looked at her again, turned and went down the stairs. Trish was not there, and he let himself out. The car motor sounded rough, and he let it idle itself into regularity while his mind sought the same adjustment. Was she still standing there by the bed? Mrs. Bardwell, Donald C. He turned around in the driveway and drove across town until he came to the discreet sign acknowledging Harney's Funeral Home.

The back door was locked so he followed the concrete walk around to the main entrance and entered the drab hallway of the converted mansion. There were no visible or audible signs of life in any of the rooms, and he wandered further into the depths, opening doors before him and closing them behind. Finally, just as he was to reach the very door that had denied him entrance from the rear, he heard from behind a side portal the creak of a chair. It was Roy Harney himself, taking his ease in his black leather lounge chair, two ounces of the finest in a clear glass in his hand, smacking his lips over the treat he had just given himself. He looked up in surprise.

"Ah, it's you, Doc," he said. "You smelled me out," waving the glass in front of him in happy guilt. "I just finished a chore. And though I've been doing it for twenty-seven years now, I still need this to wash the taste from my mouth. Would you join me?" He made as to rise.

"No, no," said Hewitt, "I've office hours ahead of me."

"The aroma of this on your breath," said Harney, "will do more for them than any chemicals you prescribe."

"Anybody ever tell you how many chemicals there are in whiskey?" asked Hewitt.

"Not in this whiskey! This is pissed by Irish elves into the blossoms of heather, which virginal maidens gather each day and transfer straight to the bottle. What can I do for you, Doc?"

"You've got one of my people here."

"No, that can't be. I've got only one case in the whole place, and it wasn't your name on the certificate."

"It's a man named Bardwell."

"That's the one I've got," said Harney, uncoiling his dark leanness from the chair. "Did I read the ticket wrong?"

"Where is it?"

"Here somewhere," he said, rummaging around in the mess of papers and empty plastic coffee containers on the desk top. "Right here." He pulled the form in front of them, and they both peered down at the signature on the bottom.

"I don't know what the hell it reads," said Harney, "but I know damn well it doesn't say Hewitt."

"It kind of looks like Shearer or something," said Hewitt.

"I'm surprised the man lived as long as he did," said Harney, sinking down in his chair and taking a slug of the whiskey. "His veins were so thin you couldn't work them with a cat's hair, and the blood was like strawberry jam. He was straight yellow by the time we picked him up at the hospital."

Hewitt was concentrating on the signature, but it told him as little as could the man lying on the slab in the downstairs room.

"I'd like to see him," he said.

Harney looked up in surprise, opened his mouth, closed it and then stood up. You didn't question doctors or priests; they all had reasons.

The phone rang as they were about to go through the door, and Harney hurried back to pick it up. "Harney Funeral Home," he said, the voice acquiring a silky smoothness that would grease the way for any ultimate departure, "may we help you? . . . Ah," he said, sinking into his chair and picking up a felt tip pen, "and what is your relationship to the deceased?" His eyes raised to Hewitt, and a nod of the head pushed him through to the corridor and the entrance to the basement. He had been down there twice before and found the room quickly, but stood outside the closed door almost as numb as she had been. Bardwell, Donald C. Was she still by the bed, the soft curve of her breast not moving, quiescent, waiting for a hand to bring it to life? Bardwell, Mrs. Donald C. He pushed open the door and walked in.

Harney had not quite finished, and there were still tubes and bottles connected to the cadaver, the sickly sweet smell pressing in on the pores with vacuum intensity. He walked over and slipped his fingers around the wrist in a professional motion as natural as breathing, feeling the dead, waxy flesh and sensing the pressure of his own life force beating against the tips.

"I have high blood pressure," he told Donald Bardwell, remembering the beat that had been in that wrist some fourteen hours before. "I am going to die, too. What is it like?" A fit of nausea swept through him, and he leaned forward to retch, the vomit rising to the back of his tongue and then down again. Through the blur in his eyes he saw his hand squeezing the dead man's wrist, his knuckles as white as the pasty flesh underneath and the beads of sweat popping out on his forehead in the chill room as he sought to keep his balance.

And though I've been doing it for twenty-seven years now, I still need this to wash the taste from my mouth.

I've been doing it for seventeen years now, he thought, and I just acquired the taste. What can bother Harney, who bears no responsibility for the people he receives? What did I miss? *Veins so thin you couldn't work them with a cat's hair, and the blood was like strawberry jam.* We're not miracle men. What did I miss? *May we help you?* That phony unctuousness that creeps into their voices. How do I sound to Mrs. Markham? Or Mrs. Bardwell? *It doesn't often show in examinations or tests.* What did I miss? Christ, is it all going, everything? The taste. That's a bitter taste.

It passed. He lifted his hand from that of the dead man and looked at the face. Bardwell, Donald C. Thirty-four years old. Blood pressure one hundred and twenty-five over eighty. Seventy-two beats of the heart per minute. Cholesterol normal, blood sugar normal. Two stones taken from the kidney. Dead. Officially dead.

But *SH*. What doctor was there whose name began with an *SH?* Sheila! That was Mrs. Bardwell's first name. Sheila. He tried visualizing the doctors' "In and Out" board at the hospital, moving down to the S's. Schmidt. Schreckhaus. Stern. None of those. Was it an *SH?* Was it even an *S?* Sheila. She was prettier than her name.

If you died with what you had, Hewitt silently told the body, I live with what I have. An omen. A good omen.

His stomach growled. With hunger! An omen. A good omen.

iv

WHAT if he should die?
The pen dropped out of her hand and she stared down at the narrow sheet of paper on the counter.

> Potatoes
> Butter
> Bacon
> Oranges
> Diet Cola
> Tuna fish

What if he should die?
Where did it come from? Who put that in her mind? But what if he should die? Would life be better? Or worse? Could it be worse? *What if he should die?* Her knees buckled slightly, and she leaned her elbows on the countertop for support, welcoming the pain of the hard surface against her bones. *What if I should die?* No more pain. No more wondering what was wrong. How many times had she wanted to scream that? *What is wrong? What have I done*

wrong? Sitting there with his drink in his hand and staring at her. Or just staring. Or reading the paper. Reading the paper as if in one second he were going to jump up and kill somebody. Her? The children? What have they done wrong? They were his children, not his enemies. *I am your wife, not your enemy.*

What if he should die? She let her mind dwell on it, all bars down. There would be peace. Even for him. Would they move down with Mama? And Papa? Not in the same house. But close by. Let the hot sun beat down all the time like it used to, bleach her hair white, no more once a week . . . I don't know how much longer we can hold this shade, Mrs. Hewitt . . . just the natural hot sun doing its job . . . oh, Mama . . . thirty-eight . . . she's only thirty-eight . . . with those big children? . . . no, really, she's only thirty-eight . . . *what if he should die?*

A shiver went through her, the whole body shaking so hard that she raised her arms from the counter and hugged herself fiercely, striving to hold firm.

Tuna fish

She racked her brain, pushing, shoving, forcing the process . . .

Tuna fish

The shivering had stopped but was still there, waiting, only a tick away from . . .

Tomato soup

She had it now. The right arm dropped to the counter and picked up the pen, wrote "Tomato soup" neatly in the line. Eggs . . . Bread . . . Olive oil . . . Grapes . . . Frozen lima beans . . . Ice Cream . . . Ice cream . . . icecream.

v

IT was a heavy day, mostly bronchial. Hewitt sent two patients to the hospital for chest X rays, two were ordered home to bed, for two he dug out samples, and eight were told not to overexert. Mrs. Moore, the office nurse, was running around with flu vaccine and urine samples and typhus and cholera shots for Mr. and Mrs. Evakian, who were going to the old country for a long visit, and answering the phone seventeen times, eleven of which had to be picked up by the doctor, and it was ten minutes to six before the last hacking cough echoed in the waiting room.

"That does it," said Mrs. Moore, picking up the folder from his desk.

"We didn't break any medical barriers today," said Hewitt. "All we needed was a big jug of honey and lemon juice in the waiting room, and they could have treated themselves."

"They feel better hearing it from the doctor," said Mrs. Moore.

"I suppose you're right. But on days like this I feel I ought to give them something extra for their money. Like dressing up in feathers and wearing a mask and dancing around them while waving a rattle."

"There are times," said Mrs. Moore judiciously, "when I think it might not be out of place for you to have a rattle in your hand." And she got the hell out of there.

"Old bitch," he mumbled, half-admiringly, and picked up the phone. He held it in his hand, unable to remember whom he was going to call. Handball! He needed a partner. And a court. Five minutes to six. Too late now. He replaced the receiver, stood and stretched, all six feet one inch, one hundred and ninety-one pounds, stomach pulled in as far as it would go, then poof, and he could feel it pushing against the belt. Jesus, he had to lose some weight. He sat down at the desk and wound the expansion rubber around his arm, slipped the stethoscope into his ears and pumped up. He could feel himself tighten as he pumped— instrument anxiety, add ten points—one hundred and sixty-two. He released the knob . . . there it was . . . eighty. It had to be the weight. The diastolic was too good for it to be anything but weight. He pulled off the apparatus and slid open the desk drawer, took the little sample bottle from the corner, unscrewed the cap and poured the bright green capsule into his palm. One a day should do it. But once you started. . . . He pulled a journal from the drawer and stared down at the headline of the lead article:

HYPERTENSION: A NEW APPROACH

The new approach boiled down to a variation of an old approach that hadn't proved successful.

"Bullshit," said Hewitt out loud, and replaced both the journal and the small bottle of pills in the drawer. You just had to run the fucking thing into the ground: Increase the

circulation, tire the muscles so they soaked up the blood,
fool the brain into thinking it had nothing to worry about.
What did he have to worry about? Just what in Christ did
he have to worry about? Nothing. Well, isn't that something
to worry about? Forty-two years old and nothing to worry
about. Might as well pack it in. Isn't that what the blood
pressure is saying: Pack it in. The body knows. He stood
and looked at the chair across from his desk. How many had
sat there today—twenty-five, thirty? Keep going, he had
said. Keep going. Who was bullshitting whom?

Mrs. Moore was still writing things down in record books
when he went through the waiting room on his way out.

"Christ, you can do those in the morning," he said.

"There's a lot of other things I have to do in the
morning."

"I want you to find a good, part-time girl to help you
with the crap."

She looked at him suspiciously.

"I can handle it."

"I know you can handle it. It's just that you're putting in
too many hours as a filing clerk. You're a nurse. I need you
as a nurse. Get a girl to do the junk."

She decided to be flattered.

"I'll see what I can find," she said. "But I don't want anybody in here who turns out to be more work than she's
worth."

"Medicine is ninety percent bookkeeping," he said.
"Look for a bookkeeper. And tell the answering service I'm
on my way home."

"Home?" she repeated, raising her head.

"Yes, home. That's where the heart is."

Betsy was in front of the sink as he came in the door from
the breezeway, but she did not hear him because of the
noise from the garbage disposal. He walked up behind her
and stood there until she, sensing a presence, turned and

jumped in shock. He saw the pupils of her eyes change as she half gasped.

"My God," she said, "how long have you been there?" and leaned her face forward and then quickly back. *A break in the pattern.* First time in seventeen years, he thought. What comes next?

He turned and walked over to the phone, where he glanced down at the pad. Two names and numbers.

"You want your dinner now?" she asked.

He glanced at the clock—six forty-five—shook his head and walked through to the living room, where he dropped his coat on an armchair. The seven-year-old was sitting cross-legged on the floor on the other side of the room, pasting something in a book, her tongue caught between her teeth. She looked up at him and gave a tentative little smile of hello, just the barely careful bit of a smile.

Hewitt turned back to the kitchen, where his wife was still at the sink. He took a large tumbler from the cupboard, grabbed three ice cubes from the receptacle in the refrigerator and filled the glass halfway up with vodka. She was watching him from the corner of her eye but was careful not to shift too far. He caught the angle of her head, and after a short pause, he tilted the bottle again and poured out another inch. The water was turned on in the sink.

He picked up the piece of paper with the list of names and walked through the living room to his den where he set the vodka on the desk by the phone, closed the door and sat down in the leather chair. The glass felt comfortably chill against his palm, and he took a long swallow, the icy burn cleaning out every crevice in his throat before dropping to his stomach right on the cold feeling that had been pressuring at him all day. He took another swallow, and another, and pulled the phone toward him.

The second reassuring "Call me tomorrow" was just passing his lips when there was a light tap on the door. He waited till he had hung up and taken another swallow before he muttered, "Yes?" and the door opened. Betsy stood there with a plate of crackers and cheese and a glass of her own. She placed the plate before him on the desk, took two of the crackers and sat down on the couch at the side of the room.

"Anything exciting today?" she asked.

He picked up a cracker with cheese and munched on it. And again. Then he took a drink of his vodka, cradled the glass in his hands and took another drink. It was almost empty.

"No," he said, as he stood up and left the room, "nothing exciting."

She was still sitting there, her tomato juice untouched, when he returned with his replenished glass. There was a frown of concentration on her face.

"I went to see them at the college today," she said, "and they told me I could get my teaching certificate if I took just four courses."

"No teaching," he said.

"I don't know that I'd want to be a full-time teacher, but it might be interesting to substitute."

"No teaching."

"Look," she said, "Bobbi's sixteen, Jeff's twelve and Jo's seven."

"I know how old they are."

"They don't need me anymore like they used to. They're on their own, even Jo."

"No teaching. No work."

"Why? So I'll always be right here?"

"That could be it."

Her mouth opened and closed, the tongue holding the even white teeth apart, almost in the same position, he noted, as the seven-year-old in the other room. She stood up and came over to retrieve the empty plate.

"Do you want your dinner now?" she asked.

He nodded.

"Where?"

He pointed to the desk in front of him. She turned to go.

"Switch on the television, will you?" he asked. She came back across the room, clicked the knob and started out again, only to halt at the door and half turn toward him.

"Do you want another drink?" she asked, her voice flat.

He stared at her for a moment, weighing, considering, undecided whether to let the rage come or not.

"If I do," he said, his voice as flat as hers, "I'll get it myself."

He watched a movie about deep-sea divers while he ate his dinner—two baked pork chops, mashed potatoes, squash, applesauce. Halfway through he went into the kitchen and opened a can of beer, which he used to wash down the rest of the meal.

His son came in without knocking, and Hewitt gave him a hard stare to show that the transgression had been noted and would be remembered. The boy looked back at him through his thick glasses, the left eye slightly askew. It was possible that the dumb son of a bitch had botched the operation and the left eye would always be slightly askew. It might be good to get another opinion. From some other dumb son of a bitch.

"Mom said I should get your plate," the boy said, moving toward the desk. Hewitt just looked at him, and after hesitating a moment, the boy picked up the plate, ignoring the vodka glass and the beer can, and left the room. His orders had been to get the plate.

Hewitt felt tight in the shoulders. He stood up and slipped off his jacket, which he flung on the couch. The tight feeling remained, and he moved his shoulders back and forth, but it was there still, nothing to do with muscles or cartilage or bones.

He pulled open the center drawer of his desk and looked down at the medical journal there. Page 43. He opened to the page and read the headline:

THE NARCOTIC ADDICTS: DOCTORS' DISEASE

Running his finger along, he quickly scanned the pages, skipping the passages his first reading had found irrelevant. The television blatted on, but everything seemed still, terribly still. He walked over to his jacket and fumbled in his pocket until he found the sample bottle, unscrewed the cap and slid a pellet into his palm. He'd prescribed it for Bardwell: one Demerol for pain. The tablet was grooved in the middle for half doses, with the initials of the manufacturer on each side. There was just enough liquid in the beer can to wash the tablet down his throat, and he replaced the bottle in his jacket pocket. Was there an exception to every rule? There was no one in the downstairs portion of the house, and he wandered through the rooms, his doctor's mind subconsciously nodding approval at the neatness of the kitchen, the soft fluorescent light gleaming over the sink and everything in its place, gleaming, ready, just as he liked it. The beer can was still in his hand, and he moved to drop it into the garbage receptacle, pulled back and set it on the counter. It stood there in lonely emptiness, contrasting with the orderliness around, a gentle touch of Alex in the night.

Betsy entered the kitchen behind him, headed for the sink, and, in passing, lifted the beer can for weight check, then dropped it into the plastic-lined pail.

"Jo's in bed," she said, "Jeff is on his way, and Bobbi's in her room studying."

"Gee, that's swell."

He was watching her whirl around from the sink, waiting for the facial expression that would indicate how far she was ready to go when it lifted, just like that—the tightness, the cold feeling, the depression—and he felt good. Physician, heal thyself. My God, how that pill worked. The beginning of the end. Pop 'em like peanuts from now on. Win or lose, happiest doctor in the race. She was looking at him peculiarly.

"What?"

"Talk," she said. "We have got to talk."

"About what?"

"About you. About me. About the children."

God, how long had it been? The looseness moving through him was like a caress, the way it used to feel on the tennis court when he was drifting over to the area where the ball was going to come, the timing just right so that the arm would be back and the legs positioned for the step into. . . .

"Alex?"

He looked at her almost kindly . . . Christ, the booze. The booze and the Demerol. Go out happy anyway. Not enough. Not enough for that kind of thing. Just enough. Just enough for this kind of thing.

"You've got to listen!" She had her hand on his arm. He looked down at it. Never touch a boy there.

"We're people," she was saying, "human beings. They're your children." There was no beauty in her face. Like a mask. A life mask. Hot and red and streaked with wet, moving, twisting, tearing, what do you want from me? It would be easier to die and sleep and not feel anything anymore. Good. Or bad. Or indifferent. He felt her arms pulling at him.

"Listen," he said, and the doorbell rang. It was two rings. The front door. Somebody was at the front door. The hand pulling at him was gone. She was gone. He still felt good. Tired. But good.

"Alex," he heard her call. "Alex. It's Dr. McCord."

Jesus, Jesus, Jesus. It's Fucking McCord.

"Sorry I'm late," said McCord from the hallway door, "but a doctor's time is not his own, you know."

The meeting. The fucking meeting. Fuck the meeting. Bed. See how it is to feel good in bed. She was looking at him. That hand was still at the end of the arm. Waiting to grab. That tongue was still in the mouth. Waiting to accuse.

"I'll get my coat," said Hewitt, and left without saying a word, leaving it to McCord to make the amenities, say the good-byes, close the door.

It was cold, goddamn cold, and he slid his hands into his coat pockets after he settled into the front seat of the big Chrysler. It took McCord two minutes to get his gloves on to his satisfaction, but they were finally rolling.

"Well, Alex, they keeping you busy?"

"Tolerable."

"Always room for a little more, eh? That's the spirit. That's why I had to talk to you tonight before the meeting. We've got a little more we want you to do."

Alex turned in his seat to look at McCord, but he kept his eyes on the road ahead, driving carefully and steadily. What the hell was going on? Alex turned back to the front and said nothing.

"There's a problem at the society, and a group of us are anxious to solve it in the right way. And we think you're the man to help us. Just what the doctor ordered."

Was the son of a bitch trying to make a joke? A little humor now from Dr. McCord.

"What problem?"

"Well, you know that they have held most of the offices for the past few years, and we think it's time some of our people. . . ."

"Wait a minute. What offices? Who's they?"

"In the society. They've been passing the top offices down to each other for too damn long now, and we want to stop it right here."

"The top offices? Like President Stern?"

"And Vice-president Hirschfield and Treasurer Mag-alener," said McCord righteously. "My God, whenever we get written up in the paper, it's more like a synagogue than a medical meeting."

"They care," said Alex.

"What?"

"These people care. They're the ones who are active, who go to all the meetings, who volunteer for crap that nobody else wants to do. That's why they're holding the offices."

"We care, too. That's why we want to nominate you from the floor tonight."

"Why me? I don't go to that many meetings. I don't volunteer for any crap. I just belong because that's the name of the game."

"That's not true, Alex. You do more than your share. And your record in Vietnam. . . ."

"Piss on that," said Alex. He was feeling a little dizzy with slight elements of nausea. Booze and pills will cure your ills. Nothing free. You get nothing for free in this world.

"Listen, Alex," said McCord, "you owe. . . . What the hell is that?" He eased on the brakes and looked to the right. Alex turned his head slowly, afraid to make any sudden moves. The wires on the guardrail were snapped and far down the bank, in the trees, were a pair of headlights shining at a peculiar angle. A figure passed briefly in front of one of the lights, and Alex had the impression it was a woman.

"That must have just happened," said Alex, aloud, but softly, really to himself. He could feel the car moving ahead and turned toward McCord. "Hey, where you going?"

"We can't afford to stop here," said McCord. "Just this week in Chicago a jury awarded eight hundred thousand dollars in a malpractice suit."

"Somebody may be hurt down there, Doctor," he said viciously.

"We'll be late for the meeting."

Alex's foot kicked McCord's off the gas pedal and jammed on the power disk brakes. The car stopped with such impact that both men were thrown forward, and Alex, who was not belted in, bumped his head against the windshield. He welcomed the pain that superseded dizziness and nausea and placed his hand on his forehead. No blood. While McCord was moving back into his seat, Alex grabbed the gear lever with his right hand and shoved it over into Park.

McCord turned and stared at Alex, his eyes wide in disbelief. Why would anyone do what had just been done? Why indeed! There was nothing but trouble outside the warm car. Who needed more trouble than he already had? But if prick-face was against it, then Hewitt was for it. That's what differentiated Presidents from people who nominated them.

"Let me just check it out," he said, and slipped through the door into the cold air. He ran back to the broken barrier and peered over the bank, which could be seen dimly in the reflections from the headlights far down. Christ, that was steep. Break a leg getting down there. Back to the car? Back to McCord and his meeting? Or just stand there peering down like a fucking idiot?

He sat down with a thump on the edge of the embankment and pushed off slowly, feeling ahead with his feet, using his rear end as a brake and his hands for balance and steering. Things tore at all parts of him, scraped, stung, prodded, pushed, pulled, and once he became entangled in a cluster of saplings that imprisoned him with venomous intensity. He finally was forced to slip out of his topcoat to release himself, and after a couple of futile tugs at it, he left it there while he continued his descent. His eyes were glued to the headlights, and several times he saw the shadowy figure passing in front of them, from different angles, once almost as if from the air, like a bird flying by. A root jammed through his pants, ripping into his skin, and he rolled up on his side, fell forward and was there.

It was a compact car, wedged between two trees with the rear end curved around some thirty degrees so that the vehicle almost formed a shallow letter *C*. It was a good three feet off the ground, and the stink of gasoline pierced through his sinuses so fiercely that he squinted his eyes in anticipation of sting.

"There's a man inside there," said a voice almost directly behind him, shrill, high, verge of hysteria, no sudden moves or the bird will fly.

"We'll get him out," said Hewitt calmly, not starting his turn until the sentence was almost finished. It was a young boy, ten, eleven, unmarked.

"Were you in the car?" asked Hewitt.

"No," said the boy, the words pouring out to hold the human companionship that had suddenly appeared from the dark, "my dad and I were coming home from my grandmother's, and this car went by us awful fast and went right off the road at the turn, and we came down here and couldn't get any of the doors open, and my dad went back up to try and call somebody, and he's been gone an awful long time."

"Not many houses out here," said Hewitt, as he worked his way up to the front of the car, trying to see into the window from the reflection of the headlights on the trees. The gasoline smell became more intense as he worked his way up, and he reflected on how long before it soaked into a hot wire or something sparked into the fumes.

"You go back up the hill," he said into the dark, not knowing exactly where the boy was, "and you'll find a doctor in a car up there. Tell him to get down here with his bag and a flashlight."

The boy didn't bother to answer, and Hewitt could hear

him start the scramble up the embankment. A good boy. That father had him a good boy.

Hewitt pressed his face against the window and made out a dark shape, masculine from the bulk, but the roof was bent in at such an angle that he couldn't see but the bottom half of the head. He inched around to the front where the windshield was shattered in jagged pieces, but something was jammed into the aperture, and he could not work his hand through to any place significant. He let himself slide down until his feet touched the ground. The car must have hurtled down the embankment and hit the trees while still in the air, wrapping itself around the pliant wood. He dropped to his knees and felt around with his hands until he found a stone, then worked his way back up the side of the car until he came to the rear side window that was almost horizontal with the ground. He tapped the rock against the glass, but it did not give.

"Can I help?" A man's voice below him.

"McCord?"

"No, my name's Garbowit. The police are on their way. I told my son to stay up there until they came."

"Did McCord come down with you?"

"Who's McCord?"

"The doctor in the car up there. The Chrysler."

"There's no other car up there. Danny said you had sent him up for another man, but there's no other car up there."

Oh, the son of a bitch, the filthy son of a bitch.

"I've got to get in there and turn off the ignition before the gas goes," said Hewitt, "but I need a bigger rock. See if you can find me one."

The man was gone so long that Hewitt could feel his left hand weakening in its hold on the frame, and just as he was about to slide down to ease the numbness, he felt a heavy object being shoved up beside him. He dropped the small stone he was holding and reached down until he bumped against the roughness. It was almost too big to be held with one hand, but he finally managed a grip with his fingers and pulled it up. No time to crap around, and he raised it high and brought it down hard. The glass shattered and as his hand bounced up from the impact, he felt a tearing at the side of one finger, a sharp pain that intensified terribly and then ceased. He raised the stone again and again, knocking the hole bigger at the edges until it seemed clear to the frame. His fingers couldn't hold any longer, and the stone fell out of his hand to the ground below.

"You all right?" bellowed Hewitt.

"I'm over here," the voice said, from the left. "What do you want me to do?"

"I'm going in there," said Hewitt, and he heard a siren in the distance, a long way off but moving reassuringly in the night.

"Can I help?"

"No, I don't think. . . ." The left hand couldn't hold on any longer, and Hewitt slid to the ground, scraping his leg against something that cut. Jesus, he'd be worse off than the guy inside in a few minutes. Hewitt staggered as he hit and fell to one knee to steady himself. A hand took him by the shoulder and held him firmly. Christ, it was one thing to play handball or run five miles and quite another to do some honest work.

"We've got to get in there and turn off the ignition," said Hewitt, hoping the other would volunteer to go through that window. He stood up and looked at the body that belonged to the hand. My god, five feet tall and five feet wide. How the hell had he climbed back up that embankment?

"I'm going to have to go in that window headfirst," said Hewitt. "Can you give me a boost until I'm over the edge?"

"Sure," said the man, and braced himself against the car. Hewitt felt himself being pushed up as easily as a baby into a cradle. Christ, five feet strong to go with the rest. He moved his head into the window frame and smelled blood, rising above the gas and car stink in heady intensity, fresh, lifesaving blood that was pouring out of some gaping vital area. The hands below pushed, and Hewitt's whole body was in the car, jammed into the rear area, which was full of debris from some section or other. There was almost no room to turn his long body behind him, but he finally managed to get his hands free toward the front. He put his fingers on the head and felt the face. A young face with smooth skin, the mouth open and slack, the eyelids down, no discernible breathing.

It was impossible to see inside the car because no light was being reflected from anywhere. Hewitt reached farther forward and encountered a metal barrier. The body was jammed into pieces of the dashboard and motor. He shoved forward as much as he could, reaching through whatever holes he could find until in one area he hooked a hand on what remained of the dashboard. His fingers scrabbled around, but he could find no key. It might be gone and only wires hanging together to keep the circuit open. He shoved forward again, squeezing as hard as he could and managed to get his right hand to the lower half of the body where he encountered a pool of sticky wet. His fingers probed. The thigh, something had gouged out part of the thigh near the groin area, possibly part of the groin, and here it was, ejaculations of wet as steady as a heartbeat, artery, ALIVE, at least the poor bastard was still alive. The first and index fingers pushed in exactly and cut the blood off. Slippery, too slippery, had to get something solid and. . . .

"What's doing in there?" said a calm voice, almost in Hewitt's ear. The windshield. It was coming through the windshield. A voice of authority. One that had been in similar situations before. Many times before.

"He's alive," said Hewitt, "but not for long if we don't get him out of here. There's a mortal wound down in the groin area with a severed artery. I've got it closed off now, but I have to get something solid in there because I won't be able to keep my fingers in too long. He may have several other wounds just as bad, but we won't know till we get him out of here."

"Are you a doctor?"

"Yes. Hewitt."

"I'm Sergeant Torchio. The doors are jammed, so we'll have to take him out over the back seat and through the window you went in."

"He's got half a ton of shit pinning him in. You'll have to cut him out."

"There's gas all over the place out here. An acetylene torch would blow us all to hell."

"This boy's going to die in a few minutes unless we get him to a hospital. You're going to have to do whatever has to be done. And quick."

There was silence for a moment.

"OK," said the sergeant. "The police emergency truck is on the way, and they have cutters and torches. We'll just have to hang in there until it gets here."

"Has an ambulance been called?"

"Yes."

"OK," said Hewitt, "I'm going to give you some things to do, and I want you to go back up to your police car and radio them in."

"I've got a walkie-talkie right here that I can call my partner on up at the car," said the sergeant. "Fire away."

"All right," said Hewitt. "We're going to need blood, lots of blood. Make sure the hospital knows that. And we're going to need a surgeon. See if they can get hold of Dr. Frank Stanton, and have him ready at the hospital."

Hewitt heard the sergeant talking outside the car, not able to make out all the words because the wind was taking them away.

"OK," said the sergeant, "the word's been passed. Now we have to wait. Are you all right?"

Hewitt could feel his fingers tiring. Blood must still be

seeping out. And from where else? How much blood was left?

"Sergeant?" he called.

"Yes, sir."

"Can you find two pieces of glass out there?"

"It seems to be all glass out here."

"Well, hand in a medium-sized piece. About the size of a half dollar."

"What for?" the sergeant started to say, and caught himself. "Here you are," and a hand pushed through the front. Hewitt pulled his hand away from the wound, reached up and took the piece of glass which he smeared with his fingers and then put back in the waiting hand.

"What the hell," said the sergeant, and Hewitt quickly slipped his hand back down to the thigh where he found the place, still spurting, some blood left yet.

"Put a piece of glass on top of the blood," he said, "just like you were making a sandwich. Then get it up the hill and rush it to the hospital. Tell them to run the tests, and then be ready to ship some out here for transfusions in the ambulance if we don't have him out or have it at the door of the hospital so we can start transfusing as he comes through the door."

The car shifted a tiny bit as the sergeant slid off the hood and started his scramble. "Just us now," Hewitt said to the boy, "just you and me. Hang in there, baby." He took his hand out again, reached up to his neck and pulled off his necktie, which he wadded together and brought down to the wound, shoving it in as hard as he could and keeping his fist tight against it. Nothing more to do, oh, skillful physician, just shove your hand against a necktie.

He gave a sudden shiver, his hand almost pulling loose as he strove to hold his body steady. Somebody walking on my grave? Cold, Jesus cold. His whole body shivering while his hands stayed nice and warm, still must be close to 98.6 in there. The first time the helicopter came in with the dozen ARVN who had been ambushed in the new drive. The same smell, arms and legs twisted, those tiny little men, and that medic, what was his name, they called him Mac, Jesus Christ, Doc, we better get going. That car accident with three people hurt when I was an intern, that was the most I'd ever seen. Jesus Christ, Doc, we better get going. Somebody always there to tell you to get going. Betsy. Betsy, where are we going? I hold life in my hands every minute, right now, and life doesn't mean anything. All I have to do is pull the plug, pull the necktie. Somebody, something has got his finger in me, has got his tie around my throat, and he's making the blood pound through my body at. . . .

"Doc?" The voice of an old friend. Who do I know down here in the bowels of black who calls me Doc? "Doc?" It was the policeman. The sergeant. Sergeant what's-his-name.

"Yes."

"How you doing in there?"

"I can't tell. What's the story?"

"We got the equipment here. We're going to cut him out of there. It would be best if you pulled out while we worked with the torches."

"If I let go, he's gone no matter what. Do your thing."

"OK. It may take a minute, and it may take an hour. I'll be down below."

It took four minutes. The torch cut through the pieces holding the door shut, and they yanked the whole section right off the frame. Two men with long crowbars wedged up the motor and Hewitt felt the body taken from his hands, gone just like that.

"Keep that pack pressed in there," he yelled through the aperture, and he could see the boy under the bright trouble light being wrapped into a stretcher with a rope attached to it, which was swiftly hauled out of sight.

"There's a fire truck up there," said the sergeant, as he

helped Hewitt ease out the side window again. The front of
the car was covered with a white foam and firemen with
tanks on their backs were spraying the roof.

"Is the ambulance up there?" asked Hewitt.

"Yeah," said the sergeant, "and there's a doctor from the
hospital with it. No blood, though. They said they'd have it
ready when they got there."

A siren started screaming from above, its whine lessening
as it moved off in the night. Hewitt stood there, unable to
move, and the sergeant fastened a rope about his waist and
gave two tugs on it.

"Just walk up slowly and hang onto the rope," he said.
"I'm right behind you."

There were four police cars, a fire truck and several other
cars lining the road when Hewitt reached the top. It was so
bright on the road that he put a hand in front of his eyes for
a moment until he could turn again toward the dark. A
fireman was unlooping the rope around him, saying nothing, only wanting to retrieve his equipment. The sergeant
came up over the bank, a short, swarthy man with bull-like
shoulders.

"Jesus, you're something," he said to Hewitt, looking
him up and down. "Where's your car?"

Hewitt tried to think where he'd left his car. Home,
that's where his car was. That dirty mother fucker.

"I don't have one," he said. "I was going to a meeting
with another . . . man"—the code, the fucking code of
honor—"and he went on."

The sergeant didn't bother to follow through on why one
had stayed and one had gone on. It had nothing to do with
his situation.

"We'll take you where you want to go," he said.

Where? Home? The meeting?

"The hospital," said Hewitt. "Take me to the hospital."
Technically, it was still his patient. A finger's worth
anyway.

He followed the sergeant over to the car. A patrolman was leaning against the side, switching a flashlight on and off for his own amusement.

"We'll take the doc to Regional Medical," said the sergeant, and then . . . "What the hell's the matter with you?"

The patrolman was standing there with his light shining on Hewitt, his mouth slightly ajar. The sergeant turned to check whatever phenomenon had turned his man to stone.

"Jesus, Doc," he said, "you are a sight to behold."

Hewitt looked down at his hands. They were covered with blood. His arms up to the elbows were drenched with blood, and there were stains on his shirt front and jacket . . . his topcoat, somewhere down there, ripped to hell and to hell with it.

"I'll wash off when we get to the hospital," he said. "I didn't think a little blood would bother you guys."

"It's not us," said the sergeant. "It's the car. This is our first new one in four years."

They proceeded to the hospital at a sedate pace, Hewitt in the back seat, the only sound that of the radio crackling out messages every few seconds about a number something or other taking place here or a suspected something or other number taking place there.

Death and disaster by the numbers, Hewitt told himself. I wonder what our number was, the boy and me. What number did they put on our little business?

They pulled up in front of the hospital emergency entrance, and the sergeant was outside and had Hewitt's door open before he'd settled back from the brake inertia.

"Park over there on the side," he told the patrolman through the open door, "and come in for a cup of coffee."

"Jesus, Sarge," the policeman started to say, and then thought better of it. The car started to move off as Hewitt was not quite out of it, and he had to jump a bit so as not to be caught by the door. The sergeant started to move off after the car, then came back. His face was flushed, but he said no word as he held the wide glass door open for Hewitt. The emergency room was deserted except for the nurse on duty behind her desk and an orderly mopping the floor.

The nurse stood up as Hewitt moved toward her. It was Lorraine Hall, one of Hewitt's favorites, and he waited for the insult with which she usually greeted him. He suddenly realized that she didn't know who he was, that the look on her face was that of a professional sizing up a situation. Then she knew.

"Doctor," she said, terribly concerned, "are you all right?"

"I'm fine. But where's the patient?"

"Patient?"

"The boy. The car accident."

Relief flooded her face. "That's his blood all over you. They took him right up to surgery. Dr. Stanton was waiting here and ordered him up. It didn't look good."

"Quiet night?"

"Except for that. Do you need treatment?"

"Don't look so hopeful. I have a few cuts and scrapes, but all I need is a good scrub."

She followed him across the room and pulled the curtain from the cubicle housing the sink. He felt the jacket sliding off his shoulders and held his arms back from his sides to facilitate the removal. Back in the chain of command where things happened to other people and not oneself. The doctor was about to scrub himself clean of a young boy with his balls torn asunder.

"Shall I get you a jacket and then you can take the shirt off and we'll throw it away?" she asked.

Hewitt turned to look at her and saw Frank Stanton enter from the hospital corridor. He was in his greens, the face mask dangling under his chin, the arms of his gown blotched with bloodstains.

The two doctors approached each other and stopped a few feet apart, reading the signs. Stanton raised his hand high in the air and then dropped it, turning his palm toward Hewitt and spreading the fingers.

"There wasn't a chance," said Stanton. "I don't know why the hell I had them take him up there; he was done when they brought him in. But that's where I work"—and his hand pointed toward the operating rooms—"and I thought maybe I could pull a miracle or something. There aren't any miracles. There aren't even any somethings."

"How'd you know I'd be here?"

"They told me Dr. Hewitt wanted me to come in to the hospital for an emergency. I was just about to leave for the meeting." He looked at his watch. "I didn't feel like going to the goddamned thing in the first place. I knew you'd follow your patient in. How was it?"

"I couldn't reach anything. Just poke a finger here or there. He was wrapped in steel."

"I almost shit when I found a necktie in there. Were you trying to plug up the artery?"

"Yeah. Did it work?"

"I don't think so. The whole chest was crushed, and he had a perforation of the abdomen. The shock factor must have been instantaneous. Just the blood you soaked up would have been enough to kill him."

"I never saw his face."

"What?"

"I never . . . I'm sorry I dragged you in, but I knew it was more than any resident could handle, and if there was a chance, he needed all the time he could get."

"Any time. Any time. We're having a bad run, aren't we?"

"What?"

"Bardwell. What the hell happened there?"

"I don't know. Adams said he'd check through, but I haven't heard anything yet."

"It's the goddamnedest situation I ever heard of. Who signed the death certificate?"

"I don't know that either. I couldn't read the name. It looked like an *SH* at the beginning of it, but I couldn't make out what it was."

"This whole hospital is falling apart," said Stanton. "I think it's time the hospital committee of the society should call a special meeting and have it all thrashed out."

"They're more worried about the laundry than they are about the medicine," said Hewitt.

"There was no indication of any coronary problems," said Stanton. "I've been going over the whole thing. We should have had an autopsy."

"He'd already been processed when I got to the funeral home," said Hewitt.

"Damned peculiar. You let me know what you find out. Good night, Alex."

Hewitt kept his eyes on him until he had passed through the connecting door to the hospital. Christ, he had to be somewhere in his sixties. Hands steady as rocks. Go forever.

Hewitt held his own hands up and looked at them. A slight trembling. And spots of blood. Sticks like glue.

"Do you want me to get that jacket for you?"

Nurse Hall, who had withdrawn beyond earshot while the doctors conferred, was now back in action.

"No. No, thanks, Hall. I'll just toddle on home."

"It's cold out there."

"I'll be all right."

"You stay right there, Doctor. Don't move."

She was back in a minute with an old windbreaker with a torn sleeve and hustled around behind him to slip it on.

"We took this off a man several months ago," she said, "and somehow it never went up to his room, and he didn't come in for it when he checked out. Just throw it away when you're through with it."

"Throw it away, hell," he said as he slipped his arms into it, "it's better than anything I can afford."

They were both still laughing as he went out the door to

the entrance and started to move toward the parking lot. He stopped still. Christ, he'd have to get a cab or ask. . . .

"Hey, Doc," said a voice behind him, and he turned to find the sergeant moving out from the wall against which he'd been leaning.

"Kid didn't make it, did he?" asked the sergeant.

Hewitt shook his head.

"I was pretty sure when we pulled him out of there," said the sergeant. "But you do it by the book. You always do it by the book."

"I didn't even have room to open the book," said Hewitt.

"You did fine, Doc, just fine. There aren't too many people would have done what you did."

The tips of Hewitt's fingers tingled as they felt again the gaping wound in the groin area, and he closed his hands into fists to wipe it out.

"Give you a ride home?" asked the sergeant.

"What?" said Hewitt, wiping his hands on the greasy-feeling windbreaker.

"You still haven't got a car," said the sergeant, "and you need a ride home. Or is there somewhere else you want to go?"

"No," said Hewitt, "home is the place. But there's no. . . ."

"No problem at all," said the sergeant. "I have to go in and write my report, and you are right on the way."

"Which way?" asked Hewitt with a smile, following the sergeant out to the police car by the side of the driveway.

"Any way where your house is." The sergeant smiled. He pulled open the front door and leaned in. "We're going to take the doctor to his house now," he told the policeman who was sitting erectly behind the wheel. "You have any more questions you want to ask?" The driver didn't answer, just reached down and turned the key.

No words were exchanged on the ride to Hewitt's house. The night was cold and clear, and Hewitt sat back in the seat, his body drained of all energy, his mind blank. There could be snow for Thanksgiving.

The sergeant was as fast in springing out for the door as he had been at the hospital.

"Thanks," said Hewitt, "I appreciate it."

"Doc," said the sergeant, "I ain't the greatest admirer of medical men that's living in the world today. But you are one hell of a guy in my book. It took balls to crawl into that car in the first place, and it took balls to stay there while the torch man worked. If you ever need anything, you just ask for Sergeant Torchio."

While Hewitt was pondering the words, unable to come up with something appropriate in return that would give the situation the right light touch, the sergeant was back in the car and the driver had zoomed into the turnaround and started down the driveway. Hewitt watched the taillight as the vehicle sped into darkness.

"Cuticles," he said aloud into the clear air, "my courage comes from cuticles." And he went into the darkened house.

vi

THE dog was waiting to greet him in the kitchen, and he held down his hand for the cold nose, but all he received was a strange whine and the sharp scuffle of claws trying to back up on a slippery surface. Hewitt looked down to his hand and saw the blackened blood on the shirt sleeve, some of it still moist after all that . . . it seemed like days had passed . . . who should have signed the death certificate?. . . Stanton? Yes, Stanton. *SH. SH.* I have two bodies lying in state tonight. Win a few, lose them all.

He walked over to the telephone on the counter.

"Dr. McCord called. He will call you tomorrow."

Not if I call him first. How would that be for an announcement at the medical society? Dr. McCord wants the kikes to be bounced. Loud applause. He also runs away from accidents. They'd probably applaud that, too, the sons of bitches.

"Mrs. Parkhurst called. Would like you to call back."

Parkhurst? Who the Christ is Parkhurst? One of the cover cases? Was anybody out of town?

He dialed the number. It was picked up on the second ring.

"Dr. Hewitt?" This house didn't get many nighttime calls.

"Yes."

"This is Mrs. Parkhurst."

"Yes."

"I am Mrs. Markham's daughter."

"Oh, yes. What's the problem?"

"Well, it's hard to say. It's just that she's been not quite herself."

"In what way?"

"Well, she had her glasses on funny this afternoon, sort of pushed on one side, and when I asked her why she was doing it, she didn't know they were on funny. And then she just sort of sat there this afternoon with her mouth hanging open a little, and once in a while spit would run out the side. She ate her supper all right, and she talked all right, but it wasn't like Mother at all."

"Where is she now?"

"She's asleep, sound asleep."

"In bed?"

"Of course, in bed."

"How does she seem?"

"Seems all right."

"How does her breathing seem?"

"What do you mean?"

"Does she seem to be breathing normally?"

"Sounds same as ever to me."

A small insult to the brain. That fine, sweet brain.

"Mrs. Parkhurst."

"Yes, Doctor."

"I think we should let her be for the night. You might check her now and again, and if anything seems out of the ordinary, call me. But I'll be over in the morning. Keep her in bed until I get there."

"All right, Doctor."

"What's your address, please?"

"Forty-six Mamaroneck."

He wrote it down. "Good night."

"Good night, Doctor."

Good night, Doctor, good night, Doctor, good night, Doctor, are you going to leave us now? His pulse was thready. Weak and thready. He looked up at the second hand sweeping across the kitchen clock. Another little tablet? He stood there, swaying a bit, ready for peaceful oblivion. It did not come, and he switched off the light and headed upstairs for the bedroom.

Betsy was in bed reading when he walked into the room, and she did not look up until she had finished the paragraph. "My God," she said, leaping out of bed and running toward him, "are you all right?"

She stopped a foot away, her hand half extended, but her mind unwilling to touch anything.

"You ought to see the other guy," he said, and started to unbutton the shirt. She fluttered around, offering little gestures with her hands but not making a definitive move. The cloth stuck to him in a couple of places, but he finally had the whole thing off and wadded into a ball.

"No sense putting this in the laundry," he said, and dumped it in the corner. His T-shirt was also soaked, and his pants had huge, dark stains. He wadded all his clothes, including his shorts, and dumped them on top of the shirt. Then he sat down on the chair and took off his shoes and socks.

She was standing in front of him in a shortie nightgown, her body still somewhat pink from a long, hot bath, smelling of the oil that had glistened the water. Her breath was coming in little gasps, and he felt his prick harden between his legs as he looked at her, the first time in over a year that tumescence hadn't been forced by the artful manipulation of her tongue, and he stood up and reached for

her, this live woman, and started kissing her on the mouth
and moving his hands over her body, tracing the swell of
her buttocks, pushing in on the large, firm breasts, down
between her legs where the wet was pouring out of her, and
they moved back till they felt the bed against them and
sank down to it, her hand squeezing him fiercely, exult-
ingly, the first time in oh-so-long since she had felt him so
strong, so at one with her, and her lips sought out the crev-
ices of his face, her tongue licking his lips, his cheeks, she
tasted the salt of . . . of . . . of blood, and she had to ask,
had to know.

"What happened?" she said, her mouth still searching for
all of him, her hand still holding him, never let go.

"An accident," he said, sensing it was a question that she
had to have answered. "A boy went off the road in his car."

"Is he all right?" she asked, her teeth feeling his tongue
slipping into her mouth, his fingers working into her, as she
pulled her mouth away and kissed his chest, moving her
tongue lightly up under his chin, the tip resting in the cleft.

"No," he said, moving over her, and she tasted the salt in
her mouth again, the salt of the blood of the boy who was
dead, and she gave a low moan of keening, a pain ripping
through her womb as she spat the saliva from her mouth,
spitting and spitting and spitting, and he rolled over and
looked at her, his eyes wide, and she saw his manhood
falling between his legs again, the bloodstains on his arms,
his body, all over covered with blood, and she jumped from
the bed and ran to the bathroom, where she fell to her
knees, retching over and over, but nothing would come up.
She sat there, her head against the cool bowl, until finally
the involuntary motions ceased, but the pain remained in
her belly, right down through her womb. As she stood and
started to brush her teeth again, working up gobs of suds in
her mouth, he came in and turned on the water in the
shower stall, stepping in before the water turned warm. In
the mirror, she saw how his body shrank from the cold

water, but he did not move aside, stood there until it was hot enough to be adjusted and then started soaping from head to toe. She spat out the foam and rinsed her mouth, then went back in the bedroom, turned out her reading light and crawled under the covers. She was terribly cold and lay there shivering, her eyes wide with nameless fear, her mind frozen into blankness. Long before he was through in the bathroom, she was asleep, her body taking what refuge it could as quickly as possible.

He barely looked at her as he slipped into clean pajamas, and he was careful to slide into bed so that he did not touch her by chance. He put out the light and stared up at the ceiling, seeing objects by the dim reflection of the digital clock on the bureau. He didn't know whether he had slept or not, whether it was a minute or an hour, when the phone on his nightstand rang, and he reached out automatically to lift the receiver.

"Yes?"

"Doctor?"

"Yes."

"I need you."

"Yes."

"I'm in pain."

With this one it was always pain. Everything in terms of pain.

"Where?"

"The usual places."

"I'd better come over."

"Thank you, Doctor."

He hung up and swung his feet over the side of the bed. The clarity was still there, the easy feel in the shoulders. A punch of the button brought the whole room into light, and he looked over to Betsy, her eyes closed and breathing regularly. In the early years each call in the night had been an adventure for her, especially the stormy ones in the dead of winter. She would lie awake with the light on, ready to quiz him about the road conditions, the bite of the wind, the condition of the patient. But now she kept herself in a semicomatose state, half awake and aware, but ready to fall into sleep again the instant the room went dark. A few times, when he had been annoyed with her or too preoccupied with the state of the patient to think about it, he had gone off without turning out the light, and she had slithered right back into sleep despite the brightness. But mostly he turned it off, as he did now.

The fresh underclothes and shirt felt soft on his skin, and he moved his shoulders to increase the sensation. The car was chilly, and he punched in the fan to push the heated air through the system faster. Lights were still on in some of the houses, and in many the colored tube could be seen glaring through the window. Fucking idiots. Watching a movie about a young doctor who is in love with a terminal cancer. Pounding somebody on the chest to get the heart started. Works every time on television. Did anybody pound Bardwell's chest? *SH*.

He swung the car into the driveway and turned off the motor. There was a faint luminescence through one of the windows but no porch light. The hedges screened the world away, and it was dark as hell. The bag seemed lighter than usual, and he swung it a bit in rhythm with his steps.

There was just enough light coming from the back of the house for him to pick his way as he pushed open the front door into the hall. He walked through to the kitchen where she was standing with a tall drink in one hand, a cigarette in the other. She was wearing a pink quilted robe, which contrasted nicely with her salt-and-pepper hair. She put the drink down on the counter and stuck the cigarette in the side of her mouth, the rising column of smoke forcing her to squint a bit.

"Oh, Doctor," she said, "I'm glad you could come."

"What's the problem?" he asked, dropping the bag on the floor.

"I hurt," she said.

"Where?"

"It hurts me here . . . and here," she said, pulling her hands into her full breasts until the pink-clothed flesh pushed through her fingers. "And down here," she continued, sliding her right hand into her crotch.

"Well," he said, pulling off his raincoat and throwing it over the counter, "I think kindly Dr. Hewitt has just the right home treatment for that."

vii

THERE was a pain in the right knee that wouldn't go away. It had started at the beginning of the second mile and was locked in just behind the patella. He went over the configuration of the knee as he ran, sorting the muscles and cartilage into ordered ranks, but the pain did not fit into any pattern.

"Take two aspirin every four hours, and let me know how it goes," he gasped into the brightening air, clouds of vapor thrust before him. The gray house with green shutters, the two-mile marker. He circled and started on the homing run. The sweat was forming in his hair under the knit cap, in his armpits, the small of the back and the pubic area. The weight of his testicles pushing against the supporter felt good, that poor young bastard having his balls scooped out by a piece of hot metal, just like Nam, shrapnel and automobiles, the curse of the young.

A car went by him, its headlights on, and he could feel the eyes of the driver, wondering who this crazy son of a bitch might be. Oh, I'm a crazy son of a bitch all right. Up half the night fucking a weirdo and participating in all kinds of deviate practices. Jesus Christ, she's something.

That first time, at the party. Alex, I don't feel well. Will you take me home? Poor dear recently bereaved widow. Betsy so concerned. Wanted to come along. No, dear, no you stay and have your good time. Helping her up the stairs to the bedroom, what can I do for you, Mary? You can screw me, Alex, that's what you can do for me. Didn't even undress, long skirt up around her ears, my pants caught at the knees, my prick so hard it. . . . And Betsy . . . Betsy. . . . Is she all right, Alex? All right? She's great. And Betsy . . . Betsy . . . calling her up the next morning to see if there was anything she could do. No, dear, Alex, took care of me fine . . . I guess I'm just. . . . And Betsy . . . Betsy . . . letting everybody. . . .

The knee eased up a bit. Nature is the best medicine. The third mile marker passed him going in the other direction. Am I running away from death or trying to catch him? Tell me, Doc, is all this exercise crap worthwhile? I mean, does it make you live longer? Well, we really don't know . . . he stumbled going up the driveway but caught himself quickly and finished on his toes by the garage door, checking the pulse, around one hundred and thirty, breathing easily, not bad, not bad.

The chill air went right through the sweat suit, and the warmth of the kitchen was a welcoming embrace. Betsy was by the stove measuring fresh-ground coffee into the filter paper, her brows furrowed to hit the line right on the mark. A glass of orange juice was awaiting him on the counter, a 500-milligram ascorbic acid tablet beside it.

"Do you or don't you prescribe vitamins?" she asked as he placed the tablet on his tongue and washed it down with the juice.

Friendly. Last night was last night, and today is today. Why not?

"I tell them they are unnecessary with a well-balanced diet."

"Your diet is balanced."

"Well, we get all these free samples and. . . ."

"But you don't tell me to take them; you don't tell the children to take. . . ."

"Well, take them. There's a whole goddamned closet full of all kinds of crap and you. . . ."

"That isn't the point."

He stopped with the glass halfway down to the counter and looked at her. "Well, what is the point?"

"The point is that you seem to be going on one track, and we seem to be going on another the last couple of years."

"Oh?"

"At first I thought it was because of your experiences in Vietnam. . . ."

"What the hell do you know about my experiences in Vietnam?"

"Only what you told me"—she wasn't going to quit—"but when I thought back, I realized it was even before you went in the Army. . . ."

"Dragged. Dragged. They dragged me into the Army."

"Well, whatever"—she wasn't going to let it shake loose from her teeth . . . lying there last night while I—"but the point is that somewhere along the line we have gotten off the track. . . ."

"Hey," he said, loud enough to stop her.

"Yes."

"You seem to be comparing our marriage to a railroad."

"Well, what I. . . ."

"They're dying, you know," he said, and went upstairs to shower.

He took his time at breakfast and was affable to everybody, asking about schoolwork and if the new brace adjustment was too tight and whether anybody was interested in a snowmobile. As he stood up from the table, Betsy told him that Jeff had a sore spot on his heel from his new shoes and she thought it should be looked at. "Soak it in warm salt water," he said, as he went through the door, "and put a piece of foam in the back of the shoe."

viii

HEWITT went straight to Jonathan Adams'
office when he entered the hospital, but before he could utter
a word, the secretary, chewing on God knew what, said,
"Mr. Adams isn't here."

Hewitt glanced at the clock, the big hand on the three
and the little hand on the eight as this dumb son of a bitch
probably read it, and said, "I know, but when he comes in,
I want—"

"He's out of town."

"When will he be back?"

"I don't know. He's at a conference."

"He must have given you some idea of when he would be
back."

"He said Thursday. Thursday or Friday."

"Did he leave any message for me?"

"About what?"

"About the Bardwell matter."

"What's that?"

"He's a patient who. . . . Do you know who I am?"

"Yes."

"Who?"

"You're Dr. Hewitt."

"Well, did Mr. Adams leave any message for Dr. Hewitt?"

"I don't think so."

"Don't you know?"

"I don't know that he left any message for you."

"Well, you tell him that. . . ." He looked down on that face, the jaws moving rhythmically—gum, she must be chewing gum—moved his hand toward her and opened the fingers . . . spun on his heel and left the office.

He was still seething when he reached his first patient on the third floor, a pneumonia, doing nicely, and the progress calmed him down to where he began to function, the hysterectomy case barely hysterical, Mr. Gold cheered by a normal bowel movement. But then he came upon a simple intravenous setup fouled up by one of the Filipino interns, and his hands shook as he ran his fingers over the blue-black marks on the patient's arm, yelling that he "never again wanted any one of those sons of bitches screwing around any one of my patients." He informed the floor charge of this in a way that made the student nurses press close to the corners of the corridors and giggle nervously in their palms. That cute Dr. Hewitt could be a bear when something went the way he didn't want it to.

Hewitt took the elevator to the basement and walked into Casey's office in pathology. The huge head was glued to a microscope, and it took three pats on the shoulder to shake him out of his concentration.

"That's the goddamnedest cancer cell I ever saw," he told Hewitt, almost not knowing to whom he was talking, just wanting someone to participate in the marvel. "Take a look."

"I can't tell one from another without a scorecard," said Hewitt. "Come on have a coffee with me."

"I just got back from having a coffee with Stern," said

Casey, pulling himself to his feet. "Is that all you doctors have to do all day?"

Hewitt took a mug of black coffee while Casey snagged two glazed doughnuts and a glass of milk.

"Jesus," said Hewitt, watching the second doughnut disappear while he was still preparing to take his first cautious sip, "you're a textbook case. Who is your doctor?"

"You'll do as well as anybody," said Casey, taking a long draw on his milk.

"Seriously, Frank, you ought to take off some of that blubber and start getting regular exercise."

"I've been thinking about it," said Casey.

"Don't give me any of that crap. I'm—"

"No, you're wrong. I've been seriously thinking about it."

"When do you want to start?"

"Whenever you say."

"Do you have any gym clothes? A jock strap? A sweat shirt?"

"I can buy them."

"Will you meet me at the Y at five this afternoon?"

"Hey, that's a little—"

"No! If you're going to start, let's start. And we'll talk over a diet and all that shit. What do you say?"

"OK. I'll be there."

"You're not going to—"

"I said I'd be there. I'll be there."

Hewitt, expert diagnostician that he was, dropped it and finished his coffee while haggling over odds for a dollar bet on the New York Giants-Philadelphia Eagles game.

"You going to that thing at the club Saturday night?" asked Casey as they were carrying their trays to the window slot.

"Yeah, I'm on the entertainment committee."

"Gerda's been bugging me. Says we never go out. Do you have room at your table?"

"Well," said Hewitt, looking him up and down, "if you will stick to the diet I am about to lay on you, there is a chance we will be able to squeeze you in by Saturday."

"You can squeeze this in right now," said Casey, holding the pudgy middle finger of his right hand up in the air. "See you at five."

There were no calls waiting for Hewitt at the switchboard. "Is Dr. McCord here?" he asked the operator.

"I haven't seen him, Doctor," she said, "but he might not have checked in. Shall I page him?" *Is shit-for-guts McCord in the house? King of the malpracticers. Archfoe of the sheenies. Protector of the divine right of doctors.*

"No," he said, "I'll catch up with him one time or another."

And what will you do? Punch him in the mouth? Yell at him? Tell him off?

He wedged himself into the car seat and pulled the slim black book from his inside pocket. There was only one entry: Parkhurst—46 Mamaroneck.

The house was set among others of its kind, a lower-middle-income development that had bulldozed the area so that all Mamaroneck and adjoining streets were divided into exactly equal parts. Someone had started a fad for flowering crab trees in the area, and birds were busily picking over the desiccating fruits as Hewitt pulled up to number 46.

Mrs. Parkhurst was her mother's daughter, tall, thin, somewhere around fifty-five, desiccating nicely in her orderly existence. Her friends would hear no complaints about what a burden it was to care for an aging mother. She was the kind who took it for granted that the umpire knew what he was doing when it was her turn at bat.

Uttering polite pleasantries, she guided him through the ritual of coat removal and disposal and then into the living room, where her mother sat in a comfortable chair by a window, encased in a blue flannel robe and with a light wool blanket thrown across her feet. Her lips moved into what she thought was a smile for the doctor, but as the thin face creased before him, Hewitt realized that she did not have the year he had predicted for the daughter after the exploratory, that the body was beginning to break into little pieces.

"Well," he said, sitting down beside her and taking the thin wrist between his fingers, "how are we doing?"

"I had a bad night, Doctor," she said, her voice quavering a bit, the brave front cracked by whatever cells had been destroyed the day before. "I woke up when it was all black and I tried to call my daughter, but I couldn't get any words out, I couldn't move. And I lay there for what seemed hours and hours before she finally came. And when I went to tell her that I couldn't talk, I could talk. And I could move. It was all like a bad dream."

"Maybe it was a bad dream," said Hewitt. "Sometimes we think we are awake when we are really having a bad dream."

"I'm going to die, aren't I?"

"We're all going to die." He looked down at his bag, wherein lay his stethoscope and his hypodermic kits and the various specifics that helped ease this or that or something else, and he could not make his hands move down to open the case. What good would it do to listen to her heart or check the dressing on her surgical scar? She was going to die. And he was going to die. She had been saying something to him. He looked around, but the daughter had withdrawn to the kitchen to give privacy to the doctor and his patient.

"What?"

"Is there going to be a great deal of pain? That's all I keep thinking about, that there's going to be a great deal of pain, and for some reason, suddenly, I can't bear to think of that."

"Do you feel pain now?"

"No, not really. It's just that I feel I'm about to have

pain, as though pain was standing there, waiting to move in."

"I have things for that," he said. "I can protect you from pain."

She put her hand around his wrist, holding him gently. He could feel his pulse against her fingertips, and he held his breath for a moment, waiting for her to tell him that the beat was sound, that he was going to be fine.

"I couldn't do this without you," she said. "You are all that is keeping me going. It is you I think of in the dark when I can't move or speak. It is you I hang onto."

"Is this your only daughter?" he asked, trying to move some of the blind faith to a shared responsibility.

"My only child," she said, taking her hand back to her lap. "My husband was killed in the railroad yard fifty-one years ago, and she was all we had."

"What did you do then?" he asked, surprised by this new facet.

"I went back to teaching. The railroad money wasn't enough to live on. Taught fourth grade for the next thirty-eight years."

"I'm an only child," said Hewitt, "but I think that's because my parents found that they didn't like having children."

"Oh, go on," she said, showing some of the sparkle that had shone so bravely in the hospital.

"No, really," he said, as much for himself as for her, because it was something he never had articulated before, "they seemed to resent the intrusion. They're private people, don't even talk much to each other or smile. They have always been good to me, didn't stint on anything. But it was all stuff that would keep me occupied and away from them."

"What does your father do?"

"He owns a jewelry store, and he spends seven days a week in it."

"Did they give you this beautiful watch?" she asked, reaching out her long thin finger and placing the point on the crystal.

"Yes, last Christmas." He looked around, bewildered for a moment, then remembered the bag and unsnapped the catch, pulling out the stethoscope. He stared at it and then placed it back in the case, lifting out instead the medicine case.

"I'm going to give you some tablets to take when you go to bed," he said, "and maybe we can at least do away with the bogeyman."

Running his fingers down the tops, he selected one with a red cover and pried it up. There were only three tablets in it. What the hell was the matter with Moore? He had told her to check the case every Friday. Pulling off the cap, he tipped the three tablets onto the table beside the chair.

"Take one of these when you go to bed," he said. "I'll bring some more when I come tomorrow."

"Oh, that's nice."

"What?"

"That you're going to come tomorrow."

Why had he said that? There was no need to come tomorrow. Or until called. It was just a matter of time. And that was all he could give her. His time. But he didn't have that much time. There was. . . . How much time did he have? No, not that kind of time. His own time. *How much time do I have?*

"Well, I thought I'd spoil you for a couple of days. And I have to bring your tablets anyway."

"I've been thinking," she began tentatively, then paused.

"Yes?"

"I've been thinking that maybe I would be more comfortable in a nursing home, after all, that—"

"Hey." It took a very small "hey" to stop her.

"Yes?"

"You'd really rather be here, wouldn't you?"

"Yes."

"If I didn't know that she wanted you, I'd order you to a home."

She looked at him searchingly, worriedly, defensively. "You mean that, don't you?"

"Doctors can't afford to lie."

"You'll see me through." Was it a question, a statement, an order?

"All the way."

A tiny tear appeared on each bottom eyelid, reflecting the sun coming through the window. Hewitt watched for a few seconds, waiting for them to fall, but they hung immobile on the edge, obeying whatever natural laws held the most potency, and he stood up and patted the woman on the shoulder, hefted his bag and walked out to the hallway. Mrs. Parkhurst appeared simultaneously from the kitchen, smoothing her dress from where it had been bound by the apron strings.

The coat was fetched, and as Hewitt slipped it on, he studied the look of polite questioning before him.

"I've left a few sleeping tablets," he said, "and she is to take one when she goes in for the night. I'll drop by tomorrow with some more."

The look was still there.

"I think," he said, "the deterioration is going to be much more rapid than I indicated to you in the hospital. It's hard to know how these things are going to go. There could be a period of remission. Or a sudden regression. My main concern is to make it as easy as possible for her. That might not be so easy for you. You will have to tell me if it is too much, if you want her to go into a nursing home. It may be that she will have to go into a nursing home anyway in order to get the right care."

The face resumed its normal pleasantness.

"My husband and I have talked this over," she said. "And we will do our best to see that Mama"—was there a slight break, a catch, a hesitation, a quiver?—"has everything she needs here even if it means bringing in someone to help."

Would I do this for my parents, Hewitt wondered. Would my children do it for me? Betsy would. Hers. Or mine. Me? Suppose the old brain cells blow and she's got a nice vegetable on her hands? She'd fertilize and water and prune the roots. She prunes my root now. Shorter and shorter and shorter. A rootless man. He thought back on the old bitch of the night before. The taste of tobacco and whiskey from her mouth, the folds of fat, the heavy perfume sloshed on the cunt to cover the stink of old pussy. And a hard-on from here to tomorrow. He felt the blood move to his penis as he stared at this nice woman who was going to help her mother die as easily as possible.

"I'll be back tomorrow," he said, and went out the door.

It was seventeen minutes past eleven. There was still that mountain of paper work at the office, but he didn't feel like doing any paper work. He stared straight out the windshield, seeing nothing, and ran his hand down between his legs where his prick was still distended from thoughts of that old bitch. Perhaps. . . . Perhaps. . . . Perhaps shit. He started the car, gunned the motor and moved out into traffic, cutting in front of one of Mrs. Parkhurst's neighbors, who was about to pull out of her driveway on the way to the market. Hewitt grinned as he thought of what she would be telling her husband at dinner that night. Probably the most exciting event in her whole week.

God, how long had it been? He took lefts and rights, slowly, carefully, grinning to himself, until finally, there it was, the two-story colonial in cocoa brown. He always thought of it as dirty brown. Dirty. Dirty. Dirty brown.

His bag felt light to him as he strode up the walk. Moore. Moore. He must tell Moore to fill the bottles. He rang the bell.

There was genuine surprise on her face when she opened

the door. Christ, it was good to know that something could move that slack jaw into another position.

"Well," she said, "well, well."

He didn't wait for an invitation but started to move forward, so that she faded back as his bulk approached.

"Well," she said again, as he closed the door behind him, "look who's here. Mr. Stranger. To what do I owe the honor of this visit?"

She was dressed in dark-blue baggy slacks that were covered with lint of some kind and a dirty blouse, a terribly dirty blouse. Brown. She reeked of brown.

"Just thought I'd see how you were doing." He grinned. "Oh, sure."

He dropped his bag on the hallway floor and walked into the living room. She followed. He looked around at the opaque curtains covering the windows, then sat down on the couch, clear of the coffee table. She stood in front of him, her face set in a stubborn mask, her lips pursed.

"Six months," she said. "Six months and now out of the blue. You're pretty goddamn sure of yourself."

"How are you?" he asked, standing again to remove his topcoat.

"What do you care? I left a dozen messages for you, and you never called once."

"I was busy," he said, slipping off his jacket and dropping it on top of the coat.

"Busy! I'll bet you were busy. Well, you can just busy out of here."

"Is the bedroom where it was six months ago?" he asked, catching her by the arm.

"I'm not a goddamned thing," she almost sobbed, turning as he pointed her, starting to lead as well as follow. "You just can't come and go as you please."

He slid his hand down her arm until his fingers were in her palm, and she tightened her grip until she was holding him firmly, pulling now so that he had to quicken his pace to keep up as they came into the hall and started up the stairs.

He knew the bed wouldn't be made and the sheets would be heavy with the odor of stale sweat, but it fit his mood exactly, and he breathed deep in anticipation.

ix

SHE must have moved her hand for some reason—it could only have been her hand that caused it—but as the cold coffee cascaded over her lap, soaking through the robe and the nightgown, Betsy leaped to her feet in realization that time had passed unknowingly again, not seconds or minutes, but a chunk, a whole chunk.

This had been happening increasingly of late, but it was only now that her consciousness pushed the matter to awareness, forced her to acknowledge and inspect it. The incidents flooded into the open—standing at the sink looking unseeingly out the window; holding the telephone in her hand, listening to the infinite buzz, unsure whether she was about to call or had just called; bending over the hamper of dirty clothes, her thumb running unendingly over the nylon panties; sitting in the chair with the cup of coffee, stone cold, perhaps one sip taken, and not remembering when it had been hot.

I must leave this man, she thought. I must leave this man before he destroys these children as he has destroyed me. They react as carefully to his good moments as they do to his bad. Has he destroyed me? Has he turned me into a thing?

She walked over to her purse hanging on the doorknob and extracted cigarettes and matches, lifted a metal ashtray from the top of the refrigerator and returned to her chair. Despite the soggy material clinging to her body, she felt comfortable amid the mess of the breakfast she had so carefully prepared so that her family would have a balanced diet, would grow healthy and strong.

But I owe them more than eggs and bacon, she thought, as she pulled the first blast of the hot smoke into her lungs. I owe them protection. Protection from what? Protection from him. But he is their father; he is their protector. Just as my father is my protector.

She stuck her cigarette along the furrow in the ashtray, lifted her purse from the doorknob and placed it on the kitchen table after shoving dishes and crumbs aside. She rummaged in the cavernous interior until her fingers closed on the thin leather case, which she carefully withdrew and laid on the table. A fingernail released the snap and the compartments unfolded.

"Open Sesame," she said aloud, and smoothed down the clear plastic covers. There was a telephone credit card made out to Betsy Hewitt of 1905 Balmoral Drive, Boca Raton, Fla. An American Express credit card made out to Betsy Hewitt of 1905 Balmoral Drive, Boca Raton, Fla. An Avis credit card made out to Betsy Hewitt of 1905 Balmoral Drive, Boca Raton, Fla. An Interbank credit card made out to Betsy Hewitt of 1905 Balmoral Drive, Boca Raton, Fla. And a Texaco credit card made out to Betsy Hewitt of 1905 Balmoral Drive, Boca Raton, Fla.

Tucked into the last of the pliofilm compartments were three checks, which she pulled out and unfolded. Each one was for two hundred dollars, each one was made out to Betsy Hewitt, and each one was signed by James Prentiss. She carefully smoothed the checks with her fingers. The most recent one was dated two weeks before, and the oldest one, which had dirt in its creases, went back to the spring of the year. She had better cash that one soon, or Daddy's accountants would be complaining to him again.

But it was so difficult to conceal two hundred dollars, as difficult as to spend it unnoticeably. Just the week before Alex had asked her about Bobbi's new pantsuit. Like a thief in the night. Suppose she bought Jeff a pair of those crazy foam ski boots. *Oh, Christ, I forgot to have him soak his foot.* Cash all the checks and throw the money right down in front of Alex. My daddy sent me that. He'll send me all I need. Or want. Keep all your money to yourself. Keep it all. Just let us live in peace.

The tears were running down her face, and she saw that the cigarette had fallen off the ashtray and made a brown spot on the place mat. Time was blanking out on her more and more, tears falling on their own; less and less control of more and more. Why? Why? Why? Why? Why? Why?

She looked down at her clenched fist going up and down on the table. Soundlessly. Even when he wasn't there, she was afraid to protest so that anybody would know. What was she afraid of? What if he did walk out? Oh, my God, what if he did?

She picked up a napkin and dried her eyes, started to stack the plates and put them down. Her fingers lifted the card case and held it before her eyes. She walked through the house to Alex's den, sat down at the desk, picked up the phone and dialed zero.

"I want to make a credit card call," she told the operator, and recited the list of numbers and letters. The buzzings and the clickings lulled her into a numbness so that she was startled into speechlessness when her daddy said, "Hello."

"Hello!" he repeated vehemently. James Prentiss wasn't used to having to say things twice.

"Hello, Daddy," she said, so close to tears again that she bit her bottom lip to bleeding.

"Betsy!" he exploded. "Mother, it's Betsy. Get on another phone. Betsy, I said. Hey there, how are ya, Betsy?"

"Fine, Daddy."

"And the children?"

Her mother broke in. "Betsy, is that you, Betsy?"

"Yes, Mama, it's me." She could hear her voice grow softer as she started to slur her words. I'll be sucking my thumb in a minute, she thought.

"How are you, Betsy?"

"Just fine, Mama."

"And the children? How are the children?"

"Gettin' bigger all the time."

"Betsy"—her father couldn't wait any longer—"when are you coming down here? I'm sittin' right now and lookin' over a swimmin' pool that nobody swims in and a boat that nobody goes out in. We need three young hellers down here for some conspicuous consumption."

"Oh, Daddy, it sounds marvelous."

"How's the weather up there, Betsy?" her mother wanted to know.

"Oh, it's cold and gray and gloomy."

"Any snow?"

"No, not yet. But any morning now we'll wake up and there it will be. For months and months and months."

"We've got the air conditioning going full blast," her father shouted. "You come on down here and warm up."

"Oh, Daddy, we'd love nothing better. But there's school and Jojo has to go to the orthodontist every other week and—"

"Come down for a weekend," her father yelled. "I'll have tickets ready for you in the morning."

"That's mighty temptin', but I think it would make the winter here seem all the longer."

"Is everybody feeling well?" her mother wanted to know.

"Fine, just fine. How about you people?"

"Oh, we're just . . ." her mother began when her father

broke in with "Your mom gave us a little scare this week . . ." when her mother said sharply, "Jim, you keep your big . . ." when Betsy broke in with "Please, please, now tell me what happened," silencing both the parents.

"Well," said her father, "she got these pains in bed the other night and we called Doc Harris, and he knocked her out, and then we took some tests, and it seems she's got some angina."

"It's really nothing," said her mother, "just that I'm getting old and worn-down. Nothing to worry about. It's all part of nature."

"What did the doctor say?" asked Betsy.

"He said for her to take it easy for a couple of weeks and gave her some pills to take every day and said there'd be some more tests. It's a mild case. Just that there'll have to be some adjustin' in the way she does things."

"You do what the doctor says, Mama, you hear now."

"Don't you worry about that. But the best medicine in the world for me would be to see you and the children."

"We'll try to work something out. How are Lorna and Fred?"

"They're fine, just fine. We'll tell them you called. Sister said she had a letter from you just yesterday."

"Did you call about anything special, honey?" her father asked.

"No, I just got . . . I just thought I'd call before you left for the office and see how everybody was."

"We're fine, just fine. Do you need any money?"

"Lord, no, Daddy. Don't you dare send me any. I've still got three checks left."

"I noticed you'd hardly been using any of those charge cards I had sent to ya. Don't they have nothing to buy up there?"

"We've got everything we need. Now just don't fret about it."

"Are the kids there? Can I talk to them?"

"No. They've been off to school for ages. I just thought I'd call on the spur of the moment. I'll call again and let you talk to them."

"Everything all right, Betsy? Everything really all right?"

"Fine, Daddy, just fine. It does my heart good just to hear your voice."

"The same for us here."

"I better hang up now. This must be costing a fortune."

"Don't you worry about that. Don't you ever worry about that. You call up every morning and every night if you're a mind. Or anything else. Anything else at all, you call, you hear?"

"I hear, Daddy. Good-bye now. Good-bye, Mama."

"Good-bye, Betsy. Come see us. Please."

"I'll try, Mama, I'll really try. 'Bye now."

She placed the phone on the cradle and sat there, the tears running down her face. Another step forward. Or back. This time even her folks had been careful not to mention Alex. Her daddy knew. Her mama knew. But now she couldn't even go home to Mama. Her mama was going to die.

X

AS Hewitt drove into the parking lot of his medical building, he saw the long black Lincoln straddled across two spaces, the driver sitting erectly in front, the visor of his cap squarely centered with military precision. When you worked for Jack Wales, whether you were one of his factory managers or his chauffeur, you did everything as exactly as possible in hopes that it would keep you from getting a kick in the ass, or transferred out of his sight, or fired. The only exceptions to the rule were the top officers of the international corporation for which he worked and his own body. For the present, they seemed oblivious to the possibility of the kick, the transfer or the firing. The body was especially recalcitrant, giving indications that it might, at any moment, blow those high-priced brains into a cerebral hemorrhage of the more spectacular sort and save those top corporate officers from being stepping-stones before their time.

Mrs. Moore was seated at her desk, studying some papers so zealously that she did not raise her head at the sound of the door opening, making it plain to whoever it might be that she was not just annoyed, she was goddamned mad.

Oh, Jesus, thought Hewitt, I forgot to call in. That filthy fucking pig. He could feel the stickiness inside his shorts, the jism clotting the hair on his thigh. Brown. He could feel the brown on him. Was brown contagious? Could you catch brown? Had he been commingling with a bubonic brown?

Moore looked up in round-eyed surprise, not quite batting her lashes, but going so far with the game as to utter an audible "Oh!" She had him by the short ones; he had committed an unpardonable sin.

"I had an emergency," he mumbled. "Is he in there?" nodding his head at the inner office.

"Mr. Wales is in there," she said, "and has been waiting for half an hour. I tried reaching you at the hospital when he called, but they said you had left some time before. He came along on the assumption that you would call in as usual and get his message. I canceled my lunch. . . ."

"Christ sakes, Moore," he barked, "I said I was sorry. Go eat your goddamned lunch and take him with you," waving his hand at the inner office. "I'm getting sick and tired of Wales thinking the whole goddamned world's going to stop whenever his eyes start pushing out of his head."

She jumped up from her desk in alarm at the loudness of his voice, glancing over her shoulder at the closed door that stood between them and the man who employed her husband, who joked with her as though she weren't just a foreman's wife but one of his own kind, who . . .

"OK, OK," said Hewitt, removing his coat, "go get some lunch and we'll start all over when you get back."

"I don't have to—" she started to say when he cut her off with a wave.

"Go get some lunch," he repeated, and went through the door.

Jack Wales was seated in Hewitt's chair making a call,

and he motioned for Hewitt to sit down across from him as he listened carefully to whatever was being said. Hewitt hung his coat in the closet and then sat down in the patient's chair, crossed his legs and waited for his turn to join the party.

"You send that slant-eyed son of a bitch a cable," said Wales into the phone, "and tell him we'll be there Thursday and he better have the goddamned figures right down to the nearest yen." He looked at his watch. "Have the jet ready at four, and we'll fly to New York and get that straightened out before we take off for Tokyo." He hung up without any indication he was through. Hewitt speculated on what the subordinate at the other end of the line might be thinking: Did I goof? Did I say something wrong?

"Well, Alex," said Wales, "you took your own sweet time getting here. Mrs. Moore burned up the wires looking for you. You out getting yourself some secret poon somewhere?"

Alex could feel the stickiness on his leg, and he uncrossed his ankles and stood up.

"Why don't you come sit over here, Jack, and let me sit over there, and then maybe we can get some order out of this mess."

They switched places and Alex glanced down at the pink slips on his desk, nothing urgent, but Picard had called. He reached out for the phone but pulled his hand back. No sense driving the pressure in front of him any higher than it was.

"Well, what can I do for you?"

Wales leaned forward, his elbows on his knees, his ruddy face creased with intentness. This was the dragon of the electronics industry about to talk, summarizing the problem briefly, concisely, accurately.

"I can't shake it," he said, moving his shoulders as though to get some burden off them. "I get up in the morning, and I'm weak in the knees as soon as I roll out of the goddamned bed, and I have this funny feeling in my chest all day, nothing hurts or anything like that, but just a strange sensation like something was going to happen. And then all of a sudden I'll get this crushing pain in the back of my head, just above the neck"—and his hand moved up to rub the spot as though it could shove the problem away —"and I don't like it, Alex, I don't like this whole fucking business one damn bit, and I want it to stop."

Alex didn't say anything but motioned Wales to take the seat next to the desk. While Wales was shedding his jacket and rolling up the shirt sleeve on his left arm, Alex was placing the stethoscope in his ears and pulling the sphygmomanometer into position. He wrapped the rubber around the flabby arm (just me and your wife and your cunt know what a bowl of jello you are, thought Hewitt) and pumped up, listened, pumped a bit more, listened, released the screw and listened all the way down. He jerked until the snaps gave and dropped the stethoscope around his neck.

Wales was looking at him tensely, hoping for good news but expecting and ready for the worst. Hewitt pulled the file folder toward him and wrote the figures under the date.

"Pretty bad, huh?" said Wales.

"Not good."

"How bad?"

"Your systolic is one hundred and ninety-eight, and your diastolic is ninety-four."

"Jesus, that's about as high as I've been. Where do we go from here?"

"Well, for one thing, I'm going to increase your dosage to two pills a day, one at morning and one at night."

"Christ, Alex, the last time you did that I was up all night pissing my brains away."

"Better that than the alternative."

"But isn't there something else we can do? There must be something else."

"Jack, they put you through every test in the book in

those five days in Boston. They even wrung your tit. You
have essential hypertension, no known cause, and you're
just going to have to adjust your life to it until we can work
something out. It's the long run we have to worry about."

"It's been two years now that you've been fucking
around with this problem," snorted Wales. "Do you know
what I would do with a research team that fouled up a job
as bad as you have?"

Hewitt began writing in the file folder again, flipped a
page for a memory check and then sat back in his chair,
rocking slightly on the springs.

"You want to fire me, Jack? Do you think that will help
get your pressure down?"

"I want to straighten out this condition. There must be
something you can do."

"We tried tranquilizers and—"

"I can't work with those things," yelled Wales. "They
made me feel peculiar. I've got to be up on my toes all the
time; my mind has to be sharp."

"We've tried nine different depressants," continued
Hewitt in the same tone, as if he'd never been interrupted,
"none of which seemed to work as well as the one you're on
now. We've tried vacations, and you come back a bigger
mess internally than when you left. I've suggested psychiatric help, and you've threatened to punch me in the nose. I
told you to give up booze, and you're drinking more than
ever."

"It relaxes me," said Jack, "more than any of your goddamned—"

"It'll relax you right out of business one day," said Hewitt. "You'll pull all the oxygen out of your brains, and
there'll be nothing but pure shit left."

Wales leaned back in his chair and smiled at Hewitt, in-
telligence taking over from fear and anger.

"Broads," he said. "How about broads?"

"If you can do it calmly," said Hewitt, "and not have

your heart start pounding when you first realize that a new one is about to come across or have shooting pains in your eyes when you're shooting out of your pecker, then you can have that in moderation. For Christ's sake, you can have everything in moderation. But the big question is, and this is the crucial question, this is the one that all those tests in Boston don't come near: Can you take your job in moderation?"

The two pair of eyes met levelly across the desk.

"Alex," said Wales, his voice full of that vibrant energy that made board meetings come alive and politicians pay attention and women moisten just a tiny bit, "this is something that would be hard for a doctor to understand. You run a piddling one-man business. Every dime you make you make with your hands. You earn a good week's pay because you've got a service that's always needed, but any day you don't work is a day you don't make a penny. I run a department that has eleven plants in four countries, and there are twenty-two thousand people under my finger. I have a fucking jet plane all for me, and I'm going to be in Tokyo on Thursday, where they start bowing even before I get in the room, and I'm going to be back here for the fucking club dance on Saturday. I am thirty-eight years old, and I am going to be president of the whole fucking shmear by the time I am forty-two or I will be president somewhere else. I like the game, Alex. I like to have the money rolling in with the options and the investments and the jet plane and everybody kissing my ass because I am who I am. And I am who I am because I do nothing in moderation. So what do we do about that?"

"We try two a day," said Hewitt, "and maybe three. It's not now I'm worried about, Jack. Your blood vessels are elastic enough now to handle this kind of thing. I'm thinking of the years ahead. How long do you want to hang onto that presidency? Do you want to be around as chairman of the board, enjoying the fruits of your labors? Or do you want to burn it out in one glorious Roman candle and to hell with the rest of it?"

Wales looked at Hewitt steadily, his mind working the bone for bits of meat that might have been missed.

"I want to live, Alex," he said. "Now and later. Not forever, but long enough to feel what the real power is like, to hold it in my hand like it was a little bird. I want to see my children well started down the path and maybe know what it's like to have grandchildren, children of my children. I don't know about retirement or any of that crap, maybe it's best to pop off in the saddle, but I do want a lot more years than I have now. There are things I want to do."

Wales suddenly realized that Hewitt was smiling at him, and he broke off, as close to embarrassment as Jack Wales was capable of getting.

"Oh, it's easy for you to smile, Alex," he said. "Nothing bothers you. You go your own way as calm as you please, spending half your time in your jock strap knocking little white balls around or fuzzy balls or black balls. You've always got your hands on somebody's balls. Life is one big ball. All you—"

Alex stood up and waved him silent.

"Go in the back room," he said, "and take off your shirt so I can listen to your heart instead of your mouth."

The beat was sound, seventy-two to the minute, strong and clear.

"Start the two pills," said Alex, dropping the mouth of the stethoscope, "and come back in a week. During regular office hours."

"I'm going to Brussels on Monday," said Wales, "and I have to hop down to Italy. Make it two weeks."

"Make it whenever the hell you want," said Alex. "Tell Mrs. Moore. It's your blood pressure."

"Alex," said Wales, and the way he said it made Hewitt turn back and look at him. "Alex, I shot up the ladder this fast because I know people, because I know who can do a job and who can't. You're my doctor."

"You know what, Jack?" said Hewitt.

"What?"

"You don't know shit." And he walked back to his own office and sat down to complete the writeup.

Wales came in to retrieve his jacket.

"Do you have enough pills for your trip?" asked Hewitt.

"I'm up to my ass in them," said Wales. "Tell Betsy to save me a dance. What's this special entertainment you had down on the program?"

"I'm bringing in a rock group from New York, complete with psychedelic lights and reverberators. The flyer said they were a favorite of Princess Margaret's."

"I heard she puts out," said Wales, and was through the door.

Alex sat there and stared at the folder. The door opened again and Wales' face reappeared. "The Moore is not here," he announced.

"When can you make it?"

"The seventeenth."

"Come at five," said Alex, "and you won't have to wait." The face disappeared behind the closing door.

Alex stood up and slipped off his white jacket, staring at the sphygmomanometer as he unbuttoned his shirt cuff and rolled up the sleeve. He sat down and pulled the instrument toward him, then shoved it back, falling in his chair.

"Cool Alex," he said aloud. "Nothing bothers you. It's probably higher right now than it is on that son of a bitch." He felt the pause, and then it knocked on his chest as if it were a door as it came back hard. Mother of Jesus. He looked down at his hands as if he wanted to put his face in them and cry, just like when his mother and father used to spend the supper hour telling him how deficient he was in whatever the fuck he was deficient in at that particular time. He could remember looking at his hands until one of them told him sharply to keep his hands down at the dinner table. Why the hands? Why did he look at his hands?

They were good hands, that was sure. What was it Wales had said? Every dime you make you make with your hands. It was true. They said Wales made over a quarter of a million dollars a year. Jesus, thought Hewitt, I've got to go see that guy about my taxes. He looked down at his hands again. You couldn't make a quarter of a million dollars with one pair of hands.

But they were his hands, his own hands, and he'd look at them all he wanted. No one would ever again tell him to put his hands down or up or sideways or any goddamned way. He'd made that vow, in blood. In blood. He could still see the bright crimson stain on the white pillow . . . how old had he been? . . . nine, it was the month after his ninth birthday and he'd waked out of a bad dream when the blood spurted out of his nose and he had screamed . . . yes, it was a real scream . . . he had screamed, and his father had come rushing in and yelled for his mother, and they put the cold packs on, and it wouldn't stop, it wouldn't stop. He could hear their voices as they argued about whether or not they should call the doctor and the cold washcloth getting soggy with blood, and he could feel himself getting lighter and lighter, and he must have dozed off because suddenly there was a doctor, old Dr. Kimball, his coat white with snow, seeming to fill the room with his bigness while he set down his bag and asked his questions quietly. There was something about the fingers as they removed the soaked cloth and carefully felt the outside of the nose, and Hewitt remembered how calm he had felt as the doctor probed the inside of his nose and explained to him about the blood vessels and their little tricks. His parents had stood there quietly, silent until spoken to, deferential, listening to the doctor, ready to follow his instructions exactly, and as Hewitt had looked at the bloodstained hands of the man who had solved his problem, who had allayed his fears, who had come out in the blinding snowstorm in the middle of the night to help Alex Hewitt, he had looked down at his own bloodstained hands and vowed that he would be like this man, this doctor, who gave orders to parents, who came alone in the night to help people, and who became a blood brother to those who needed it. He was master of his own. . . .

The phone rang, and he waited for Moore to pick up. It rang four times before he realized she wasn't back from lunch yet.

"Dr. Hewitt," he said into the mouthpiece.

"Alex?"

It was Picard. "Yes, Emile."

"I just got the results on the Peters boy. Coarctation of the aorta, You hit it right on the nose."

"Well, the symptoms seemed to indicate. . . ."

"Maybe for you they did, but I wasn't that sure until I had all these test results."

"Are you scheduling surgery?"

"No, I'm going to hold off a bit. It's such a borderline condition that I want to make sure it's an optimum situation before I go in. Even after all these years I get a little nervous working that high in the chest."

"OK. Keep me informed on the situation."

"Listen, baby, I wouldn't make a move without checking with the best diagnostician in the area. You have to be using a crystal ball on some of these."

Hewitt laughed. "Don't give me away, Emile."

"Hey, Alex, the grapevine says that you were the passing doctor who gave first aid in that fatal car accident."

"I wasn't able to do much good."

"From the writeup in the paper, it must have looked like Vietnam to you again."

"Not quite."

"Well, thanks again, Alex. You're a hell of a doctor."

He kept his hand on the phone for a moment after he hung up, savoring the good feeling in his chest. Emile Picard was not one to hand out compliments lightly. He lifted both hands and held them before his eyes, the long, strong fingers steady as a drum. It was enough to work with your hands and screw the jets to Tokyo. The boy had a chance. Because old Hewitt was right again . . . *the best diagnostician in* . . . the buzzer rang.

"I have a roomful of patients out here," said Mrs. Moore.

"Be right there," said Hewitt, buttoning his sleeve as he stood to put on his white coat. Time for the best diagnostician to perform his magic. He reached down and pulled his penis clear of his leg. Filthy fucking pig. That filthy fucking pig.

xi

AS Hewitt was waiting for his locker key, he glanced up at the clock over the reception desk, broke into his usual grin as he read the little sign under it that said "Jesus Has Time for You" and lost it as he saw that he was twenty-five minutes late.

Mrs. Moore had gone home early because she was having her canasta (who still plays canasta? Hewitt had asked himself. Mrs. Moore and her friends still play canasta, he had answered himself) club for dinner, and Hewitt had trouble finding the right tablets for Mrs. Markham in his treasure trove of samples. He was on the verge of driving to his house, where he knew he had some bottles of the particular brand he wanted, but then he found some foil packets that contained almost the right dosage and let it go at that.

A man answered the door to Hewitt's ring, a tall, spare man who could have been brother instead of husband. He looked down at the bag in Hewitt's hand and then stepped back without uttering a sound. Mrs. Parkhurst came in from the kitchen, smoothing down where the apron strings had been (only those allowed to see her naked can see her with her apron on, thought Hewitt), and gave him a small smile of welcome.

"Mother is asleep," she said, "but I was going to wake her soon for her supper."

"No, let her sleep," said Hewitt. "Let her body dictate her hours. I just brought these along," and he handed her the packets, held together by a rubber band. "Did she sleep the night through?"

"I think so. I went in there twice, and both times her eyes were closed and her breathing seemed steady."

"Is she eating anything?"

"She ate some Wheatena this morning and a couple of spoonfuls of soup at noon, but I have to keep after her."

"Don't worry about a balanced diet or anything; just whatever appeals to her."

Mrs. Parkhurst nodded. Her husband stood to the side, tall, bony, silent, alert, ready to fetch or carry without a word.

"I'll be by over the weekend," said Hewitt, "but call me if there is anything extraordinary." He nodded at the man and turned toward the door.

"Thank you, Doctor," said Mrs. Parkhurst.

Hewitt turned back. "Even if it isn't extraordinary," he said, "even if you think it will do her good just to see me," and he went out the door.

It wasn't until he had gone three blocks that he realized he wasn't heading directly for the YMCA. Dark was taking over subtly, and here and there lights began to appear in the houses as he pulled up across the street from the Bardwell house. There were two cars in the driveway, but nothing could be seen within, the windows palely reflecting the gray from the sky. The funeral would probably be the next day, or would it be the day after? There had been nothing, no indication at all. With the Peters boy there had. . . . He could feel the tension in his shoulders, the perspiration under his arms . . . sticky . . . and Wales in New York al-

ready, chewing somebody's ass . . . Tokyo . . . and back
on Saturday. Jesus, what a life. *SH. SH.* A light in an upstairs
room, was it her bedroom, caught his eye and like a thief,
he quickly started the car and left.

Casey was sitting alone in the lounge room, clad in his
brand-new gym clothes, the creases plainly visible on trunks
and shirt, the sneakers blindingly white. He was leafing
through a *Sports Illustrated* magazine, and he kept rubbing
his hand along his hairy thigh as though he were cold.

"I'm out of my mind," moaned Casey.

"It will only hurt when you move," yelled Hewitt, digging through his locker until he came up with his old pair
of handball gloves. He brought his new pair to Casey.

"Work your fingers into these and soften them up," he
said. "I'll be dressed in a minute."

Casey followed him back to the locker area and stood
there, working the stiffened sweat creases out of the gloves,
while Hewitt undressed. The room was full of discarded
towels, scattered on the floor, on chairs and overflowing the
containers. The air was warm and humid from the adjoining sauna room and the number of showers that had been
taken. Hewitt liked to come at this time of day when the
place was usually empty, most men hurrying home for dinner and the nighttime users not due until seven.

Casey was pinching masses of blubber between his
thumb and forefinger, making sounds of disgust. Hewitt
stopped his tying of a shoelace.

"Why the big change of mind all of a sudden?" he asked.
"You trying to get some insurance?"

Casey looked around the room, seeming to study each
towel individually, as though there might be a person hiding under it.

"I'm having a problem," he said, in the tone of a little
boy who can't hold his urine.

Hewitt resumed tying his shoelace, being careful not to
look up at Casey's face.

"It's sexual," continued Casey. Hewitt knew it was going to come out, that nothing could stop the flow of words that was about to engulf him. His mind automatically switched to the case history of Frank Casey and readied itself for the information, which to sort into fact, which to be stored in the memory bank, which to be interpreted in terms of the personality.

"I can't keep it hard," said Casey.

Hewitt looked up, startled. Visions of Casey and Gerda, both like stuffed pandas, trying to couple, enveloped him. Her smooth, creamy, rose-tinted cheeks, the fat arms and heavy thighs, the massive outthrust of flesh that had to divide somewhere into two separate tits, and the belly, that soft underbelly that looked as if it were going to burst its restraints at the first hard bounce. Gerda had learned well at her mother's elbow, and those lucky enough to dine at the Casey table experienced the delights of Lentil Soup with Sausage and Sauerbraten and Roast Duck and Potato Pancakes and Liver Dumplings and Linzertorte and Dobostorte, nine goddamn layers high with a chocolate frosting as thick as Gerda's pudgy fingers. Christ, thought Hewitt, they eat like that every night, not just when company comes. Casey had been talking and Hewitt pulled his mind open again.

". . . and by the time we can work something suitable out, it's gone, just gone, and she's there crying, not loud, just kind of sniffling, and I feel like a goddam fool, and then I get mad and start yelling that we're both just too goddamned fat and we're going to go on a diet, and the next morning we both have black coffee and one slice of toast, and I eat a poached egg for lunch, and I come home at night and she's in the kitchen with eight pots steaming away, and the goddamned smell drives you right out of your mind with hunger, and she's standing there smiling and giving me a kiss, and we both eat like pigs and go to bed. And I don't touch her for a week, and then we try it again and it's a goddamned mess. I told her last night that this time I meant it, that when I got home tonight I expected a lamb chop, one goddamned lean lamb chop, and some cottage cheese and tea."

Casey's face was red, various shades of pinkness showing through the folds, and Hewitt stood up, pulled a ball from his locker and started off, not looking back. Casey followed him through the underground labyrinth until they came to the courts, all of which were dark.

"Look," said Casey, "we're the only idiots in the world. Let's take a steambath and let it go at that." His color had returned to normal, but he was still embarrassed. Hewitt figured they would fool around a little, and then maybe they could talk about the situation in more objective fashion.

"I'm paying a three-dollar guest admission fee for you," he said, poking Casey in the arm, "and I'm going to get my money's worth if it kills you. I know you're not the type to do calisthenics or run by yourself, so we're going to get you interested in a game. If this game doesn't appeal to you, we'll try another one. And another one. Until we find one you can enjoy and that will do you some good. We'll take it nice and easy today because right now you are nothing more than a blivot of shit, but inside three months I am going to take thirty pounds off you and you'll be screaming about people who don't take care of their bodies."

"Sure, sure."

They went into Court 1, and the light went on automatically as Hewitt slammed the door that pushed in the button.

"Have you ever played this game?"

"Yeah, I fooled around with it a little bit when I was in college."

"Do you remember how it's done?"

"You keep hitting the ball against the wall until your opponent comes close enough for you to hang one on him by mistake."

"Hey! That's pretty good."

Hewitt leaned over, bounced the ball on the floor and hit it against the front wall. It came off softly and landed right at Casey's feet. He stood there looking at it, not raising a hand, and it sailed right past him, tapped the back wall and rolled on the floor toward the front of the court.

"Well, you don't need any instruction on how to lose a point," said Hewitt, retrieving the ball. "Let's see if you can hit it." He threw the ball to Casey who caught it in his right glove.

"All right, you son of a bitch," said the bulky figure, "let's see how good teacher is."

He bent over and bounced the ball on the floor. Hewitt went up on his toes in readiness as he saw Casey's arm draw back with the ball coming up from the floor, and Casey leaned over a bit more and kept right on going until he landed on his face in a crumpled heap, the ball going up and down and up and down and up and down in diminishing force . . . and Hewitt knew. The slackness of the body, the unnatural sprawl of the limbs. He knelt on the floor and picked up an arm, his fingers feeling for the pulse. He could feel nothing and looking down he saw that he had his gloves on, that he was holding Casey's wrist with his glove on. He jumped up and fumbled open the door, the gloves impeding every move, and he tore them off as he ran up the stairs and into the office of the phys ed director.

The tiny Scotsman was seated at his desk, painstakingly drawing a basketball elimination chart on a large rectangle of white cardboard, and he looked up in surprise, his eyes blinded with lines and dots.

"Call an ambulance," said Hewitt. "There's a bad one downstairs."

The hand went out immediately for the phone and

started dialing as Hewitt headed back down. As he approached the doorway, he stopped, unable to go into the dark where death lay, and he could hear his father's tired voice saying, "Boys your age don't need a light, boys your age don't need a light, boys your age don't need . . ." when his shoulder was shoved, and he whirled to find the phys ed director trying to move past him. They both went in, and the little man slammed the door. In the moment before the light went on Hewitt had a wild feeling that there would be no body on the floor, no Casey, safe at home with his Gerda and children, no problem, no . . . the light went on.

The phys ed director went down on his knees beside Casey and tried to pull him over on his back, but the weight was too much. The man looked up at Hewitt, who was able only to look back down. Then the director, Doc, they called him Doc, these people were always called Doc, stood up and pulled at Casey, the veins standing out on his neck, and finally had the chest portion over, the legs crossed sideways. He dropped to his knees again and pulled Casey's cheeks together with his fingers, placed his mouth over the lips and began to blow with mighty, steady bursts. He continued this for about a minute, his face scarlet with effort, and then sat back on his haunches, hands by his side.

"He's done."

Hewitt stood there, stonelike, unmovable. He could feel the slow, measured beat of his heart, pumping steadily, easily, no strain. Jesus Christ. He looked down at his hands, spreading the fingers wide, and saw the ball through the gap between his index and third fingers, round and black and still like a deadly weapon in repose. The sound broke through to his ears, a light treble, like Jojo's when they had almost gone off the road, you never know when . . . the little man was looking at him strangely, and had obviously been asking him something.

"What?"

"Who is he, Doctor?"

"Frank Casey. A friend of mine."

The director said nothing more. He did not rise but stayed on the floor close to the body, assuming jurisdiction in his domain. They remained that way until the police came, maybe ten minutes, neither saying anything, an official vigil.

The police had quite a difficult time getting Casey up the stairs once it was agreed that they should take the body to the hospital rather than wait for the medical examiner.

"We haven't established death yet," Hewitt kept saying to the patrolman. "There may be something they can do there."

"Come on now, Doc," said the patrolman, who had been informed by the phys ed director of Hewitt's status, "this guy's starting to stiff already."

"Do you want to hang around here?" asked Hewitt, knowing that he had to get Casey out of these alien circumstances, a place he should never have been.

"OK," said the policeman, who was already almost two hours past the regular end of his shift and who knew how long it took sometimes to get the medical examiner there and how many forms would have to be filled out once he got there, "but you come along in the ambulance just like he wasn't dead already."

Hewitt threw his coat on over his gym clothes and scrambled into the back of the police ambulance with Casey and one of the patrolmen. They headed for the hospital with siren full out and drew up in front of the emergency entrance with a lurch that threw Hewitt against the side of the vehicle and banged his head sharply. The policemen quickly wheeled the stretcher into the foyer, and as soon as the resident on duty saw the face on the stretcher, all hell broke loose.

Casey was placed on the emergency table and an oxygen

mask clamped on his face. The resident did everything in the book—stimulants, direct injection into the heart—but they all knew he was dead. It was just that they didn't want him dead and postponed the final moment as long as they could.

White coats began appearing from everywhere within a minute of the ambulance arrival, and Hewitt found himself being moved, by pressure rather than flesh, farther and farther to the back of the room. He stood there leaning against the wall, seeing and not seeing.

"Alex? Alex? Alex?" He heard the voice and didn't hear it.

His shoulder was shaken firmly and he turned to look. It was Irv Stern.

"What happened?"

"We were going to play handball. He leaned over to hit the ball and keeled right over. Didn't even swing. Heart."

"No. It looks like it might be a massive cerebral insult. Everything at once. What about his wife?"

"What?"

"His wife, Gerda?"

"Yes."

"Somebody has to tell her."

"I suppose I. . . ."

"Where are your clothes?"

"What?"

"Your clothes. Where are your clothes?"

Hewitt looked down at his gym outfit showing between the flaps of his coat and then around at the people in the room. Two of the nurses had obviously been talking about him because they quickly averted their eyes. How long would it take to get through the hospital that Prick-face Hewitt was down in emergency cavorting around in his jockstrap? Killed off poor Dr. Casey and then displayed himself in his skivvies. Jesus Christ.

"They're at the Y."

"Why don't I drive you there and wait while you change and then we'll go over together?"

"Over where?"

"To Casey's house."

"Yes. I'd appreciate that."

"Fine. Let's go, Doctor."

There was enough emphasis on the "Doctor" to make Hewitt bring his head up quickly. All the nurses and aides were still staring at him. He buttoned his coat, looking each one in the eye as he did so, making the rounds in Dr. Hewitt style. They dropped theirs, or turned aside or moved somewhere else. Sons of bitches. He looked at each one again. *SH. SH. SH.*

xii

THERE was no one in the kitchen, and before he took off his coat, he drew a glass of water and washed the tablet down. Betsy came in as he was standing at the sink, the glass half lowered, looking out the window into blackness.

"Hey," she said, "what have you been up to? A dozen of your noted colleagues have phoned. Are you planning a convention?"

"Frank Casey's dead."

She searched his face, looking for a sign to tell her that there was a joke or a perversity of spirit, but there was nothing. She finally realized that he wasn't going to speak unless spoken to.

"What?"

"He came to the Y to work out with me and keeled over. Cerebral, they think."

"But was there any indication that—"

He whirled on her, his face so furious that she put her left hand in the air between them, as though to ward off an impending blow.

"Christ, do you think we're miracle men?" he yelled. "We do the best we can, you know that. If Bardwell. . . ." He stopped and turned back toward the sink, spilling the rest of the water from the glass into the drain.

Bardwell. She knew she had heard that name somewhere, but was unable to place it. What did it have to do with Frank Casey?

"I was talking to Gerda about four," she said, trying to fill in the gap with sound. "They're going to sit with us Saturday. . . ." Her hand came up to her mouth, the fingers stopping the words.

"I just came from there," he said. "She seems to be doing all right."

"Who's with her?"

"A couple of women came in. I didn't know them."

"I'm going over there."

"All right."

"Jo and Jeff are in bed. Bobbi's in her room. If you have to go out, let her know."

"Were there any calls for me?"

"Just those doctors. It's all written down."

She was gone in a few minutes. He took off his coat and dropped it on a kitchen chair. The red indicator light over the oven caught his eye and he pulled down the door to find a casserole sitting snugly in the warmth. His stomach felt empty, but there was no desire for food. He took another tablet out of the bottle in his pocket and washed that down, sticking his mouth under the spray nozzle of the faucet. The heat from the open oven door washed over his face as he turned around, and he rotated the dial to Off. Using a dish towel for insulation, he removed the casserole from the oven and set it on the counter. When the top was removed, a mixture of ground meat and noodles was revealed under the steam. He took a fork out of the drawer and began to shovel large chunks into his mouth, tasteless gobbets that slid down greasily. He stopped, fork in midair, dropped the whole thing into the dish and headed for the bathroom, where he bent over the bowl and vomited the mess into the water, a seemingly endless stream that came up through his nose, as well as out of his mouth. Paroxysm after paroxysm seized him, and he shoved his right hand into his belly as hard as he could, feeling the muscles ripple with each heave. It stopped. In the middle of the brown and tan chunks he could see a white pill floating by itself, an island of content. He flushed and reached for a hand towel, checking his jacket to see if he had splashed. As he turned toward the door, Bobbi, her face a mixture of disgust and—Jesus Christ, it was a smile; it couldn't be anything else but a smile—stepped back.

"Frank Casey's dead," he muttered, it being suddenly important that she know it wasn't booze. He never puked from booze.

"What?"

"Dr. Casey. Frank Casey. He's dead."

"The fat one?"

He threw the towel on the seat of a chair.

"Yes," he said wearily, "the fat one."

"Why are you throwing up?"

"It's the food around here, I guess."

"I made that."

"What?"

"The casserole." She pointed at the dish on the counter.

"It's very good."

"Yeah, it makes you throw up. Everything I do makes you throw up."

"What do you mean by that?"

She thought for a moment. "I don't know."

"Sit down," he said, pointing to one of the kitchen chairs.

"What for?"

"Because I told you to. Your father told you to."

"I have homework to do."

"That can wait. It's early yet. Sit down and we'll have a little father-daughter talk, a little generation ungapping."

She pulled the chair back a bit with her left hand, her eyes never leaving his face, and slid onto the seat carefully.

She's frightened, he realized, and almost went back into the bathroom to look in the mirror, to see what it was that had this sixteen-year-old practically shitting her drawers. When the hell was it they'd last had a nice chat like this, him not knowing what the hell to say and her with her legs pulled together tight enough to choke a man to death? Boys. There never were any boys. Christ knows she's pretty enough, her mother to a T; Jojo, too.

"Do you smoke pot?" he asked.

"What?" Her eyes grew bigger before him, pretty eyes, pretty blue eyes. What if he'd told Casey that he had trouble getting it up for his wife, too, even with her pretty blue eyes? All Gerda had to do was go . . . worked every time. Jesus! At least I can tell where the hole is. Old Gerda must have to piss to give you a hint. He laughed out loud, the sound ringing clear in the background afforded by white enameled machines that reflected . . . and he laughed again, liking the clarity of the tone, the way it . . . she was looking at him strangely, her mouth agape. . . .

"Go to bed," he said.

"What?"

"Go to bed!"

"What for?"

"Because I told you to."

She looked at him, then at the casserole on the countertop and then at him once more. Without another word, she left.

Suddenly he felt nauseated again and went quickly into the bathroom. As he stood over the bowl, a cold sweat came over him, and he retched once, undecided as to whether to push it or hold it back. Flecks of vomit were still in the bowl and he watched them swirling idly in the current, trying to see if the white tablet had gone down or not. He took the little sample bottle out of his pocket and dumped the two remaining tablets into his palm, which he turned far enough so that they fell into the bowl with tiny plops, scarce two drops being spattered from each one. He flushed and watched the whirlpool pull them down, putting his right hand against the wall to hold him firm against the noise of suction. It took the persistent ring of the telephone to break his watery trance.

Betsy didn't come home until ten thirty. There had been six calls from doctors wanting to know if what they had heard was true and one from a patient with a pain in the right side of his chest. He had told the doctors that it was true and little more than that; he told the patient it was probably indigestion but to call back if it persisted.

He was just finishing up with Dr. Picard when Betsy came into the room. The television was going without sound, and she stared at the colors, her mind absorbing them as colors only rather than people or things.

"Yes, Emile, quite a shock. No, no medical history that I know of. I suppose, like the rest of us, he never bothered with checkups. You're right. Absolutely right. OK. I'll be in touch. See you then."

She had sat down in the chair across from his desk, still in her coat, while waiting for him to finish the call. She turned her head from the television as he replaced the receiver, but neither said a word as their eyes met and held. She considered it no victory when he was the first to speak.

"How did it go?"

"Pretty bad."

"She was doing quite well when we left."

"It took about three hours for it to sink in. Death had no place in her life right now."

"What does that mean?"

"She's thirty-six. He was thirty-eight. Their children are

all under ten. The parents are living on both sides. Nobody dies in a world like that."

"But he was a doctor."

"He wasn't your kind of doctor. He went to the hospital in the morning and came home every night. Their phone never rang in the dark because somebody was dying. He never had to make any house calls while she lay there wondering where he was, what he was doing."

"Is that what you do?"

"What?"

"Lie there wondering what I am doing?"

"Sometimes. All the time in the early days."

"What did you think I was doing?"

"It was always pretty dramatic. And I wanted to be there with you, helping, sharing." Their eyes met again and held.

"Did anybody say anything?" he asked.

"About what?"

"About me taking him to the Y, making him play handball."

"No. Not to me anyway."

"It would have happened anyway."

"Of course."

"But I wish to hell it didn't happen this way."

"Let's go to bed."

"What?"

"I'm cold. I want to go to bed, and I want you to hold me until I am warm."

Their eyes met again for a moment, and without saying a word, he stood and went upstairs, undressed and slipped into bed while she scraped out the casserole and put the dish to soak, locked the doors and turned out the lights, checked the children, all of whom were asleep, Bobbi with a book on her chest and the high-intensity lamp drilling into her face. She came into the bedroom softly and scurried into her nightgown quickly, her eyes darting toward the bed every few moments. Habits die hard, and after much internal debate, she went into the bathroom and ran the electric brush over her teeth, rinsing quietly, no spitting, and crept into bed beside him.

"Put out the light," he said, and her heart gave a jump in her chest. Alex insisted on sex in the dark, and in the instant of black that followed the click his hands reached out for her, running over her large breasts, between her legs, her back, pulling her close. She placed her lips on his and while they kissed, she moved her hand down between his legs, feeling the semihardness, and there was such a softness in her, that wet burning softness that this man always induced, this unbearable desire to have him inside her, and she slipped down in the bed and sucked the softness out of him, her eyes closed and her head moving from side to side in a rhythm of music unheard, until he threw back the blanket and moved her under him, pounding the flesh harder and harder until suddenly his hand came over her mouth and she realized that her moans were in danger of waking the children.

They sank back on the bed, not quite touching, and she placed her clamped fingers on her vulva, pressing down hard to retain as much as she could of the sensation, the moment.

"Are you all right?" she asked, as she always asked.

"Fine."

"I'm not cold anymore."

"Fine." He was already drifting into sleep as he always did. Sex drained all his life (oh, no, God, no) from him, and he could not stay awake for more than a minute. Even on their honeymoon, when she had wanted to talk and he had tried to answer her questions, her oohs and gurgles (she smiled in memory) and wasn't-this-wonderfuls. But right now it was enough to hear him suddenly start that slow, deep breathing that made everything seem so normal, so safe, so permanent. She pulled the blanket around his shoulders, which roused her from her drowsiness. Perched on an elbow, she chuckled.

"By the way," she said into the dark mass of his head, "this reminds me. I am just about out of pills."

"Some sample packets in my case," he muttered, half asleep, half awake. "Remind me to get them out of the car in the morning."

"I hope they're the right kind this time," she said. "Isn't it bad to be switching around?"

But he was in deep sleep and didn't answer. She moved her hand a bit, contentedly, between her legs. What had it been? Four weeks? Something like that. She rubbed a bit more to keep the feeling of contact. Should really get up and go to the john. Should really get and go to . . . warmthwarmthwarmth.

THEY all knew. Even the guy in the parking lot was obviously aware who had helped Frank Casey through the gates. The women at the information desk thought they all said good morning as usual, but so overcome were they by the bedazzlement of the tragedy and the real, live participant in front of them that no sound issued from their mouths, except for a slight clicking of dentures when they waggled their jaws in the belief that they were uttering words.

The staff were all careful not to mention the incident, but Hewitt could tell they were primed for him to bring up the subject, that one word would unleash the torrent. He did not utter that word but made his rounds as always, taking each case at a time, letting his work wash over him in cleansing absorption. So engrossing was the mysterious mass in Mr. Riley's large bowel that Hewitt suddenly found himself walking in the subterranean corridor that led to Casey's laboratory. You can't have coffee with a dead man.

The sweat pooled under his arms as he leaned against the cinder block wall, and there was a tightness in his head that didn't go away even after he took several deep breaths. Medication was definitely indicated. But not that shit from last night. Not that route. It was only good for scaring the hell out of your oldest daughter.

Another wave of dizziness passed over him, and he turned to look down the corridor—*last night in the emergency room in his skivvies and today hanging on a wall in a cold sweat outside Frank's office*— But no one was—it came again, accompanied this time by a fierce throb in the back of his neck. The fingers of his right hand moved to the opposite wrist. Steady. A nice steady beat. The rough cinder block felt cool against his cheek, and he rubbed against it, sandpapering the weakness away. A dark streak of moisture remained where his head had been, and he knew that if he stood there much longer, he would fall down on the floor and lie there crying, like a baby, like a weakling, all done, all done. Get out, Hewitt, he said, not quite aloud. Get out. Get out. Get out!

Up the stairs. Through the double doors. To the parking lot. Into the car. Out, away. Away. Away where? Today was . . . today was . . . Wednesday. He pulled over to the side of the street and turned off the motor. A shiver swept over him, and he reached into the small back seat for his topcoat, which he started to struggle into, becoming so entangled in the narrow space that he finally opened the door and stood in the road in order to get his arms into the sleeves. Wednesday. He reached into the inside pocket of his jacket and pulled out his engagement book. Wednesday . . . Wednesday.

A.M.—Huber
   Slotnick
P.M.—Squash. Atherton.

Nice and neat. Nothing like a day off.

When he arrived at the Casey house, there were so many

cars clustered around it, parked every which way, that he had to go halfway down the street before he could squeeze in. The front door was slightly ajar, and women were dashing about everywhere, including Betsy Hewitt, who paused in surprise. He was caught by her beauty, a soft gray wool dress reflecting the pale blond hair and smoky blue eyes. In her right hand was a red kettle with water for the plants, spout full, and she sloshed some liquid on the rug as her wrist tilted unknowingly.

"Hey," she said.

"How's it going here?"

"Pretty well. Too many cooks for the broth, maybe, but at least it keeps things lively."

"How's Gerda?"

"Well, that's a major problem. She's not doing well at all. Kent's upstairs with her now, and I think he's going to knock her out. She didn't sleep a wink last night apparently."

"Kent? Kent McCord?"

"Yes. He's the family doctor."

As if in response, he came down the stairs, the precise little man with the trim mustache and an oversized bag that rendered him askew.

Hewitt was waiting for the face to dissolve into fear, for the legs to start backpedaling up the stairs, for the bag to come sailing at him as the weasel tried to scurry out the door.

"Ah, Alex," said McCord benignly, giving him a friendly smile and dropping the bag on the floor with a jangly thud.

If there was anything in Hewitt, it was perhaps a touch of admiration. The son of a bitch not only was not going to acknowledge that he had run out on an emergency situation and abandoned a fellow member of the kike-ridden medical society, but was probably not even thinking about it. "Ah, yes," he would indubitably say, if it were brought forcibly to his attention, "you made me three minutes late for the meeting."

"How's she doing?" asked Alex.

"Not too well. I put her out. On top of everything else, she has a bad cold and quite a bit of congestion. This happened at a bad time."

"What's a good time?"

"What?"

"Is there anything I can do?"

"No, no, I don't think so. You've done quite enough already."

"What?" said Alex, moving a step forward.

McCord was reaching down for his bag and looking around for his coat. "She'll be fine," he said. "There are all these women here to take care of things. She needs rest. She was up all night with her parents, and she needs rest."

Betsy had shifted the kettle to her other hand, and she and Alex stood there silently while McCord slipped into his coat and rubbers and left. It didn't bother him that a boy might be dead because he had forsworn his oath. It didn't bother him that Alex had taken Casey into that handball court. Nothing bothered him, the slimy son of a bitch. His blood pressure right now was probably one hundred and twenty-five over eighty. Hewitt waited until the door was shut and then started toward it.

"Alex?"

He almost kept going but finally stopped with his hand on the knob.

"Is there a chance you might be home in time to have dinner with all of us?"

"I don't know." He half turned toward her.

"We're having a rib roast, and that doesn't taste as good when it has to be warmed."

"I don't know."

"You haven't eaten with the children in ages."

"I'll see," and he was out the door. McCord was gone.

The son of a bitch. What if he'd been there? Knock the little shit on his ass? Ask him what the hell he meant by that crack? Did he mean anything? Did the little shit even know what he was saying? *I try. At least, I try. I tried with that boy. Maybe I should have tried with Frank. But he was gone. Gone. Gone. Gone.*

He drove over to the Bardwell house. There was one car parked in the driveway, but no one answered when he rang the bell and then knocked. He tried the knob, and the door opened easily. "Hello," he called in, "hello!" Nothing. Where . . . Wednesday . . . Monday . . . funeral day. A lot of them two days now. They were all out burying the mistake. Was it a mistake? Ask Bardwell. Or SH. He turned quickly, not wanting to be caught there now, and headed for the Hubers.

She must have been watching for him because the door opened while he still had his finger on the bell.

"Good morning, Doctor," she said, her head tilted to one side, the eyes so big in the thin face.

"Good morning, Cindy," he answered, moving into the foyer and dropping his coat over the final swerve of the hall banister. He lifted his bag and headed up the stairs, hearing her soft footfalls on the rug about two steps behind him. How many times had this procession taken place? How many more to go?

The smell hit his nose even before he reached the door, the thin, acrid, cloying stink of rot. He knew it wasn't possible, maybe there wasn't any odor at all, but each time it grew stronger for him. Always bearable, but stronger.

His eyes went to the inverted bottle on the stand—drop by drop by drop by drop—before they fell to the figure on the bed. So still. Living drop by drop by drop by drop.

Hewitt sat down on the side of the bed and lifted the limp wrist with his fingers, steady as a drum, beat by beat by beat by beat. He looked up at Cindy standing across the room, so thin, her sharp little breasts and hard hips jutting out from all that thinness. But live thin, not dead thin as this still figure on the bed with the heart pounding away so grandly, as if forever, as if it would never permit this stick of flesh, this bag of bones ever to quit its labors.

"I told him all about us," she said from across the room, the reedy voice breaking the stillness like a sonic boom.

He held onto the pulse, the firm, steady beat reassuring in his hand, something around fifty a minute, the drugs would hold it down, but solid, a testament to the miracle of the cells.

"I told him the whole story," she continued, her hands behind her back, a quiver of a smile, "every filthy thing you made me do."

"What?" he said, knowing what she was saying, but really hearing only the pulse, its vibrations setting up complementary overtones in his own body, moving up his fingers into his head.

"I sat where you are right now," she said, "and told him about every single time, from the very first when he was in Cleveland for three days for that regional sales meeting and every time after that. I told him about every one."

She looked like a little girl reciting in school, her hands behind her back, the hair pulled tight, no makeup. Except for the breasts, those sharp points, she was just like a little girl reciting in school.

"Cindy . . ." he began, his voice low and patient, like an adult talking to a little girl who had already or was about to commit a nuisance.

"I did it twice. I wanted to make sure, so yesterday I sat down and told him again, all about us, all about his good friend Alex Hewitt and what Alex Hewitt did to his friend's wife when he was out of town or playing golf or working at the plant, how Alex came and did things to his wife."

"Cindy, this is crazy." Sharp, louder, adult to adult.

"I wanted him to know. I didn't want him to die without knowing what you did."

"What *we* did."

"Whatever you say. Whichever way you want it to be. But I wanted him to know that it was he who had been the fool, not I, his own friend, I wanted him to know about it, all of it."

Hewitt laid the wrist back on the cover.

"When did you tell him?"

"Last week. Right after you left I told him."

"Has Mrs. Maven been coming in regularly to give him his shots?"

"Twice a day. She comes in the morning and puts on a new bottle and cleans him up and gives him a shot and then comes back in the afternoon and gives him another shot."

"Then he didn't hear a word you said. I've got him under too deep."

"He heard. He heard all right. He opened his eyes. Both times he opened his eyes."

Hewitt lifted a lid. The pupils were so small you could barely distinguish them.

"You're lying," he said.

"He heard. He knows about us. His head is jammed full of it. It's the last thing he'll know."

Hewitt looked at her across the room, her hands in front of her now, the fingers twined, twisting, unable to keep them from twisting around each other, the rest of her life, twisting. Christ, there was a year when his own fingers had twisted every time he thought of this woman, of how those thin legs would twist around him in furious strength, striving to crush something out of his body while her teeth gnashed together, the eyes growing larger and larger, and he could feel the swelling between his legs, the unbearable pleasure as he. . . .

"You're out of your mind," he said. "You're crazy. You

need treatment." Christ, treatment! Would she be blabbing
this whole thing to the psychiatric brethren, Henderson or
Morris or Goldfarb—she'd probably use Henderson—or
one of those other dizzy bastards who always had pipes in
their mouths and fingers up their asses? Would the whole
fucking medical society have a classic case on their hands?

Did you hear about old Hewitt? He was banging Huber's
wife.

Even after?

I suppose so. Why not? What's the difference? Does it
make any difference if you bang a man's wife while you're
treating him for cancer? He was banging her while he was
treating him for the flu. For sinus. For tennis elbow. What's
so sacred about cancer? A bang is a bang is a bang is a drop
is a drop is a drop. Alex looked up at the bottle. Functioning perfectly. He stood up.

"Listen, Cindy," he said, "you are understandably in a
terribly emotional state right now, but there is no justifica-
tion for what you have done. Who are you trying to hurt?
Sam's beyond anything you might do to hurt him. You're
not capable of hurting me. . . ."

"I'll tell Betsy next," she flared. "You haven't got her all
doped up. I'll tell her about her precious Alex."

"Do you want to hurt Betsy? Even if she would believe
you. Will that give you some kind of satisfaction? Will that
make everything all right?"

The hands raised a little, palms turned toward him, im-
ploringly.

"Oh, Alex, I don't know anymore what I want to do. It's
nearly three months now with him just laying there and the
nurse coming each day to change the bottle on the stand
and empty the one on the floor and give him his shots. Why
don't you just let him go? Or help him go? Why don't you
just help him go?"

He looked down at the figure on the bed . . . had that
eyelid just flickered? . . . was there a movement? . . . and

the skin almost translucent under the stubble of beard. His golfing partner. Part of the pleasure had been that it was good old Sam's wife. Fuck you, Sam, by fucking your wife. And here we are finally, the three of us, the traditional showdown. Everybody is about to know. Do you know? Did you hear her? Are you hearing us now?

Hewitt leaned down and picked up the wrist again. Strong. So incredibly strong a beat. He placed it down carefully and lifted an eyelid again. Impossible to hear anything. The pupils so tiny. That's quite a monkey on your back. But not as big as the one in your system.

"He's going to go," said Alex. "He'll be going soon enough. He doesn't need any help from me."

"It's me that needs the help," she said. "He's beyond help. He doesn't care one way or another. But I'm chained to this bed. For what? What good does it do? I have to get out."

"I'll put him in a nursing home," said Hewitt. "I don't know why you insisted on this whole rigamarole."

"I told him I'd see him through," she said heavily. "You remember that. You remember when he made me promise that."

"But that was when you both thought he was going to make it," said Hewitt, "that he was going to beat the rap. We all uttered nonsense then."

"It may have been nonsense to you," she said, her fingers clenching into fists, "but it wasn't nonsense to me."

They had come back to the house from the hospital that day, Hewitt remembered, he following some ten minutes after, and made love on this very bed, was that the last time? Was that the last time they had done it, with her crying and refusing to let him go, and he barely able to keep from hitting her, wanting to snap those thin wrists so they would let him go. Forever. Nonsense. Nonsense. She was right. There was no sense to the whole fucking mess.

"Then get another woman to come and stay with him,"
said Hewitt. "You don't have to be here all the time."

"It isn't that. It isn't that at all. It's that I'm in between.
I'm not a wife; I'm not a widow. I'm nothing. I can't stand
being nothing anymore."

He walked over and took her by the arm. She sagged as
both remembered how this was once the beginning of something else, the prelude of bodies coming together, of lips
and tongues and hands and bare skin merging, rubbing
against each other, demanding, demanding, demanding
. . . it was either drop or tighten; he tightened.

"Look, Cindy," he said, "you've come this far, and you
can go the rest. Don't think about anything else; just that
you've come this far and you can go the rest. It can't be too
long now."

She closed her eyes. His hand was still holding the soft
part of her arm.

"Do you promise?" she asked, her eyes still closed.

"I'm promising nothing. I'm just telling you the way it's
got to be. Don't quit now when the game's almost over."

Her eyes opened, those immense eyes in that thin face.

"It's all a game to you, isn't it?" she said. "All of it. What
happened before and what's happening now. It's all a
game."

"It's no game," he said crossly, annoyed that an unfortu-
nate choice of words should move to her advantage. "Nobody's playing any games. Now why don't you get out of
here and let me do my work and I'll see you downstairs?"
He turned her by the arm and started her toward the door.
She moved slowly, but she moved and was gone.

Hewitt turned back to the bed and looked down at his
patient. There was no discernible rise or fall of the chest,
but the breathing was steady, that solid piece of muscle
pounding away. Reaching down, he opened his bag, withdrawing the bottle and the syringe case. He rubbed the top
with an alcohol swab and inserted the needle. Inverting the

bottle, he slowly withdrew the plunger until the fluid reached the correct mark. The correct mark? The right mark? He pulled again until the fluid was three more marks down, then withdrew the needle. Huber lay there; his patient lay there; and Hewitt's thumb exerted pressure so that a tiny fountain rose in the air (celebrating what?) and the thumb did not cease its pressure until the fluid level was at the correct mark again. The right mark. Then the doctor carefully searched until he found a pitifully small vein that receptively ballooned a bit under the restraining rubber, and he gently slid the easing balm into the ravaged system. Once more he checked the bottle on the stand, drop by drop by drop, replaced the equipment in his bag, snapped it shut and headed for the stairs.

Cindy was not in the foyer, and he could hear no sound at the rear of the house. Mrs. Maven would be there in the afternoon after her morning off, but he had no new instructions to leave for her. He put on his coat and went outside, quietly closing the door behind him. It felt as if it were going to snow, thin bracing air but with a heavy monotone of grayness to it. He took a deep breath and turned around to look at the big house with the wide expanses of lawn on each side. Huber had enjoyed mowing all that grass with his little tractor, dragging the three banks of reels behind him. Golf and tennis and mowing lawns and running around the country to sell whatever Jack Wales was pushing that week. Friend. She had used the term "friend."

"I have no friends," Hewitt told his car as he turned the key to start. A tiny snowflake settled on the windshield and hung there for a moment until the forward motion of the car melted it in the air. There were no others.

xiv

SHE lay facedown on the bed with her nose pushed into the spread, able to get air only by pulling through the corners of her mouth. A few times she didn't attempt to breathe, listening to the pound of her heart until she could feel herself blacking out, a strange, almost delicious sensation; but then her chest moved, and the air came in.

It was so good to be alone. *Alone.* Frightened, she lifted her head in the air and looked around the room, seeking comfort from anything. The photos of her parents caught her eye, the placid smiles and white hair, the hands folded so comfortably in the laps. It had always been so comforting in those laps, the hands held protectively around your tummy, making a warm spot. Her head dropped down again, sideways this time, so that the left cheek rested on the smooth bedspread and the air passed easily in and out of the nostrils.

Decision. She would have to make a decision. Soon. But some said not to hurry the decision. Take your time. Decision in haste, repentance at leisure. She could feel a tear in the corner of her eye, puddling up on the bridge of her nose, but made no motion to disturb it. Where had it come from? You would think there would be no more tears left. Had she drunk a glass of water? No. Her mouth was dry, parched. But still enough for a tear. It was time to go; they would be waiting for her. But a move would disturb the tear, and since this was the last one she would shed, she had better protect it for a while, let them wait while she protected the tear, her last one, there could be no more. No more tears. No time for tears. Too much to do.

That pleasant man from Mr. Wales' office . . . Mr. . . . Mr. . . . She hadn't really listened when he gave his name. Nothing to worry about, Mrs. Bardwell. Just sign here . . . and here . . . and here . . . and here. Mortgage insurance. Company insurance. Personal insurance. Army insurance. Masonic insurance. Nothing to worry about, Mrs. Bardwell. Nothing to worry about.

The tear spilled over the bridge, and she could feel the moisture spreading, thinning, evaporating in the air. The last tear. No more tears. Time to go downstairs and watch them eat . . . the bile rose in her throat and she swallowed quickly, but the sour stink remained there, fogging her brain with the horror of rotting garbage . . . flesh . . . nothing to worry about.

Oh, Don, she moaned silently, help me, help me, help me.

She raised her head again and looked around the room, passing over the bureau with the smiling pictures on it, her face moving right and left and back again, nothing, nowhere, no help.

Trish. Trish was downstairs with the rest of them. Trish would need help. She sat up and looked across the room into the mirror on the wall, staring at the pale face in the rumpled black dress. She saw her bare breasts in the mirror, her full bare breasts, and how his hand would come around from the back, fingers spread wide and . . . she scrambled off the bed and stood on the floor, her breath coming in labored motions, the pain in her side . . . her hand went down and pressed in where the pain had been since early the night before, dull and heavy and demanding. Probably from not eating. But it hurt, it hurt terribly. Maybe Dr. Hewitt . . . she had kept expecting Dr. Hewitt at the cemetery. Not at the church. Why should he come to the cemetery? He was a doctor, not a friend. She thought of his face, of Dr. Hewitt's face. Was it a friendly face? There was something in it . . . trustworthy? . . . concerned? . . . friendly? Was Dr. Hewitt her friend? He must have so many friends.

She ran a comb through her hair and went down to the breads, the baked beans, the egg salad, the cakes, the cookies, the relatives, the neighbors, the friends and Trish. She went down to see if Trish needed any help.

XV

"YOU'VE got a *goyishe kop*. Do you know what that is, Doctor?"

Hewitt shook his head from side to side.

"It means you're a dope, a dummy, a *shlemiel*. Do you know what a *shlemiel* is?"

"It means sort of a jerk, doesn't it?"

Slotnick cocked his bushy head to one side, considering the definition. What's right is right; he grunted an acceptance.

"Well, then," he said, "you must pardon my effrontery, and this is no reflection on your ability as a doctor, but when it comes to money matters, when it comes to looking out for yourself, and for your family, you are a *shlemiel* . . . and there is nothing personal intended . . . a *shlemiel*."

Hewitt grinned and stretched his legs in front of him. It felt good to be on the opposite side of the desk for a change, catching hell and being read out by an expert. Nice way to spend a day off.

"Do you know what your net income is going to be this

year?" the accountant asked, bouncing up out of his chair and then sitting down again. "Do you know what your net is going to be?"

Hewitt shook his head slowly from side to side. If put to it, he could have come up with a figure that wouldn't have been too far off, but that was the job of this excitable little man. Let him tell it.

"Seventy-two thousand dollars. Your taxable income is going to be approximately seventy-two thousand dollars."

"Sounds about right," acknowledged Hewitt.

"Sounds about right, he says," moaned Slotnick to the ceiling. "He says it sounds about right. It sounds about wrong, that's what it sounds about. Twelve thousand dollars of that you could have put in your own pocket if you had used your head, if you had listened to advice, if you had asked advice. That twelve thousand dollars is going to the government, and the government is going to take that twelve thousand dollars and give it to some smart cracker for not raising soybeans. We are lucky if you keep forty thousand of that seventy-two thousand dollars."

"I can get by on that," said Hewitt mildly.

Slotnick stared at him, quietly, calm of mind, all passion gone.

"Doctor," he said, measuring his words, "suppose someone came to you and said, 'Doctor, I want you to take care of me. I am putting myself in your hands.' And you said, 'Good. I want you to do such-and-such and such-and-such, because otherwise, God forbid, you are going to get cancer.' And that person went away and came back some months later, and you examined him and found he had cancer. And you said, 'But I told you not to do such-and-such and such-and-such. Did you?' And the person said, 'Yes, I did.' How would you feel, Doctor?"

Hewitt thought about it. "Why, I guess the way you feel about me now, Maury. But money is one thing and cancer is another."

"It's not the money," cried Slotnick, jumping up and down in his chair again; "it's not the lousy twelve thousand bucks. But when you came to me in May, when you told me you wanted someone to take care of everything from then on, you were putting yourself in my hands, right?"

Hewitt nodded, almost enthusiastically.

"And then I don't hear another word from you until all of a sudden last week you send in that whole bale of crap for me to wade through. And when I go through it, I get sick. You didn't do one of the things I suggested when we first talked."

"Listen. . . ."

"No, you listen," and the little man was sitting straight in his chair, head up and eyes boring in. "I can do your tax return for you this year, do a few things here, a few things there and maybe save a couple of dollars. I'll do the best I can for you. But if this is your attitude, if this is how you are going to act, that's the first and the last one I do. You can take your business elsewhere."

"Listen, Maury. . . ."

"No, you listen. When I go to a doctor and he gives me advice, I take that advice. Because I figure he knows his business and I respect his knowledge and experience. He's a professional man. Well, I'm a professional, too. And if someone comes to me and asks for the use of my knowledge and experience, I give him the best I've got. And if that's not good enough for him, then I want him to go elsewhere."

"Listen, Maury, I apologize. We're so busy filling out government forms nowadays that we just get buried and don't have time to take care of our own business. I've got to take on an extra girl in my office just because of Medicare and Medicaid and Blue Cross and all the other health plans. I promise you I'll do better in the future."

Slotnick was more than mollified; he was pleased. In addition to the fascination of working on a case so crying for improvement, he was attracted to this big, white, Anglo-Saxon, Protestant American. And that wife. What a looker!

"Which reminds me," said Slotnick, getting right down to business, "I couldn't find any record of life insurance payments. I need your total financial picture."

"I don't have any life insurance," said Hewitt, starting to cross his legs and then bracing in alarm at the look on Slotnick's face. Cyanotic. The eyes were actually bulging.

"You must not play games with me," cried Slotnick. Perplexed, Hewitt began looking for other medical signs, but a huge sigh seemed to relieve the pressure, and the color began returning to Slotnick's face. He picked up a ball-point pen, drew a piece of paper before him and poised, almost birdlike, ready to write down the amount of the insurance.

"I really don't have any insurance," said Hewitt.

"This includes term insurance," said Slotnick. "I happen to know from the case of the doctor who referred you to me and from a few others that there is a very good deal on term insurance through the medical society."

"I don't know about that," said Hewitt. "I've just never bothered with any insurance."

"But that's criminal," said the accountant. "It is one thing to be insurance-poor, and I am always careful about this very point, but everybody has to have some insurance, some straight life, some term, enough to see his family through in case of, God forbid, death or even worse."

Hewitt became entangled with the "or worse" and did not hear the next sentence or two.

"I'm sorry, Maury," he said, "I didn't get that."

"You are a man with a large income," repeated the accountant. "You have a big house, cars, high expenses. If something happened to you"—Hewitt felt his heart stop, then THUMP—"your family would be stuck with a pile of bills and no money coming in. Your wife would have to sell off everything and get a job just to exist. How would your children go to college? What would happen to them? This is madness. Crazy! How can you sit there and smile?"

Hewitt laughed. Christ, it felt good to be a patient instead of a doctor, to induce exasperation rather than endure it, to hear the words fall over you and just pick out the ones you wanted.

"Maury," said Hewitt, "do you know my wife?"

"I've seen her here and there," said Slotnick, "a most beautiful woman."

"Yes," said Hewitt, "you could say that. She comes from the South, and, I suppose, if she had been a poor girl, she would have entered beauty contests and maybe become an actress or a model." He thought for a moment. "Or a whore." Slotnick wasn't sure he had heard correctly, and in case he had heard correctly, he wanted to believe he had not heard correctly."

"My wife," Hewitt continued, "is from Boca Raton, Florida. And her daddy"—(he slurred it just a bit)—"builds things down there. He builds condominiums and shopping centers and marinas and highways and byways. You name it, and one of his companies will build it. He's one of those Gentiles, Maury"—(Hewitt's eyes held Slotnick's in a vise)—"that scares the hell out of Jewish businessmen. Because whoever he works a deal with, he holds him right by the cuticles." Hewitt laughed out loud while Slotnick stared in bewilderment. There was strangeness here, a tenseness that didn't belong.

"He's got two daughters," said Hewitt, as Slotnick tried to think of ways to get the talk back to taxes and insurance and write-offs, anything that would stop the flow. Hewitt's eyes were pointing directly at him, but the accountant did not feel the same about the words. "The older one," said the doctor, "a nice-looking girl, is married to a former half-back from Vanderbilt University, who is a vice-president in several of Daddy's"—the slur was a bit longer this time—"companies and who lives in a white stucco mansion on the

Inland Waterway. They have no children. This big, beautiful, almost All-American is incapable of fathering children. This has been verified by clinical tests."

"But, Doctor," said Slotnick, picking up the first two papers he could grasp with his fingers, "we—"

"The younger daughter," continued Hewitt, "the beautiful one, is married to a brilliant internist and they live way up in the cold, cruel Nawth, away from Daddy and Mommy and Sissy and all that bullshit. Once a year, in the winter vacation time, Daddy sends up first-class plane tickets so that beautiful daughter and her kiddies, the only grandchildren in the bunch, can come down and roll in the sand and swim in the Olympic-size pool, and once a year, during the summer months, Daddy and Mommy come Nawth to see beautiful daughter and the kiddies. Daddy keeps trying to shove goodies on daughter and kiddies, but they keep getting shoved back."

"Yes, but . . ."

"Wait a minute, Maury, I'm just getting to the point of the whole goddamned . . . you people have a special word for it . . . I heard it from a patient of mine once . . . something like—"

"*Megillah?*"

"That's it, that's the very one. He told me to remember that it rhymes with guerrilla. Anyway, if something happened to that brilliant internist, beautiful daughter and only grandchildren would be so smothered in goodies for the rest of their lives, which they will someday anyway, that the few dollars of life insurance that might come in would be more in the way than anything."

"You know, Doctor," said Slotnick, "talking to you is like talking to someone from Mars. You don't understand anything. You are so independent of your father-in-law's money, but you are ready to let that money take over your responsibility in case something happened to you. Suppose something happened to his money or just suppose he didn't leave your wife and kids a dime. It is up to you to take care of this, not your father-in-law. I am talking about a way of life."

"You people are more family-oriented, Maury. You worry too much about things like this."

"Like what?"

"Like dying and not leaving a pile of dough for your wife and kids to get fat on."

"Everybody dies, Doctor, you know that. Even doctors." Hewitt felt the dizziness out there, just beyond, ready to move in.

"Especially doctors, Maury," said Hewitt. "You ought to see the actuarial tables."

"Dead, shmed," said Slotnick, "the important thing is to live happily while you're here and take care of your family when you're gone."

"Agreed," said Hewitt. "I'll follow your instructions exactly, Doctor. What's the prescription?"

"First of all, don't buy any more of that crappy stock just like all the other doctors who are so smart."

"I do that for fun."

"Fun! The amount of money you dropped on stocks is not a matter of fun. It's more tragedy than fun."

"OK. Agreed. What else do you want me to do?"

Slotnick scattered the pile of papers in front of him with his fingers and then spread his hands in the air.

"Let me go over these again," he said, "and work out a plan of action. If you think you can follow it, if you are willing to follow it, then we are in business. If not, then we'll shake hands and part friends."

"I'll do it, Maury," said Hewitt, standing up. "Whatever you say. You're the boss."

Slotnick laughed, stood up and walked around the desk.

"They tell me you're a smart doctor," he said, "so who am I to know different?"

"Stern told you that," said Hewitt, "just like he told me

you were a good accountant. Do you think he lied to both of us?"

"There's a man," said Slotnick, waving his finger in the air, "who would have made a hell of an accountant."

"Gee, Maury," said Hewitt, "I hope you'll say that about me someday."

"We should all live so long," sighed Slotnick. "I'll call you when I make some sense out of this mess."

Hewitt went out the door, and Slotnick returned to his desk, looked down at the stack of papers and then gathered them together in a pile. Not only was the wife beautiful, he mused, but she was rich as Croesus. Everything. Some people had everything.

xvi

SHE could hear them talking in the kitchen, the soft murmur comforting to the ears, especially when she closed her eyes and let the sound dominate all the senses, not thinking or seeing or smelling or feeling, but just the buzz, the low buzz.

Maybe it was the medicine that Dr. Hewitt left for her. The grogginess had been there all morning, as though sleep were reluctant to leave. No dreams. There had been no dreams. He had promised her there would be no dreams, and there had been no dreams. He had promised her there would be no pain. Why was there such fear of pain? Was it that it was unknown pain—that once it made itself felt, once she knew what she had to deal with, the fear would go? Pain had always been a companion in one form or another, especially on the winter nights with the wind howling and the little girl in the next bedroom, and no one to tell what the day had been like or to ask about tomorrow. Life had been one day after another, and even when the girl had said she was going to be married, it had been hard to figure out where the days had gone in between, where the little girl

had become a big girl and then a woman. Nobody talked
much. Charles. Never a word more than was needed. Salt.
Why would that stick in the mind? Salt. No matter how
much had been poured in the pot it was never enough. Salt.
Married eight years and the only word that sticks in the
mind is "salt."

Perhaps it was the babble. Fourth graders are probably
the worst babblers of them all. Those earnest little faces
hunched over the desks, the tongues between the teeth, the
pencils gripped with deadly intent. The good ones and the
bad ones, all with deadly intent. Where now? Where are
they now? Were there any Hewitts among them? Were any
Hewitts helped on the way, given the beginnings of skill
and understanding? Where do the healers come from, the
special ones who devote their lives to helping others? Does
any of it come from the Mrs. Markhams, or is it all in there
to begin with, from their mothers and fathers? How could
they not pay attention to him? Did the girl feel that no attention was paid to her?

The noise of a door closing broke into the buzz. Or had
the buzz still been there? The fuzziness would not go away.
Perhaps only half a tablet would be enough to keep away
the bogeyman. Save up the rest, and when the time came,
take them all. No more pain. When would it start? It was
there, somewhere, close by. But when would it start? He
would see her through. He had promised. A man like that
did not make promises easily. He had promised. He wasn't
only a doctor, he was a friend. There never were any
friends, not even the girl. But he was a friend. There would
be no pain.

xvii

TWICE Hewitt almost pulled into a restaurant parking lot, but each time there was some trifling impediment—a car waiting to leave, two people chatting in the driveway—and he had rolled on, smug in the resolution of skipping lunch, of starting the diet right now.

This didn't keep him from looking through Moore's desk drawers in hopes of coming upon a jar of peanuts or a box of cookies, but there was nothing. The cupboard was as bare of edibles as it was of people. Pulling the phone to him, he dialed the answering service.

"Dr. Hewitt here," he told the voice, one he did not recognize.

"A message from your wife, Doctor, asking if you intend to attend Dr. Casey's wake tonight."

"Thank you. I'll be here at my office the next couple of hours, but I won't be picking up."

"Thank you, Doctor."

He held onto the reciever, listening to the buzz, the only contact with the outside world. What if he decided to never pick up again? Attention, world! Dr. Hewitt is no longer picking up? Why had he picked up on medicine in the first place? Was it those Dr. Kildare books? Long before the movies or the TV. Could TV influence children toward medicine as well as violence? Or were they one and the same thing?

The buzz.

He looked at the receiver. She never bothered trying to reach him anymore, just left messages with the answering service. That had been quite a session, her screaming that some men, including doctors, lawyers and Indian chiefs, called home several times a day to keep contact with their wives and children.

"Suppose I need you," she had yelled, "suppose for God's sake that I really need you one time?"

"My answering service always knows where to reach me."

"Why can't your wife ever know where to reach you? You go out of this house in the morning and you come back at night. You don't even have the courtesy to tell me whether you'll be home for dinner or when you might be home for dinner. Do you know how much food has simmered away in our oven over the years?"

"Have I ever complained about warmed-over food?"

"It's not the food, for God's sake. You don't even know what I'm talking about. I'm talking about a marriage, a husband and wife and children. A family. It's no different on weekends. You go in the morning, and you come home at night. Your buddies know where you are. Sam Huber knows where you are." The buzz.

At least she wasn't leaving crazy messages anymore.

Your wife called. The washing machine broke down, but the man came and fixed it.

Your wife called. She said she filled the station wagon with high-test gasoline.

Your wife called. She said they were having fish for supper.

Your wife called. She said you knew what you could do.

In the beginning she had looked at his face when he came home, hoping he was going to say something. But then she didn't look for that anymore. And then she stopped leaving messages. Too bad, they were kind of fun. This was the first one in . . . the buzz.

His mother always knew where his father was. The store. He was always at the store. Daddy called. He said he was leaving the store and coming home. Daddy called. He said he was leaving the store and going to the post office and then coming home. Daddy called. He said he was leaving the store and . . . Daddy? I think he's in the bathroom. Daddy? I think he's in the backyard raking the leaves? Daddy? I think he's in the cellar . . . the buzz . . . the buzz . . . the buzz.

He replaced the receiver and walked into his own office, noting the stack of papers on the desk that Moore had left for him to sign. They'd have to get somebody in. Moore couldn't take this much longer. Betsy wanted to work. That would be something, really something.

Maury would probably know somebody who would be good at this sort of thing. Twelve thousand dollars. That's a lot of money to piss away. Probably goes directly to James Prentiss for his soybean condominium. The son of a bitch must be worth twenty million dollars. Ten anyway.

Hewitt sat down in his chair and shoved the stack of papers away, his hand bumping into the new tape recorder, scattering a few of the sheets on the floor. Twelve thousand dollars. How much did he piss away each year on crap like this machine just because it could be written off? Two electric typewriters, and Moore used one finger. The tape decks in both cars to listen to the medical cassettes. The photocopying machine for the bills. And now this. To dictate case histories. To capture random thoughts for the betterment of medicine.

He punched in the two buttons that started the record system. "Hewitt here," he said, "Dr. Alexander Hewitt.

Case history." The whirring of the machine was not unlike the buzz, filling the mind with a batting of sound that kept out all else. Hewitt pressed the stop button. Then the rewind and then the replay. "Hewitt here," he was told in a fairly close replica, "Dr. Alexander Hewitt. Case history." He pressed the stop button and regarded the machine with new interest. It was time to stop acting like a patient and begin functioning like a doctor. He suddenly realized that he had been thinking of his symptoms and actions in nonmedical terms, using the phrases that the patients used when they described their ailments to him.

"Ninety percent of medical conditions are psychological," he intoned as he pressed down the two buttons for recording. "Everybody says so."

"I am having a menopause at the age of forty-two," he told the machine, "and it is not refreshing. It is manifesting itself in a heightened systolic pressure and tachycardia. No medication has been prescribed, although reserpine and a thiazide in conjunction with quinidine sulfate might be indicated. The subject is six feet one inch tall and weighs approximately one hundred and ninety-four pounds, some fifteen pounds over desirable level for his particular bone structure. There has been no medical rundown, and a full checkup is indicated for blood, heart and assorted vital organs. There is also trouble with the most important organ, which is erratic in tumescence and superrapid in detumescence. Patient has also slowed down a bit in athletic competitions and has lost that all-important step to the right. He is burdened with a spoiled wife and three spoiling children. He is a man of sweet, even temperament, much put upon, good, nay, great at his work, and has been known to drink more than was good for him. As a matter of fact, more than was good for everybody. He is tired. Physically, mentally, morally. Pooped out. In failing condition. He no longer wants to pick up."

The finger went out by itself and pushed the stop button.

Hewitt looked at the handsome little machine and read off "Solid State TC-90" as though it were the answer to something. Once more the hand went out and punched down the record buttons. Hewitt listened to the hiss of the tape passing through the cassette.

"Psychiatric evaluation," he said finally, and then was silent again. The hissing of the machine was pleasant in a way, but it had an insistence of its own.

"Mother," said Hewitt. "And father. Patient had . . . has a mother and father. The mother has thin lips which almost disappear when she is angry. The father . . . the father . . . the father has no distinguishing characteristics. The patient was . . . is . . . an only child. The patient was a good student. The patient was a good boy. The patient never had to make a choice. There was no choice. There is no choice. There can be no choice. The patient was a virgin until. . . . There was no choice. There is no choice. The mother has thin lips which almost disappear when she is angry. The father. . . ."

A finger punched in the rewind button while the ear listened for the whirring to stop. When it did, the finger punched the stop button and then the replay.

"Hewitt here" sounded through the office and he listened all the way, nodding his head now and again even when the sound stopped and the whirring took over, nodding to the whirring as though it were making sense. It was impossible to tell how a half hour tape could have played through in such a short time. Was it such a short time or was it a half hour? He punched in the stop button and looked around for the little plastic pick that you stuck in the microphone jack to erase the tape. Although he pawed through the plastic bag three times, he could not find the gadget. The tape could not be left for Moore or anyone else in the world to hear. One could record over what had been recorded, substituting new words for old, but he could not think of one thing to say, or sing, or read from a book. There was not enough strength in his throat even to read from a book. Pushing the eject button, he watched the cassette leap in the air like a sailfish that has been hooked, jumping in the first rage and frustration of containment. Holding the strip of tape with his left hand, he pulled on the cassette with his right, so that a long strand of tape dangled in the air. The scissors were in his center drawer, and he began to cut the tape into little strips, carefully piling them up on the desk in front of him and then cutting each piece in half again, lengthwise this time. Some of the tiny pieces he dumped in his own wastebasket, and some he took out to Moore's basket, where he carefully splattered them among the wadded papers. The men from the cleaning service should have them out of the office by Monday into the big dump truck and then scattered to the sanitary landfills of the world. The secrets of Dr. Hewitt would once more be locked in the earth.

Returning to his desk, he looked down at the scattered papers that Moore had assembled so neatly. Not today, Cleo, not today. Maybe Atherton would be at the club early and they could get in their game of squash. Or paddle tennis. Or any goddamned thing. "We who are about to die," he told the unloaded tape recorder, "really don't give a shit."

xviii

HEWITT slid his gym shorts past his thighs and executed the little wriggle that dropped them to his ankles. Hooking both thumbs into the elastic, he shoved the supporter to the same level and then nimbly stepped out of both. Looking down at them expectantly, he waited to see if they would walk into the locker by themselves. When he remembered to bring them home for washing, Betsy always went through this ritual of gagging and holding her nose as she dropped them straight into the washing machine. Once she had dropped them into the garbage bag, loudly maintaining that her machine was not capable of handling this much stink.

The brown spot on the inside of the right leg caught his eye, and he bent over to inspect it. The mole looked as if it had darkened and grown somewhat. He poked his finger into it, and the whole mass seemed harder than it ever had before. Hardly a day went by that he wasn't prodding or pinching the damn thing, and he ought to have it out immediately, if not sooner.

"Come to me, my melanoma baby," he crooned softly as

he shoved his socks and sneakers into the locker. A skinny length of sweat ambled over and regarded him with baleful eyes.

"Hey, Gus," said Hewitt, "take a look at this thing, will you?" He put his foot on the stool opposite him and turned the leg so that the mole was plainly visible. Gus Atherton bent over the leg, prodding the protuberance with one finger and then gathering it between two.

"Well," he said, "as an obstetrician, all I can tell you is that it isn't pregnant. As a doctor, all I can tell you is that I don't like the looks of it. As a friend, all I can tell you is to go to someone who knows about these things and have him cut it out."

"Melanoma, huh?" asked Hewitt with a grin.

"Only the good part of it. I hate to tell you about the rest. But if you will grant me another opportunity in the court next week, I will proceed to knock it off your body and save you all the fuss and bother."

"On your best day," said Hewitt, "you couldn't knock a pimple off my ass."

"I believe in deeds rather than vulgar expressions," said Atherton, heading for the shower.

"You owe me a drink for today's deeds," said Hewitt, following after. They walked silently into the tiled cubicle and took long, latherful showers, faces held up to the hot spray, each lost in his own nonthoughts as his body recovered from the physical exertion. Both men had played to win every moment, had given all they were capable of. The game of squash was as the game of life to them.

The courts were in a separate building off the clubhouse, and they had used Atherton's car as a jitney. He glanced at his watch as they pulled into the main parking lot.

"You're not going to welsh on that drink, are you?" asked Hewitt.

"No," said Atherton, "but I've got a young girl with an

interesting pelvic structure who is about to go into labor, and I thought they would be calling me about this time. You'll get your drink."

They walked into the men's bar, where some half dozen stalwarts were pressed against the mahogany, two of them talking with enough decibels to show where they had spent the entire afternoon. Loud greetings were exchanged all around.

"Your pleasure, Doctors," said Mac, the barman.

"I'll have one of your very special vodka martinis," said Hewitt. "No, make that a double. Dr. Atherton is paying."

The barman smiled.

"And I'll have a Virgin Mary with a lot of ice," said Atherton.

"For Christ's sake," said Hewitt, "it's your afternoon. . . ."

"Hey, Gus," bellowed one of the bulls from the end of the bar, "this call is for you."

Atherton moved down to the phone on the wall, and Mac poured out the drinks. Alex looked at the pale liquid in the frosty glass for a moment and then carefully lifted it by the stem for the first sip. The raw burning went right from the tongue down the throat into the belly, and the body, which had been crying for liquid replenishment after the fierce exertion, reacted with a jolt. Jesus Christ, Almighty God, in Heaven Above, Bless Them, Every Fucking One of Them. He started as Atherton touched him on the shoulder.

"That pelvis is in action," he said, "and I'd better get over there to check its rotation." He took a long gulp of his tomato juice, signed the check that was by the glass and started out. He stopped, turned and came back.

"Next Wednesday," he said pleasantly, "I am going to give you cancer if you haven't already got it," and he was gone.

Hewitt could feel the damn thing pulling on his leg. Best to have Stanton just cut it out. Tomorrow. Cardiac, cerebral, carcinoma? You pays your money and you takes your choice. He drained the glass and ordered another.

"Double?" asked Mac.

He started to shake his head but turned it into a nod. Wednesday, beautiful, beautiful Wednesday.

A bulky body moved onto the next stool, crowding just a bit.

"Hey, Alex," said a familiar voice, "let me get that glass filled for you."

Hewitt looked down in disbelief. Christ, it was empty. The ubiquitous Mac was standing in front of him, both hands flat on the bar, his face reflecting the patience of his profession—we will stick it out on this front if it takes all summer.

"Well, thanks, Charlie," said Hewitt, turning to his benefactor, "I think I just might have a small one," and he made a sign to Mac that indicated a single on this occasion. Wednesday or no Wednesday, somebody might fall down and break his goddamn neck.

Charlie Rivers had fetched his own drink with him, and he kept his eyes focused right on it while Mac flourished his way through to a fresh martini. There was nothing strange about Rivers buying the doctor a drink. Although they did not socialize outside of bumping into each other at the club or a party here or there, Hewitt's malpractice insurance was underwritten by one of the companies represented by the Rivers Insurance Agency, and the premium was a princely sum, almost a fucking king's ransom, as a matter of fact. Prick-face McCord was at least right about that. But the drinks had always been bought in group good-fellowship, never with the plunking of an ass on an adjoining stool. The man had obviously clapped his bell and wanted a cleansing injection that even his own personal physician wouldn't know about. Did he think that the eminent Dr. Hewitt could be bought with one lousy martini? It would cost him at least three. . . .

"Alex, I. . . ."

Hewitt waited him out. It isn't easy to tell a comparative stranger in a bar that you fear your pecker is falling off, but if you want to save your pecker, you have to piss it out. How would you like to have a cancerous mole eating your leg off, Mr. Malpractice? No penicillin shot is big enough to wipe that out, you beady-eyed fuckface.

"Alex, you were in the Nam."

Hewitt very deliberately put his drink down and turned with a frown. Who the hell was this old fart to talk about the Nam? That was for the veterans to use. All those hard-nosed kids and yours truly, Captain Alexander Hewitt, hero. Nam! Where'd he come off with that shit?

Rivers was still peering down his glass, searching for what? He didn't want to see the expression on Hewitt's face —good, bad or indifferent. Whatever he was about to say had to be said in a vacuum, as if it were not being said, as if it would disappear once it was said and nobody would ever know about it, including the man who said it and the one who heard it.

"Yeah," said Hewitt, lifting his glass and taking a sip—he could feel it in his knees now, holding the cancer below the knee—"I was in the Nam."

"My youngest boy was there," said the insurance man.

Hewitt drained the glass. Rivers had obviously made some kind of signal because Mac was right there with a fresh one, taking away the old glass and sliding a bowl of peanuts between the two gentlemen. Hewitt pushed his fingers into the dish in a scoop and stopped—salt. Take it easy on the salt, man. He removed his hand and wiped the fingers on the tiny napkin. Rivers was still talking.

". . . dropped out of school and disappeared for three years. Not a word. Then last month he showed up as if nothing happened. Dirty. Jesus, he was dirty. Beard. Mustache. Hair down to his ass. She moved him right into his old room. Crying, Christ, I thought she'd never stop crying. With joy, she told everybody. With joy."

Hewitt took a handful of nuts and chewed on them. You can't drink on an empty stomach.

". . . and he just stays in that room and listens to tapes all day," said Rivers. "Eats when he feels like it. Disappears without saying where he's going or when he'll be back—sometimes for two, three days. And he's on drugs."

"Drugs?" said Hewitt.

"Marijuana, for one. When we asked him whether he was smoking it in there, he pulled a tin box out of his pocket and offered us some. Just like that. I told him to get that stuff out of the house, and he just looked at me and smiled. My wife said maybe we should smoke one with him and then we could talk about it."

"Might not be a bad idea," said Hewitt reflectively. "At least it would give you a starting point."

"Are you crazy?" said Rivers, shifting around in his seat. "It's bad enough having one dope fiend in the family without everybody starting up."

"Is he on anything else?"

"What?"

"Is it just marijuana or is he taking something else?"

"I don't know. How should I know? This is bad enough."

"Most of them were on grass over there," said Hewitt. "I used it myself." Christ, he'd finally said it. And to this asshole, of all people. Dr. Hewitt smokes pot. Dr. Hewitt smokes pot. Dr. Hewitt smokes pot.

"He told his mother he'd killed a woman."

Christ, he hadn't even heard him. He was so busy getting it out of his own gut that he wasn't even listening to what old Doc Hewitt was saying. He waved to Mac for another one and threw a fistful of peanuts into his mouth. How many would this make. Five? No, six. There were the two doubles. Don't forget the two doubles. This and out, you dumb shit, while you can still stand.

"They were going through a village, and he saw this guy run out of a house, and he shot him, and he turned out to be a woman."

"Most of the time," said Hewitt.

"What?"

"Most of the time it was a woman or a kid or a goddamn dog or something. Or they'd go up in the choppers and spray bullets like it was rain."

"What the hell am I going to do?"

"Wait him out."

"What?"

"He's young. He can brood only so long. He's got too much juice in his body. The young can't sit still that long even on pot. Wait him out."

"How long?"

"How long has he been home?"

"About a month."

"It shouldn't take much longer."

"I don't know if I can take it."

"What else are you going to do?"

"What do you mean?"

"You going to throw him out? You going to turn him in?"

"My wife. . . ."

"Exactly. Exactly. You still have a lot of years to live with your wife. And this is her baby. You have to consider your wife as much as the boy. Maybe more. You're dealing with two, not one."

Rivers uttered a long sigh and took a swallow of his drink.

"You know," said Hewitt, sliding off the stool—Jesus Christ, knees—"it isn't easy walking around and knowing you wiped out somebody. *SH. SH. SH.* Especially when the somebody turns out to be an innocent party."

He signed his tab and walked away from Rivers without

looking back. Just as that kid had probably walked away from that God-forsaken slant-eye. Don't look back, that ballplayer had said. Somebody—or something—may be catching up.

He had trouble remembering exactly where he had left the car, but he drove home with no trouble because he knew he was drunk and took care accordingly.

xix

FOUR startled faces, two with mouths agape far enough to display partly chewed beef, gazed up at Hewitt as he entered the dining room.

"Well," he said pleasantly, "I thought I had been invited for dinner. Did I get the wrong night?" And he turned to go.

"Alex," said Betsy, louder than she intended, scrambling out of her place and running toward him, "here's your plate, right here. When I didn't hear from you, I assumed you were tied up."

"Nothing would keep me from the bosom of my family," he said, "especially when there is such a nice-looking roast as this." He sat down at the head of the table.

"And how are you, one and all?" he asked, looking around at the circle, pausing a moment at each face. Jeff and Joanne were still staring at him, but Bobbi had resumed eating, carefully cutting a tiny strip of meat off the slab on her plate.

"Jeff?"

"Yes." A most careful yes. They smelled the booze. The tiger's in the bag. Watch out!

"How are things progressing at school?"

"All right."

"Jeff doesn't seem to have much appetite tonight," Betsy interjected, hoping to get a general conversation going, to fill the room with harmless words.

"Why is that?" Hewitt cut in, closing all mouths, focusing all eyes on Jeff.

Jeff, his face bright red, wavered, uncertain which was worse, words or silence.

"I guess I'm just not hungry," he finally managed.

"Then get up to your room," snapped Hewitt, despite himself, knowing it had all turned around on him, the alcohol heavy in his system, the weight of his head almost more than he could sustain.

Jeff looked at his mother, who opened her mouth and then closed it again, an action he had witnessed innumerable times. His eyes welled up with tears, but before one of them escaped its confines, he was off his chair and out of the room.

"I don't want any more to eat," said Bobbi, scrambling out of her seat and heading for the door.

"You stop right there," commanded Hewitt, and the girl stopped. But didn't turn around.

"I'll tell you when you've had enough to eat. Now get back to your place."

She returned to her chair and sat in it, but made no motion to pick up her fork. Hewitt contemplated her for a moment and then decided it wasn't worth pushing any further. He turned his attention to Jojo, who was looking at him as though he were a strange but interesting specimen on a slide. Miss Cuticles. There was hope for this one. She took things as they came along, one at a time.

"All right," said Hewitt, "now everybody is going to eat

his dinner, nice and friendly. Including me, if anybody ever gets around to giving me some."

Betsy stood and came to take his plate, filled it with beef, roast potatoes and broccoli and set it down before him. She did not look at him once while she was doing this, nor did she speak to the children. Hewitt cut his meat and bit into the lukewarm piece. For one wild moment he thought he was going to retch, and the effort of getting the food past his throat caused his stomach muscles to tighten into a band of iron.

He got up from his place and walked through to the den, where he half filled a glass with vodka, took it to the kitchen and loaded it with ice cubes. When he came back to the dining room, he found only Betsy still at her place. He set the glass down by his plate and looked at her. She was waiting for him to ask where the children were, and she could dry up and blow away in dust before he did. They could run, but they couldn't hide.

"I read in the paper about a Bardwell funeral," said Betsy. "Wasn't he one of your patients?"

"The food's cold," said Hewitt, pushing away the plate and lifting the glass of vodka.

She ignored the challenge. As far as she was concerned, there was no food on the table. There were only a husband and wife having a chat at the end of the day, catching up on what had happened.

"Wasn't Mr. Bardwell one of your patients?" she persisted.

"How do you know that?"

"You left that name when you went on a house call. It was a Sunday, the Sunday we were supposed to go to the Scott's."

"Starting next week," said Hewitt, "you will have twenty dollars extra for household money."

"What?"

"You've been bitching you haven't got enough money to run your house, and I'm upping the ante, that's what."

"Alex, why can't I have my own checking account?"

"Because you'd piss away all the money inside of two days."

"You wouldn't have to worry about that."

"You think your daddy'd keep it loaded up for you?"

"It's just that it's so . . . so demeaning. I have to come to you for every little thing. It's a bother. . . ."

"I don't mind being bothered."

"I'm talking about me, Alex. *Me!* I have to come and stand before you like a little girl and tell you that I need five dollars for this and three dollars for that and six dollars for the other thing. . . ."

"That's fourteen dollars so far."

"What?"

"You've just pissed away fourteen dollars, and you weren't even started. Money doesn't come as easy in this household as it did in yours. I am working my balls off so that you can keep your hair the right shade of yellow and Jo can have braces on her teeth and Jeff can turn up his nose at prime roast beef."

"You made that decision for him."

"I make all the decisions around here. It's not going to be like it was at my house." He took a long drink of his vodka. It burned coldly, and he could feel the beads of sweat on his forehead.

"What was it like at your house?" she asked softly.

"What?"

"Your house," she repeated. "What was it like there? I've known your parents for nearly twenty years now, and I really don't know them at all. They come every year and spend Christmas Eve, and we all sit around and talk about nothing, and then they go away the next day. And I know the same thing about them that I knew the year before. They have never once in twenty years invited us or their grandchildren to visit them. And I know in my heart that if I don't call them to come this Christmas, they won't come, and they probably would hardly notice."

"What the hell has all that got to do with anything?"

"I don't know. Maybe everything."

"What's that supposed to mean?"

"Alex, why don't we go talk to Jim Henderson, the two of us? Lay it all out on the table, your problems, my problems?"

"I have no problems," said Hewitt. "I have no problems. Maybe you have problems. But that's your problem."

"You do have problems, Alex. You just won't acknowledge them. Our whole marriage is falling apart."

"Oh," he said, taking another swallow from the glass. He had the weak feeling in the knees again. It could be the blood pressure and not the booze. One click in the brain and all over. Or a vegetable. Like good old Sam. One giant cancer cell. Henderson. Dr. Henderson, for Christ's sake. *Oh, yes, Betsy. You're not the only one having a problem with Alex. Cindy Huber was just in and wait till you hear this.*

". . . and it's having a terrible effect on the children, too," Betsy was saying, had been saying, had said.

He looked at her—the beginning of the lines at the corners of the eyes, the breasts down a peg . . . or two . . . or three, the down on the arms noticeably darker, the hair, no, you couldn't tell a thing about the hair. Still prettier than anyone else in the circle.

"Do you want a divorce?" he asked.

"What?" She seemed really surprised.

"Is all this bullshit leading up to a request for a divorce?"

"Do you want a divorce?" she asked.

"No. Why should I want a divorce?"

"Do you still love me?"

He thought about it, seriously. He took another long pull on the vodka and thought about whether he still loved his wife. Had he ever loved his wife, even when the hair was golden to the roots and the mouth tasted like the small fragrances of his mother's lingerie drawer? Love. What is love? Come to me, my melanoma baby. *SH. SH. SH.* There had to be a reason why nobody called. Wasn't Mr. Bardwell one of your patients? Was he? Yes, he was. Then why hadn't somebody called to tell of his. . . .

". . . nor is it that simple," she said.

"What?"

"I don't want a divorce," she said. "I love you and our children and what we have. I want to hold onto them, all of them. You've seen what happens to families when the parents are divorced."

"Some of them, it's the best thing that ever happened."

She stared down at her plate, at the half-eaten slice of beef, the congealed gravy, the graying vegetable—there's my life, she thought, all on a plate.

"You may be one of the lucky ones," he said.

"What do you mean lucky?"

"Well, you're still fairly young, you've got most of your looks, you're a pretty good lay. . . ."

"You wouldn't know it from the way you've been acting," she said, not sure as she said it whether to be glad or sorry, but having to say it out loud.

"Oh? I haven't heard any complaints."

"This week was the first time in five weeks. And it was four weeks before that. And I don't know how long before that."

"Just weeks?"

"What do you mean just weeks?"

"You don't know how many hours, how many minutes, how many seconds between each one? You just know how many weeks?"

"I just know something's wrong."

"But you don't know what it is."

"No, I don't. I know there's something wrong between us

but I don't know what it is. I go over and over everything in my mind, but I don't know what it is."

"Maybe it was the war. They say war does things to people."

"No, it started before you went to Vietnam. You were different when you came back, you've been different ever since, but whatever is wrong between us started happening long before you went in the service."

"I was dragged in," he said woodenly, his arm suddenly too weak to lift the glass to his mouth. "Why do people always talk about it as though I volunteered?"

"Oh, Alex," she sighed, "why must you try to be so cynical all the time? About me, the kids, medicine, the war? What about your medal?"

"Did I ever tell you how I got that Silver Star, Betsy, my wife?"

"I've read the citation."

"Is that how you think I got it, the way it reads in the citation?"

"Well, I assume that's—"

"That's your trouble, Betsy, my wife. You're always ready to believe what you read in the citation." He finished off the vodka in the glass, sucking at the ice cubes for bits of moisture.

"Let me tell you why I got that medal, Betsy, my wife. I got that medal because one night the colonel, the regimental commander, got blind drunk and beat his whore into a coma. Beat the living shit right out of her. And I patched her up as best I could and shipped her back to the hospital. And do you know what I marked on her tag? Do you? Did you read that in the citation?"

"It doesn't say anything about—"

"No, of course it doesn't. It doesn't even mention the colonel or his whore. I'll tell you what I marked on that tag. I wrote down that she was a victim of a hit-and-run truck accident. He was a big bastard, my colonel. Getting racked up by him was the equivalent of being run over by a truck."

"But how did—"

"I didn't know a thing about it until the medal came through. He had them write it up so that one of those helicopter rides I took, one of the joyrides where they let me spray the trees with the fifty-calibers and who gave a shit what you hit, he had them write it up so that one of them sounded like something out of a John Wayne movie."

"This all sounds—"

"But I'll say this for him. He didn't have the balls to present it to me in a formal parade. He just came in the tent and handed it to me and said, 'Thanks.' He thought he was paying off a debt, the son of a bitch."

"Alex, I'm sure you did many things over there that were worthy of—"

"Can you imagine what the enlisted men were thinking, the ones who had to write up that shit? And fatasses in bars wonder why they came back smoking pot and sticking needles in their arms."

"Alex, I think—"

"Shut up, Betsy, my wife. I haven't finished talking. I was talking about divorce. If you want a divorce, go ahead. Take the kids, take two of the television sets, and take a flying fuck at the moon. But as for me, I still believe the citation the minister read to us. I don't want a divorce. I'm perfectly happy the way things are now."

He stood up and started to walk out of the room, turned and came back for his glass.

"Where are you going?" she asked.

"We're going," he said, "you and me. We're going to a wake. We're going to go look at our friend Frank Casey lying in a box. And we're going to tell everybody, including the widow, how terrible it all is. And we're going to let everybody look at me, the finger man, the one who set him up for the kill. Then when they've all had their fill, we'll come home. And if it isn't too late, maybe we can diddle a bit to make up for all those weeks you've gone without."

She stood up abruptly, almost knocking over her chair.

"No, no, no," she cried, halfway between despair and rage, "you're not going to do this to me anymore. Do you know how degrading it is to have a man not speak to you all day, to treat you as if you were a faceless thing, and then have him expect sexual satisfaction before he turns over and snores away the rest of the night?"

"Sexual satisfaction?" he said evenly, rotating the glass in his fingers. "Where the Christ did you come up with that? Your problem is that you're a horny broad who uses words like 'vagina' and 'penis' and 'sexual satisfaction.' What you'd really like to say is—"

"Must you degrade everything," she sobbed, "turn it all into filth? We're all faceless things to you, with no more significance than the chairs or the cars or the dog. Have you ever stopped to think how little time you spend with us, any of us? The children see you for one hour a day at the most, and if ten words are exchanged, it's a lot. And how many of those words are nice words?"

"I do a lot of things with the kids," he said, moving a step toward her, holding the glass as though it were a weapon.

"Only the things that you want to do. And then it's more as a drill instructor than a father. You teach them how to ski or swim or throw a ball because you want someone to go skiing with or swimming or to play ball. There's no joy in anything you do with our children. There's no joy in anything you do with me, even the sex. Especially the sex."

He dropped the glass on the floor and moved in to her, grasping both arms above the elbows and holding her straight out before him. She looked into his face, somewhat fearfully but too exhausted really to care about what she might have to endure.

"What do you know about me," he grated, his teeth barely apart, "what do you really know about me? What have you learned in seventeen years?" The strength in his fingers seemed linked directly to his brain, and he knew that if he closed his hands, they would go all the way, crushing through flesh and muscle and bone until his fingers touched his palms and this woman would be destroyed forever.

Her eyes widened as she felt the iron in his grip and sensed the latent power, but it also served to stiffen the core within her, and as her shoulders spread in reaction, she lifted her head the half inch that put her eyes directly on his.

"I know you are lonely," she said, "and I have tried to fill that loneliness. The first time I saw you, that very first time, I thought to myself how tall, how attractive, how lonely. And I wanted to fill your whole being with love right from the start, from that very second. You had all of me right then. All you had to do was open your hand."

She turned her head so that her eyes rested first on where he was holding her right arm and then her left. The grip tightened for a moment and then slackened, but he held her firm, still undecided as to what he had in mind, perhaps needing the steadiness of her body to hold himself upright.

"When things started to go wrong," she continued, "I looked at me, never at you. Where was I letting you down? You were a doctor, a healer. You were devoting your life to helping others. It couldn't be that you weren't trying to help me or your children, that we meant less to you than any other human being.

"I'm your wife," she said, "and I believe there must have been a special reason why you married me, why you wanted me for your own. And they are your children, and I believe you must have had a special reason for wanting them, for wanting three of them for your own. I believe you must have had special reasons, and I lay awake nights wondering what those reasons were."

Hewitt dropped his hands to his sides. The white marks on her arms caught his eyes and held them, mute testimony in the case against him.

"One day," said Betsy, "after you'd left the house in one of your rages, Jeff, he couldn't have been more than two, walked over to me and stuck out his little finger and started to shout, the gibberish pouring out of him, and I suddenly realized he was imitating you, and he looked so funny, his little face all screwed up, that I started to laugh, and then I began crying, and I couldn't stop, I just couldn't stop. And he became frightened and held onto my knee and was crying away, and I knew then what was wrong with us, with our marriage."

Hewitt bent down and retrieved the glass from the floor, never taking his eyes off her.

"You never had to share," said Betsy, "you've never known what it is to share. You're an only child, and I know you were a lonely child, and you grew up without having to share anything with anybody—your toys, your thoughts, your good things or your bad. And you became a doctor because you don't have to share anything in that either. Your patients, the nurses—they all take orders without having to know the reasons. And me. You've never once discussed anything with me. I'm allowed to do all the things that you're not interested in, but you decide everything else, everything."

He put both hands around the glass, squeezing them together with a fierce pressure that could conceivably smash it into pieces, hard, sharp pieces that could cut through flesh and into bone.

"It was the children, wasn't it?" she said, not expecting an answer. "It was the children finished it off. The adults do everything you want, but the children are a different matter. As their demands grew greater, as they sought more and more of me because they were getting less and less of you, you couldn't take the competition. You're a bigger baby than any of them have ever been. If you can't be the center of attention, you won't play."

"Life is not a game," he said, holding the glass up in his left hand and waving it for emphasis.

"What is it then?" she pursued, suddenly aware that she was dominating the conversation, the room, the person in front of her. "What is life to you? You run our lives by your rules, and God help anybody who breaks one. What do you want from us? What can we do to make you like us?"

He stood there drained of all strength, all emotion, barely able to keep the glass from slipping through his fingers. One truth stood out from all the words with which she had assaulted him: alone. With a mother and father he had been alone. With a wife and three children he was alone. How did other people break through to each other? Suppose he said to her now, right now, *I have hypertension and extra systoles,* would a new look come over her face, would a new bond be forged? Would there be a look of pity, compassion, love? Does this woman love? Can anybody love?

"I like you," he said, "all of you, including the goddamned dog. Tomorrow I will ask Frank Stanton to cut out my heart, and I will wear it on my sleeve, so that all of you, including the goddamned dog, will know how much I like you. Meanwhile, get ready to go to the funeral parlor. You can tell Gerda how lucky she is not to have problems like yours anymore."

She didn't bother to look at him as she walked out of the room. A piece of toast. Another piece of burned toast.

He placed the glass down on the table, scanning the food that was oxidizing into its next stage. There was almost the smell of rot in the air as nutrients dissipated and bacteria performed their prescribed function. This is life, he thought, the breaking down of everything into nothing. Had he broken down his marriage this night with his parcels of truth? The colonel's whore. What about Hewitt's whore? Why hadn't he told her about Hewitt's whore, too, if he was going to be so truthful? And what was the special reason for marrying Elizabeth Prentiss, the belle of the ball? Because she was pretty and rich? Rich and pretty? Pretty rich? Because there was all that security right there if you ever needed it? Truth, Hewitt, truth! And three children? What special reason for three children? The only special reason is that you don't have one child, you never have just one child, to be alone, alone, alone. One child is. . . .

He heard the rush of feet coming toward him and winced at the thought of the funeral home and the hours ahead with Casey on the platter and the bacteria working. The nausea was still there in the back of the throat, and it might. . . .

"Alex," she moaned, coming through the door so quickly she stumbled on the rug, "there's something wrong with Jeff. I can't wake him up."

She didn't have her coat on; she wasn't ready to go. He couldn't remember when he had felt so tired, so drained, as if. . . .

"Alex!" Hysteria, he noted, just this side of hysteria. She was pulling at his sleeve, and as he looked at her arm, he could still see the mark where he had held her. "Alex! His face is scarlet, and he's making noises, and he won't open his eyes!"

He followed her out of the room. It was easier to do that than argue about her not having her coat on.

XX

BETSY was already kneeling beside the bed by the time Hewitt came through the door, and his eyes focused on the gold of her head before they shifted along the line of her arm to the cheeks she was caressing with her fingers. The boy's face was bright-red, and his chest was moving up and down in spasmodic jerks. Peripheral vasodilatation with hyperventilation, a part of Hewitt's mind was noting as he reached out his hand and took the boy's left wrist between his fingers. The skin was so hot that the rapidity of the beat was almost a secondary sensation. The noises were interfering with his concentration, and he was about to shout for Betsy to shut up, for Christ's sake, when he saw that the sounds were coming from between the boy's teeth, low animal gutturals of primitive intensity.

He dropped the wrist and straightened up, closing his eyes. I am drunk, he told himself, I am drunk, drunk, drunk, and this boy is about to go into shock. *This boy is about to go into shock!*

"Alex, what's wrong? What's wrong with him?"

He took a deep breath through his nose and exhaled through his mouth. Again. And again.

"Get his clothes off," he said, reaching down for a shoe while she started unbuttoning the shirt. He smelled infection somewhere, tasted it in the back of his throat, and as the shoe slipped off, his other hand reached out and pulled the sock with it. The body shivered as he held the heel—high fever, chills, rapid heart, hyperventilation: His mind ticked them all off—and he dropped the foot and reached for the other one. The shoe came off, but the sock stuck, and as he lifted the foot higher, he noticed an area of dark wetness at the heel. It took both hands to work the cloth off and there it was, bright red, gleaming, suppurating thick masses of greenish yellow pus from the edges. Bands of red radiated from the wound up the leg as far as the trousers allowed vision, and the bands widened as Hewitt shoved the cloth higher.

"Oh, my God," Betsy moaned beside him, as she turned to pull the shirt from under her son, "the shoe. I forgot about the shoe."

Hewitt placed the leg back on the bed and undid the boy's belt, zipped down the fly and pulled the pants down to the knee. His fingers pressed into the groin where the glands had already swollen to twice their normal size. The area was hot, and the boy moaned a bit as Hewitt probed the area.

Betsy's hands returned to Jeff's face as if in answer to his cry, and she moaned in return, a sound as hot and sick as the one that had called out.

Hewitt pushed her aside and gathered the bedspread around the boy before lifting him up in his arms. The weight caught him by surprise, and he stopped for a moment. When was the last time he had held this boy in his arms? When was the last time he had touched him?

As he carried his burden through the door, Hewitt was thinking ahead to procedures, and it wasn't until he reached the bottom of the stairs that Betsy was able to run around them and stop their progress.

"What is it?" she cried, her tear-streaked face twisted in pain. "What is wrong? Where are you taking him?"

"Listen!" said Hewitt, and his voice was such that she stepped back a half pace. "Call the hospital and ask for admitting. Tell them I am bringing my son in with bacteremic shock and a severe infection. Can you remember that?"

She nodded.

"Bacteremic shock with severe infection," he repeated. "Say it!"

"Bacteremic shock with severe infection," she said.

"Tell them to call the pediatric floor and arrange for isolation," he said.

She nodded again, and he started toward the door.

"Don't go without me," she yelled as she turned for the phone in the kitchen, "don't go without me."

Hewitt didn't hear her as he twisted the knob awkwardly with his left hand while Jeff almost slipped from his grasp. He pulled the knob sharply and wrestled the bulk back into full control. The garage spotlights had not been turned on, and Hewitt, his mind full of medical procedures rather than concrete steps, was almost pitched to his knees by the first one down. He was still in a half crouch when he glided off the last one and didn't straighten up until he was halfway to his car.

His left hand was almost to the doorlatch when he snarled in rage and whirled around, looking for the station wagon. She had pulled it into the garage, and he ran into the dark exterior and laid the boy down on the hood while he yanked open the rear door. As he was backing out after placing the boy across the rear seat and tucking the spread into the slot for restraint, he bumped into Betsy, who was standing there with her hands making little motions in the air, helplessly trying to help Hewitt with his burden.

"The woman said she would inform the pediatric floor of

your instructions," said Betsy as she moved to open the door again and get in with her son. Hewitt grabbed her shoulder and held firm, not knowing why, squeezing his eyes shut as he tried to force the reason for his action into consciousness. Betsy bucked, wanting to get her arms around Jeff, protecting him from whatever was burning inside him, but Hewitt's hand was locked into her shoulder, not to be released until the key was revealed.

"Stanton," he yelled, pulling her around until she faced him. "Call Frank Stanton and tell him what's happened. Bacteremic shock with severe infection. Tell him I need him at the hospital for a surgical consult." The hand unlocked.

"Wait for me," Betsy pleaded as she ran for the house, "wait for me."

As Hewitt's hand turned the key in the ignition while his foot pushed delicately on the accelerator, the motor caught with exactly the right amount of fuel in its carburetor and the tension poured out of his shoulders and moved into the horsepower with grateful release. The headlights clicked on, the gearshift moved into reverse, and the car was backed out into a tight arc that fitted it exactly into the pattern for moving down the driveway. Dr. Hewitt was now on an emergency run with a patient.

His eyes swept the dials automatically as he turned right toward the hospital road, and he noted that the needle of the gas gauge was sitting exactly on Empty. She'd done it again, the stupid bitch. One of her daddy's blacks had always seen to it that Miss Betsy's car was always right full up and washed and swept, and she'd been stranded on every goddamned street in town every goddamned year they'd been married. Six miles. The tank held two or three gallons when it first registered Empty, but the question was how long it had been on Empty. Would it be better to keep the speed down and hope there was enough to squeak through or go like hell and take the chance? Hewitt's foot answered the question by pressing hard, and the powerful wagon burst forward toward the downtown section, the skilled hands whirling it around cars without even a warning blast. Hewitt ran two lights at intersections, slowing slightly on each occasion, but moving swiftly enough to get across before the waiting traffic had a chance to move. There were a couple of horns blasts, but nothing close enough to involve braking or swerving, and in nine minutes he zoomed through the hospital gates and around the driveway to the main door, where he braked smoothly to a full stop. Not once during the trip had he looked into the back seat.

As he slid out of the car, he saw the hospital door open and a figure in white moving fast toward him. It was Junie Hall, one of the residents in internal medicine, a chunky towhead who never seemed to tire physically or of asking questions that he felt would increase his knowledge.

"We've got a stretcher available, Doctor," he said, as Hewitt was reaching into the back seat for Jeff, who seemed not to have moved an inch during the trip. Hewitt tugged the boy out and folded him in his arms once more before moving toward the door. The resident said not another word but trotted ahead to pull the glass panel open. Both the woman at the switchboard and the one at the reception desk were standing up as Hewitt came past them heading for the elevator. Some people were browsing in the gift shop, and a few were seated in chairs in the waiting area, and all turned to stare at the figure of the tall man with the child in his arms, a corner of the red bedspread trailing on the floor behind them. An orderly was standing at the elevator holding the door open while a man and two women stood waiting four steps away. Hewitt strode into the elevator with Hall close behind. The orderly released the door as Hall punched three, and in ten seconds they were on their way up. He set it up, Hewitt noted, looking at the intent face of the young doctor before him, who was scanning what was visible of Jeff's face. He told the guy to hold the elevator as soon as he saw the car.

The elevator bumped gently to a stop, and the door slid open. A nurse's aide was standing there, frozen in a sentinel position, and as Hewitt and Hall emerged into the corridor, she turned stiffly and moved down the hall in fast march time around the corner to the second door on the right, where she stopped dead and swiveled to face them.

Hewitt stepped over the threshold and deposited his burden carefully on the bed, stood back and looked. His arms ached with such weariness that he dropped them to his sides in an attempt to alleviate the pain. Hands reached out and started to tug the bedspread from beneath the boy, and Hewitt moved forward again to lift where it was necessary. The nurse was capped and gowned and it took him a moment to pull a resemblance out from behind the gauze mask. Driscoll. Sophie Driscoll. A surge of relief went through him as he nodded to the old pro, and she inclined her head briefly in acknowledgment. He stepped back a couple of paces and let his jacket slide to the floor behind him as he pulled his tie from his throat and unbuttoned the shirt.

Another gowned figure came through the door holding a green smock for Hewitt, and as he slipped his arms into it, he looked full into young Hall's blue eyes, which were bright and clear and anxious to get going on what might be an interesting case. As he pulled on the cap and slipped the mask over his face, Hewitt thought back on that night in Vietnam when he had stood on the mountain and watched the 371st in the valley three miles away take an all-night pounding from heavy mortars. It had seemed so strange and exciting to be safe from harm while those men below had been digging into the dirt with their teeth or cowering in their bunkers while the shells screamed in one after another and the explosions rocked the ground. The Cong had hit a gas dump within the first fifteen minutes, and the whole area was light as day as Hewitt and some of the others stood there and mumbled to each other about "Poor bastards" and "Jesus Christ" and "Maybe we ought to . . ." while each one of them thanked God he was where he was and shit his pants for fear that somebody would order somebody else to get the hell over there and see what you can do. There had been seventeen men killed and a hundred and fourteen wounded in that barrage, and Hewitt had worked all the next day and night trying to clean up what was salvageable. "That's my son," he wanted to say to the resident, "not just an interesting case. That's my son."

"Let's get the vital signs," said Hewitt, moving to the bed. The nurse turned the boy on his side and inserted a rectal thermometer while Hewitt took the pulse and Hall leaned over to time the respirations. The heart rate was one hundred and forty, and Hewitt was about to announce this when Hall said, "The respiration is thirty-two."

"One hundred and forty," said Hewitt.

The resident took a sphygmomanometer and stethoscope from the stand and handed them to Hewitt while the nurse removed the thermometer and let the boy fall gently on his back. She twirled it in her fingers to catch the murcury column right while both doctors regarded her intently.

"One hundred and six," she said.

Hewitt heard a long sigh coming out of himself and tried to stop it before the others noticed, but the nurse was busily shaking down the thermometer and the resident moving the IV stand closer to the head of the bed. Wrapping the black elastic around Jeff's arm, he pushed down the snap and started to pump up. Son of a bitch. He unscrewed the aluminum disk and listened to the hiss. Both faces were looking at him as he removed the stethoscope from his ears and dropped it on the bed.

"Eighty over sixty," he said.

The nurse was slipping a hospital dickey over the boy's arms, not bothering to tie it at the neck.

"Let's start with a d/five w," said Hewitt, "and I'll use an intracath so we can get some blood cultures going."

The nurse turned and went out the door after removing her gown.

"Do you figure staph or strep, Doctor?" asked Hall as he moved Jeff a little higher on the bed. The boy was quiet now, and except for a slight trembling of the limbs and the rapid breathing, he seemed to be sleeping easily. Too easily, too easily, said Hewitt to himself.

"I want a catheter in his bladder," said Hewitt, "and we'll put him on the urinometer." The resident went to the door and called for a nurse, who appeared instantly and listened intently while he detailed instructions. As she disappeared down the hall, Driscoll walked in with her package and handed it to Hall before gowning up again. The resident tore open the seals and exposed the intracath, the steel needle gleaming around the white plastic tube. He looked inquiringly at Hewitt, who held out his hand, and the resident handed over the apparatus almost with reluctance. He'd love to have me the Christ out of here and work it up himself, thought Hewitt as he watched the nurse swab Jeff's arm with alcohol and then iodine. She took a rubber tube and tied it just above the elbow. Hewitt watched intently to see if any extraordinary measures would be needed, but the vein ballooned nicely and he slid the metal in smoothly, carefully threaded the plastic after it and then pulled the needle back. The nurse handed him a syringe, which he quickly attached, pulled the small wire, and the blood pumped into the tube. When it was two-thirds full, he clamped off and removed the syringe. The resident was right there with the IV tube, which he snugged over the needle, and all three looked up at the bottle, which was now dripping dextrose into the veins.

Hewitt corked the tube of blood and held it out to the nurse. As she started to move away, he called, "Wait," and she stopped and looked at him. "Let's get some samples from the ankle down to the lab at the same time," he said, "so they can get working on both. How many people are down there?" They all knew there was only one lab technician on at night, and the question did not have to be answered.

"I can probably roust somebody up to help out," said Hall, but Hewitt did not bother to acknowledge the suggestion. By the time somebody could be "rousted out," the one man in the lab would have everything under control.

Hewitt let the resident take the samples of pus while he considered the next move. Where the Christ was Stanton? He walked to the door and saw Betsy leaning against the wall across the hall. She looked shrunken, her shoulders hunched into her body and her coat twisted to one side. She was thinking her own thoughts and did not see him at first, but when recognition dawned, she ran the few steps to reach him.

"How is he?" she said, her voice so low he almost couldn't make out the words.

"Where's Stanton?"

"He and his wife went out for dinner to a restaurant. I left word with the answering service, and then I called all the restaurants I could think of, but he wasn't at any of them. I've left word everywhere. How's Jeff?"

"He's in shock, but I don't know how deep. We're having some tests made, and then we'll know more. I'm pretty sure it's a strep infection, and if it is, we're that much ahead of the game. He'll be all right once we can get some stuff into him."

"Don't let my son die, Alex," she said softly.

Although his mind registered the implication, there was not enough adrenalin left in his system to permit more than a lifting of the head. Her eyes were there to meet his, straight on, held for a moment, and then she turned to go back to her wall, her back an unseeing target.

"Let's piggyback three grams of Methicillin," said Hewitt as he turned back into the room, and Driscoll took his place at the door, relaying the instructions to the nurse in the hall.

The resident was inspecting the lesion in Jeff's ankle, his nose close enough to sniff the rot.

"Did it start with a blister?" he asked.

"It was a new shoe," said Hewitt, "but I don't know if it was a blister or a lesion."

"I think maybe there should—"

"Dr. Stanton is on call," said Hewitt, "but nobody seems to know where the hell he is."

"We could get one of the surgical residents," said Hall, "or I could do it. It's a fairly simple—"

The phone rang, and the resident broke off to answer it. He listened intently, said "Thank you, George," and hung up.

"Beta-hemolytic streptococcus," he said to Hewitt.

"That was fast."

"He knows it's your son."

Jesus, thought Hewitt, it's the same in every business. Everybody is somebody's son. Or daughter. Never kill a cop because the cops work harder on cases like that. If you're going to need fast blood tests, make sure you're a doctor's son.

The nurse in the hall handed Driscoll a small bottle, and she and Hall rigged the IV stand for the Methicillin to piggyback through the dextrose.

"We'll use twenty million units of aqueous penicillin," said Hewitt just as Frank Stanton came breezing through the door, a nurse close behind him with a green gown in her hands but stopping at the threshold with it held before her.

Stanton moved right over to the bed and looked down on Jeff.

"What have we here?" he asked.

"It's my boy, Jeff," said Hewitt, not certain whether Stanton had ever seen him the few times the surgeon had dined at their house. "Beta-hemolytic streptococcus."

"Hmm," said Stanton, moving back to the door and letting the aide slip the gown on him, then the cap and the mask. "Let me see the chart."

Hewitt felt his body sag in relief as Stanton accepted the chart the nurse handed him. The booze. The booze had drained his body of all its strength. One thing about the goddamned surgeons; they moved right in and took over. No sense asking a lot of questions one at a time. You looked over the chart, and you knew right away what everybody else knew. Goddamned surgeons. He could see Hall looking at Stanton with all the love and hate that every medical man feels toward the special breed. Damn the torpedoes and full scalpel ahead.

Stanton walked to the foot of the bed and picked up the foot, bending over it as close as Hall before him.

"Looks like a lot of fluctuance," he said. "I think the first order of business is to get a drain in there. Get me a surgical I and D kit," he said to the nurse. She was halfway out the door while he was saying it.

Stanton replaced the foot carefully on the bed and walked up to the head, where he pinched Jeff's arm with his thumb and forefinger.

"No need for any anesthesia," he mused, as much to himself as anybody.

"We'll want to get some blood samples," he said to Hewitt. "BUN, electrolytes, CBC. And we'd better check the ph and the gases." He turned to the resident. "Call down to the lab, Doctor, and tell them to send up a heparinized syringe."

Christ, thought Hewitt, this all could have been started

long before he got here. He looked down at his hands, which seemed firm and steady, but he could feel the tremble underneath, fatigue or blood pressure, and he was finding it impossible to concentrate, to focus in on the problem and analyze it correctly.

"Doctor," said Stanton, and there was the same ring to it that Stern had used when Hewitt was bombed out over Casey dropping dead—Jesus, they must be wondering why we're not at the wake—"Doctor," Stanton said again.

"Yes."

"I want to check the venous pressure as soon as we lance."

"Yes, of course." Stanton was looking at him, head cocked a bit.

"Right, right," said Hewitt, in answer to no question.

Driscoll came in with the surgical kit, followed by another nurse, and the two of them began to drape the area around Jeff's leg. Hewitt felt like a stranger among them, all these people going about their work, and he was uncertain about how much he should be doing himself. Twice he started to move forward toward the bed, but each time either Stanton or Hall was in the way, and he stayed where he was.

The nurses stepped back a bit, and Stanton moved in at the foot of the bed. Hewitt saw the flash of reflection as the scalpel was lifted and then the spurt of the greenish yellow pus, some of it splashing on the floor. It seemed to take only seconds for the surgeon to affix the drain, and then the nurses moved in again to tidy up.

"The syringe is here, Doctor," said Hall, and Stanton peeled off his gloves and took the case in his hand. He moved up to Jeff's thigh and took a sample from the femoral artery.

"Tell them we're in a hurry," he said to the nurse as he handed it to her. "What's the blood pressure?"

"Sixty over forty," said Hall, who had just taken it.

"I think we ought to give him five hundred milligrams of Solu-Cortef," said Stanton.

Hewitt could see the resident staring at him, his eyes narrowed. Just the week before Hewitt had discussed the use of cortisone IV's with the young doctor, and had stated strongly that they didn't do a damn bit of good and maybe had a detrimental effect in the long run.

Stanton turned to see the look on Hewitt's face and knew immediately what was going through his mind.

"Think about it," he said, "while I get the venous pressure. I've found they do a lot of good. Where the hell's the catheter set?"

Nurse Driscoll handed him the kit, and he moved farther up to the chest, where he quickly inserted it in the subclavian vein.

"The reading is four," he announced.

Hewitt's stomach spasmed with almost unbearable pain. He'd been hoping for a seven, would have settled for a six.

"How about the cortisone?" Stanton was relentless. Hewitt nodded, and the other nurse left the room for the pharmacy.

"I want to get that blood pressure up," said Hewitt. "I'm going to give him five milligrams of Aramine intramuscularly." Stanton nodded in his turn, and Nurse Driscoll left on her errand.

The phone rang, and Hall picked it up, listened, grunted an affirmative in what he thought sounded like true senior fashion and hung up.

"Metabolic acidosis uncompensated," he said, "and the white count is twenty-nine thousand with a shift to the left. He thinks the BUN and the electrolytes are normal, but he needs more time."

"We'll give him forty-five milliquivalents of sodium bicarbonate," said Hewitt, and the resident moved a new IV stand into position on the other side while the junior nurse went for the dosage.

"Wait," said Hewitt, and all turned to look at him. "Is bicarbonate compatible with Methicillin?" he asked Stanton.

"I don't remember," said the surgeon. "We'll have to look it up."

"Does it make any difference, Doctor?" said the resident. "It's going in a separate IV."

"Of course," said Hewitt wearily, "of course."

He stood there and watched the other two doctors and two nurses work around the bed, some with the arms, some with the legs, moving here and there and back again so that there were only little glimpses of the boy, the face so tight and strained and frail-looking without the glasses. It was the first time Hewitt had really looked at him, what with trying to keep his head clear for procedures, and he could see a thin line of down on the upper lip—My God, he's going to be twelve soon and. . . .

"Blood pressure sixty over forty," said Driscoll.

"I've done all I can, Alex," said Stanton, "and I'm going to leave him with you now if there's nothing more you want me to do."

"Thank you, Frank," said Hewitt. "I appreciate it. I wanted him to have the best."

"He's going to be all right. I'd like you to keep up that cortisone. And maybe some Lev-o-phed. Get that blood pressure up."

"All right."

"I'll be by first thing in the morning. Never did get to eat my dessert. We were going to drop by the Casey thing, but it's way too late now."

Time. Time had gone. Hewitt looked down at his watch and saw that it was thirty-four minutes past nine. The Casey thing. The Bardwell thing. *SH*. *SH*. He looked around the room wildly, so strangely that even the nurse who had her back to him turned around because she sensed something wrong. Not my son, he thought to himself, not my son. He doesn't disappear in the night.

"Alex. Alex, I'll see you in the morning," said Stanton, and left.

"Is there anything more I can do, Doctor?" asked Hall, and Hewitt looked up, surprised. Had he missed something? What was the resident trying to tell him?

"We've covered it all, haven't we?" he said. "We'll continue the penicillin and try to get that blood pressure up."

"I haven't had any sleep in forty-six hours," said Hall, "and I'm beginning to see double."

"I never got to bed once during my whole residency," said Hewitt with a soft smile. The lines on Hall's face were most noticeable now, and the stocky shoulders were definitely sagging. Everybody dies, thought Hewitt. If not today, then tomorrow.

"I appreciate your help, Doctor," he said. "It's good to work with a man who knows what he's doing."

"I've been getting some excellent instruction," said Hall, with a small grin. "I can be here in a minute if you want me for anything."

As Hall walked out of the room, Nurse Driscoll went over to the bed and checked the blood pressure again.

"Still sixty over forty, Doctor," she said. He's holding, thought Hewitt. At least he's holding. He walked over to the other side of the bed and looked down at the plastic bag with the urinometer. Empty. Not one drop. The IV's were all delivering their solutions into the body drip by drip by drip—no, the boy's face had life in it, not like Huber. He put his hand on the stomach, still burning, but burning with life, burning with life.

"I think the regular shift can handle from here on in, Doctor," said Driscoll, "and if you don't need me for anything special, I think I'll—"

"Were you off shift?" asked Hewitt. "Did you stay over for—"

"I happened to overhear the call when it came in and—"

"Jesus, Driscoll," said Hewitt, "I sure appreciate—"

"Really, Doctor, I—"

"No, but—"

They looked at each other and smiled, their eyes crinkling above the masks, two professionals who appreciated and liked each other.

"You're a good nurse, Nurse."

"You're a good doctor, Doctor. He's going to be all right. I'll stay on if—"

"No. No need of that. I'm going to be here, and there will be plenty of help if I need it."

"Good night, Doctor."

The other nurse was moving around the bed, checking the IV's and making little motions that indicated there was really nothing more for her to do but that she didn't want to just stand there in the presence of the doctor.

"Are you on regular shift?" asked Hewitt.

"Yes, Doctor."

"No sense leaving them short on the floor," said Hewitt. "I'll call for anything I need."

"We could dig up a special somewhere, Doctor."

"No, no reason for it. Thank you for your help."

"We'll be watching, Doctor," and she was gone.

He moved in and checked the venous pressure as soon as she was out the door. Four. Four, four, four, four, four! Come on, Jeff, he pleaded, you've got to try.

Out of the corner of his eye he saw the nurse come back in the room and move to the other side of the bed opposite him. Her hand went out to the boy's forehead and rested there, checking . . . checking what?

"Is he all right? Is he all right now?"

It was Betsy. Someone had gowned and masked her . . . Driscoll . . . the family that. . . .

"He's burning up. Is he all right?"

"It's too early to tell. He's not going any deeper, but he's not showing any signs of coming out of it yet."

"Isn't there something more you can do? Can you call anybody else in? Couldn't Dr. Stanton. . . ."

It was always the same. Most just looked the questions at him, but some had the courage or the anger to speak up. There was somebody lying on a bed with his life possibly draining out of him, and they wanted something done that would bring instantaneous results for the better. She wanted Jeff to wake up and smile and say "Hello, Mom," and get out of bed and go home and everything would be just fine. Just fine.

"There aren't going to be any miracles," he said. "We have to get the poison out of him and start his system functioning again so that the body can do its own cleaning out. It can't be done in a minute."

"Is there anything I can do?" she asked.

"Yes, you can go home."

"I want to stay here."

"There's nothing you can do here. This is a hospital. You go home and take care of your other children. I'm going to be here. Once we get him out of the woods, then he'll need you. But right now I'm all he needs, and you'll just be in the way."

"In the way? Your son has to practically crawl through death's door for you to pay attention to him, and you tell me I'm in the way."

Her voice had risen almost to a shriek, and he looked at the door to see if any of the nurses were there. She was close to hysteria, and it might not be a bad idea to give her something. But he could see that she would take nothing from his hands—a tablet, a suggestion—and it might be best to just let her run her course.

He slipped the stethoscope in his ears and pumped up the tube. Sixty over forty.

"Look," he said, removing the instrument from his ears,

"I'll level with you. Jeff could go either way at any time. I'm pretty sure he's going to be all right, but it can still go either way. There may come a moment when all hell is going to break loose, and I'm going to need people to do things fast. If you're here, standing like a zombie or a wrath of the gods, you may throw someone off. Maybe just a second or two. But that second or two might be the difference of whether Jeff makes it or he doesn't. I leave the decision up to you whether you want to hold that responsibility."

She looked at him levelly, trying to measure how much was truth and how much was bluff. This was James Prentiss' daughter now, measuring the opposition. Truth or bluff, she couldn't afford to take the chance and moved toward the door.

"You'll call me if there's any change?" she asked.

"Yes."

"Alex!"

"Yes."

"If anything happens to Jeff, I don't even want to see you again."

He put the stethoscope back in his ears and pumped up again. Sixty over forty. He'd give him an ampul of Lev-o-phed. When he turned to pick it up from the stand, his eyes swept the doorway. She was gone.

xxi

THE phone was ringing, and he reached out to the side of the bed to pick it up, but it wasn't there and Betsy must have. . . . He sat up straight, bewildered by the whiteness of everything and realized he was in a hospital room. . . . His eyes wildly scanned around, and there was Jeff on the bed, and the phone was ringing. He leaped to his feet, and a wave of dizziness passed over him that almost brought him crashing down. The phone rang again, and he rushed over to it before it woke up Jeff . . . he stopped and let it ring while watching the boy. If only it would; if only it would.

"Dr. Hewitt here," he said into the receiver.

"This is the service, Doctor. You had a call from a Mrs. Parkhurst about a Mrs. Markham. She said it was an emergency."

"How did you know I was here?"

"I called your house, Doctor, and your wife. . . ."

"Of course. Thank you very much."

"Do you want the number, Doctor?"

"Oh, yes. Yes."

"Four-four-seven Seven-three-one-one."

"Thank you."

"Will you be going home from the hospital, Doctor?"

"No, I'll be here the rest of the night."

"Thank you, Doctor."

He hung up the receiver and looked at his watch. Ten minutes past two. Couldn't have been asleep more than five minutes. Jeff felt a little cooler. Or did he? The nurse had sponged him at one. You're going to make it, he silently told the boy. You're going to make it. Would she leave him if. . . . What would it be like to be alone again? No hassles. Come home to silence. And darkness. And no hot meals, he thought wryly. No wife in the bed on the occasions when . . . . Pigs. "I'm sick of pigs," he said aloud, and looked quickly at the door, where the nurses had been poking their heads in inquiringly about every fifteen minutes.

He lifted the phone, asked for an outside line and dialed the number. It was answered on the first ring.

"This is Dr. Hewitt."

"Doctor"—there was fear in the voice—"my mother must have tried to go to the bathroom by herself, and she fell down, and she can't talk, and her right arm and leg seem lifeless."

"Did she take her sleeping pill before she went to bed?"

"Yes."

"That's probably why she seems so groggy."

"Doctor, it's more than just groggy. There's something wrong. If you could just. . . ."

"I'm on an emergency at the hospital, and I don't know when I can break loose. Why don't you wait an hour and see how she is and then. . . ."

"Doctor . . . my mother. . . ."

He could feel the sweat gathering in his palms. One at a time. One at a time.

"I guess we'd better get her in here where I can check her over," he said. "I'll call the ambulance service and arrange for admittance."

"Oh, thank you, Doctor. I'll have the porch light on. Should I come with her?"

"No, there's nothing you can do, and it probably won't be until morning before we have something definite. I'll call you when I have something."

"Thank you, Doctor."

He disconnected and then jiggled until the switchboard came on. Instructions were given for the ambulance and the admissions office.

"Would you ring Dr. Hall's room?" he asked. It took five rings before the receiver was lifted and a muffled grunt received.

"I'm sorry to bother you, Doctor," said Hewitt, "but an emergency has come up. . . ."

"Your boy?" asked Hall, wide awake now.

"No," said Hewitt, and he told him about Mrs. Markham, the exploratory operation and the present situation.

"Sounds like a stroke would be the best thing that could happen to her," said Hall.

"Will you work her up when she comes in and then give me a call here?" asked Hewitt.

"Certainly, Doctor. How is your son?"

"No change. Blood pressure same and no urine passed."

"He should start to show improvement soon."

"I think I'm going to double the cortisone dose. How do you feel about that, Doctor?"

The pause was significant. Something rotten in the castle when the king asked advice of the head of the stable.

"I suppose there's nothing to lose, Doctor," said the resident.

"Fine," said Hewitt. "I'll wait your call. And, Doctor . . ."

"Yes."

"This Mrs. Markham, she's . . . I'd appreciate . . ."

"I understand, Doctor."

Hewitt looked down at the phone for a long time after he hung it up. How could young Dr. Hall understand when old Dr. Hewitt didn't really understand? How many old ladies had he helped over the edge? Why should this one be something special? Why did you decide that this is the girl you want to marry? Why Betsy? Why Mrs. Markham? Were they both going to leave him? He turned to Jeff and checked everything once more right through to the piggy-backs on both IV's. The temperature was down to 104, but that was the only positive sign, and who could really tell if it was a positive sign? He could slip off just like that, gone while Hewitt was dozing in the chair or . . . I will not sleep, he silently told the boy. I will not leave you alone.

"Alex?"

He turned and found Stern standing in the doorway, bloodstained green gown in the wildest tie-dye fashion.

"How's the boy?"

"He's static," said Hewitt, moving over toward the door. "What the hell are you up to?"

"I just delivered a baby. A boy, to be exact. An eight-pound three-ounce boy, to be even more exact."

"You don't do obstetrics, for Christ's sake."

"You go tell Mrs. Perenucci that. I delivered her daughter hale and hearty twenty-two years ago, and I was damned well going to deliver her daughter's baby, too, and that was all there was to it."

"How did it feel?"

"I'll tell you. The last baby I delivered was something like fifteen years ago, and it felt good to whack the little *pisher* in the ass. It wasn't necessary, but I noticed they still do it on television."

"Were you nervous?"

"Why should I be nervous? Besides, just between us, I had a deal with Pekola and he's the best in the business.

When Mrs. Perenucci called me that her daughter's time was come, I called Pekola and told him his time had come, too. He stood there beside me during the whole business and talked like a football coach. It's easy to deliver with a real OB for an assistant. The nurses told me about your boy. Is there anything I can do?"

Hewitt looked at the president of his medical society, the man he was not about to succeed.

"Yes," he said. "Will you come in and check over the whole procedure and see if I'm missing anything? I've gone over it and over it, but I'm not sure anymore. I'm not sure of anything."

"Let me get sterilized, and I'll be right there," said Stern, and in five minutes he was back in the room. Hewitt watched him as he carefully retraced all the steps that had been taken that night, consulting the chart from time to time, mumbling incomprehensible oaths or chants and finally closing his eyes with his head cocked to one side for what seemed five minutes.

"Nothing, Alex," he said, "you've missed nothing. This will do it if anything does. But why fool with that cortisone? I don't think it's necessary."

"You're probably right, but I was at a stage at one time tonight when I would have handed needles to an acupuncture man."

"It isn't easy to treat your own. You either don't listen to them in the first place or you try to do too much in the second place."

"I'm all screwed up, Irv," said Hewitt. "I've been having a bad time myself, and it's thrown me for a loop."

"What do you mean bad time?"

"I've got hypertension out of the blue, and the past few weeks I've been having some extra systoles."

"What do you mean out of the blue, Doctor?"

"I mean all of a sudden I began feeling tight, and I took my pressure, and there it was."

"Why shouldn't it be?"

"What do you mean?"

"I mean the statistics say one out of four, and why shouldn't you be one of those ones? What makes you so sure that you should be the other three?"

"Nothing, but—"

"Doctors die just like everybody else."

"I know that, Irv, but—"

"No buts about it. We get so caught up in trying to keep other people from dying or trying to belittle death so that they won't be so feared of it that we begin to think of ourselves as outside the limits, as beings apart from human breakage and decay."

"In medical school," said Hewitt, "three-quarters of the students thought they had some fatal illness."

"That's true," said Stern. "Every time you turned a new page in the book you thought you had that particular disease. And by God, a couple of them sometimes did. But we had youth on our side in medical school. And when we were interns. You'd work three days without sleep and say, 'My God, I'm going to die if I don't get some sleep,' and you'd get two hours and bounce right back. It's going to take me a week to get over this one night."

"Go on," said Hewitt, "you're like a bull."

"A bull?" said Stern. "I am sixty-two years old, and I've had angina for fourteen years, come Tuesday, though I never think about it. I pop nitroglycerin like Mrs. Perenucci's husband eats spaghetti. I've got a kidney that's disintegrating on me, and my flatulence produces enough energy to get a rocket to Mars. And all that is no bull."

"It's not that I'm afraid of dying," said Hewitt.

"Everybody's afraid of dying. It's a way of life. But you're a young man yet. And you're a doctor. Have somebody put you through the ropes—I'll do it myself if you want—and work out a treatment that will keep you going as long as possible under the most comfortable circumstances. But don't worry yourself into the ground. After a certain point your body has to undergo changes. As a doctor you know better than most how to cope with those changes. Use your skill and knowledge for yourself as you are doing for this boy."

"It's strange," said Hewitt, as much to himself as to Stern, "the one thing I have completely trusted in this whole world is my body, and now it is betraying me."

"No," said the older man, putting his hand on Hewitt's shoulder, "it is you who are doing the betraying. Your body is acting naturally. You know, if I didn't know you better, I'd say you were acting like a spoiled child who can't have his way."

Hewitt laughed. "That's what my parents used to say."

"They probably both have high blood pressure," said Stern.

Hewitt turned and stared at him. He had no idea what his mother and father might or might not have. There had never been any outward manifestations one way or another when he was a child, and neither ever discussed any present symptoms during the Christmas visit or the infrequent phone calls. They could be running two hundred over a hundred and forty for all he knew and still going their merry way at sixty-eight and sixty-seven years of age respectively. With premature ventricular beats right through their assholes.

"I've inherited a few of their strange ways, I'm sure," said Hewitt, "and that may be one of them."

"The main thing right now," said Stern, "is to get your boy straightened out and home to his pretty mother. How the hell did he get that lesion?"

"A new shoe."

"The classic case," said Stern, "just like President Coolidge's boy. Only his was a sneaker."

"Oh?" said Hewitt. "How'd he make out?"

The pause was long enough to send a tremor through

Hewitt, his shoulders tightening straight across and his heart pounding as though to a starter's gun.

"Well," said Stern, waving his hand at the apparatus clustered around Jeff, "they had none of these things in those days. A bacteremia then was treated with hot packs and little more."

"Christ," said Hewitt, spinning around and staring at the boy laboring on the bed, "the whole thing is unreal. I stand here waiting for miracles, for somebody to come in and say everything is going to be all right now. I've done everything I can possibly do, and I know I just have to wait, but I keep wanting to take him by the shoulders and shake him out of it."

"He's going to be all right," said Stern soothingly. "His body has had a tremendous shock, but he's young and strong. You just have to—"

The phone rang and Hewitt picked it up quickly.

"Yes, Doctor," he said.

"Alex?" It was Betsy.

He wracked his mind for something. "His fever has gone down," he said.

"Oh, thank God. Is he awake?"

"No. He isn't out of it yet. The fever is only one factor."

"But he's all right?"

"As far as we know."

"Shall I come back?"

"No, there's nothing you can do here. I'll call as soon as there's any significant change."

"But couldn't I—"

"I have to hang up now, Betsy. I'll call you when I can."

Stern had been doing the fifteen-minute check points while Hewitt was on the phone and he straightened up from the last one with his brow furrowed.

"What was the temperature when you last checked it?" he asked.

"It had dropped to one hundred and four."

"It's back up to one hundred and five now. What time did you first start treatment?"

"Around eight o'clock."

Stern sighed. "He should be making some kind of turnaround soon," he said. "But the damn urine isn't coming through. Those glands are really up there. We might try a bolus of Isoproterenol."

Hewitt's hands were up to his cheeks, rubbing hard, and he could feel the bristles biting into his palms. Christ, how could she let the goddamned ankle get that messy without noticing it? The phone rang, and Stern picked it up, listened, said, "Just a minute," and handed it to Hewitt.

The resident reported that Mrs. Markham had definitely thrown some embolisms and was paralyzed completely on the right side. He had started an IV, and there was no necessity for Hewitt to come down.

"I'll be right there," said Hewitt. "Wait for me."

"Irv," he said, "I have a patient down on the third that I have to check. I'll send Dr. Hall up here, and then you go home."

"I'm fine," said Stern. "No sense to send that young punk up here. I'll wait till you get back."

"You go home and take a nitroglycerin," said Hewitt, with a smile, "and thanks for everything."

"You're a good doctor, Doctor," said Stern, "and I feel that when you grow up, you might even be a better one."

Hewitt told the nurses where he was going to be and ran down to the third floor, thinking about whether the Isoproterenol should have been used instead of the goddamned cortisone. Fucking surgeons.

He sensed death in the room as he walked through the door, and a surge of happiness passed through him. There had been none of that upstairs. But down here you could almost smell it, like at Huber's, the feeling pressing in at you from all sides—in your nose, your ears, your eyes—every sense telling you that there was nothing more to do, that the decision had been made. There was none of that upstairs. He looked at the thin figure on the bed, the eyelids twitching ever so slightly, and guilt replaced the joy.

There had also been no death in Bardwell's room that night, the two of them discussing convalescence periods and restriction of calcium and the weather, they had discussed the weather, but nothing about dying, there had been no death in that room. Witch doctor, he told himself, you're being a witch doctor.

As he was moving around the bed to take the pulse, Hewitt started with surprise as a great white blob suddenly confronted him from the corner. It was Dr. Hall seated in the creased, fake-leather easy chair, holding the metal chart case, while his lips pursed in and out in even beats that indicated sleep of a highly enjoyable nature. The lines in the young face indicated how much that sleep was needed, and the grayness of the pallor almost equaled that of the woman on the bed. Hewitt edged carefully around and checked the pulse. Thready. Death was there, ready to pluck the string at any moment. Looking up, he saw his face in the mirror of the medicine chest in the corner, the pallor matching those around him. We're all dead, he thought, some a little more than others. If oblivion comes at this moment, right now, what has been lost? Day after day after day of doing the same thing. What did I have before that I don't have now? he wondered. Why is everything so flat, so dead? Has it happened already? What was there before that isn't there now? The challenge? The challenge of what? Of flu and cancer and kidney stones and coronaries and housewives moaning that they don't feel good, they just don't feel good. How do you tell a woman of twenty-eight that she's had all the excitement she's ever going to have, that from now on it's getting the kids through school and the husband through his working days into retirement and the aches and the pains and death in the night, and day, will come with increasing frequency? How do you tell Dr.

Hewitt that he is no better off than a twenty-eight-year-old woman who's having the vapors?

"Dr. Hall," he said harshly, wanting to bring another human into the circle.

The resident leaped to his feet, his face red from the adrenalin surge, confused, exhausted, but alert and knowing within two seconds.

"Yes, Doctor," he said, flipping open the top of the metal chart and handing it over for inspection. Hewitt checked through all that had been done and all that had been ordered for the morning. There was nothing to add.

"Exactly right," he said snapping the cover down and handing it back. "Did you get through to her?"

"I think she's aware," said Hall, "but there were no visible indications."

Hewitt leaned over and took both her cheeks in his palms.

"Mrs. Markham," he said loudly in her ear, "it's Dr. Hewitt. I'm here with you now, and we'll take care of you. It's Dr. Hewitt. There's nothing to be afraid of."

The eyelids moved a bit, but there was no way of knowing if this was a voluntary action. Hewitt placed the head gently back on the pillow.

"I'm going to be busy as hell," he said, turning to the resident, "and I would appreciate your following through here to make sure we cover everything between us."

"No sweat, Doctor," said Hall, moving toward the door. "I'll handle it as though I were the only one on the case."

As they came out in the hall, Hewitt saw Mrs. Markham's daughter standing against the wall, almost in the same position that Betsy had been in several hours before. The sense of imminent loss. Why didn't he feel that? What if Jeff did die? What if that eleven-year-old boy up there, the product of his loins, died? What would he feel? Would it be an insufferable loss? A loss of any kind? Or just a numbness? I'm scared, he told himself. I'm scared and I don't know what I'm scared of. Am I scared of dying? Is that what it is? To lie there like Bardwell on that slab with the tubes running in and the bones locked tight? Or Casey? No more worries about getting it up or sticking it in. What is there to be afraid of? When it's over, it's over. You don't know a goddamned thing. Why can't I. . . .

Mrs. Parkhurst was saying something to him. He could see her mouth moving, and his head went from side to side trying to pick up the words.

". . . all right?" she said and stopped.

All right. She had asked if her mother was going to be all right. That was what she must have asked. No more drinking. Too tough. Too tired. No more drinking. If I can pull Jeff out of this, he told himself, there will be no more drinking. She was still looking at him expectantly.

"She's paralyzed on the right side," he said, "and it's too soon to know if it's going to be a permanent condition."

"Might it . . . might it . . . get worse?"

"That's a definite possibility. I'm not going to minimize the situation, Mrs. Parkhurst."

"I don't want her to suffer. I just don't want her to suffer."

"She's feeling no pain. I guarantee you that."

She lifted her hand, held it in the air for a moment and then dropped it by her side, as though it were too heavy to sustain.

"I just don't want her to suffer anymore," she said. "I'd rather . . . I'd rather . . . that she. . . ."

He knew she would be unable to finish the sentence and broke in with what help he could.

"We're going to keep her as comfortable as possible," he said. "Right now I don't know exactly what is going to happen, but I am fairly sure she is going to have more of these. And she can't take too much more. However, she could regain use of all functioning, or at least part, within the next few days. Right now all we can do is wait."

"I suppose you're used to waiting in situations like this, Doctor, but it's all new for me and terribly difficult. I'm all that's left. No brothers, sisters, cousins. I'm all that's left."

"Your mother is still here, Mrs. Parkhurst."

"But she's eaten up with cancer inside. I want her to live, but I want her to die. I don't want my mother to suffer, Doctor."

"I promised her she wouldn't, and I promise you that, too, Mrs. Parkhurst."

"Oh, it must be so easy to be a doctor," she said, looking up at him in fear and frustration and hatred, her thin face screwed up in tight circles or wrinkles, her whole wrinkled life combining to make her speak up once without worrying about embarrassment or being out of place.

His hands reached out and grasped her by the arms, exactly where he had held his wife some hours before, but this time his touch was soft and comforting rather than harsh and unyielding.

"Your mother is very important to me, Mrs. Parkhurst," he said. "I have done everything within my capability to steer her correctly through this part of her life, to keep her going as long as possible when she was no longer able. I am not going to wash my hands of her now. I am going to see her through to wherever this might lead."

The wrinkles broke into jagged lines, and tears flowed from the eyes down the cheeks.

"I know it, Doctor," she said, and he could tell from the slight push against his hands that she would like nothing better than to fall against his chest and weep out loud, wailing for her mother who was about to die, the last barrier against her own death, and for the helplessness of all who must witness the breeching of the fortress walls.

"I know it," she repeated, and with a slight movement of her arms indicated that she would stand alone now. "May I see her?" she asked, as his hands dropped by his sides.

"Of course. You might talk to her, too. There is no way

of knowing how much she hears or understands, but there is the possibility that she can hear and understand everything. Just talk naturally about things. Give her the news of what you are doing, and assume you know what her answers are. I'll be in touch with you."

Hewitt gave the charge nurse instructions and told her where he would be. As was always the case in hospitals, she seemed to know as much about Jeff's situation as he did. Probably Driscoll on her way out had. . . . Christ, he should have asked her about Bardwell. She had been charge nurse that night. She would know who SH was, who had signed the papers. She could. . . .

"Doctor? Doctor?"

He looked at the nurse. She was looking peculiarly at him.

"Yes?"

"Do I call you or Dr. Hall if there is a question?"

"Dr. Haw . . ." He had made a promise. "You call me first, and if I am not obtainable, you check with Dr. Hall."

He turned and looked in the door of the room. Mrs. Parkhurst was holding her mother's left hand in hers and was talking earnestly, telling her the news of the day as she had been instructed. It's so easy to be a doctor. You just tell people what to do and they do it. Get well, Jeff. Ignore the poison in your system and get well. Do what the doctor tells you. Do what your father tells you. It's so easy to be a doctor. Easier even than being a father.

He climbed the two flights of stairs slowly, aware of how little strength there was in his body and how much more he might have to call on it. There had to be something terribly wrong. He had never felt this weak before. Perhaps there was a clot already lodged in one of the smaller vessels, blocking off a link to. . . . There were no nurses in the hall and he could hear movement in Jeff's room. He hurried to the door and saw Stern and three nurses clustered around the bed, moving something with. . . .

"What is it?" he called as he rushed through to them.

Stern looked up. "Put your mask on," he said. "We're just lowering the head a little to see if that will stir something up."

"Any change?"

"No. All signs are the same."

The nurses bustled about for a moment more and then left the room.

"He should have been out by now, Irv," said Hewitt.

"That's a father talking and not a doctor," said Stern. "He could go like this for several more hours just on the natural course. You know there aren't any miracles involved."

"If you're lucky, there are. You can't deny that. I need some luck. All my life I've had to do without luck. Everything I've ever done has been with my mind and my body. Nothing else. But I've used them up. I need some luck."

"Why don't you go home and let me work it out here," said Stern.

"You know I'm not going home."

"Then flake out somewhere on a cot. We'll call you if we need you."

"No. You're the one who's going home. I appreciate everything you've done, and I thank you. But you're going home. You've got your regular day tomorrow."

Stern opened his mouth to protest and closed it again. "To tell you the truth," he said, "I can hardly stand up. I just took my second nitro since you were gone. Ah! I'm not much good to anybody anymore."

"Tell that to Mrs. Perenucci," said Hewitt. "I'll talk to you tomorrow."

"It's going to be all right, Alex," said Stern, as he paused in the doorway. "I have the good feeling here," and he placed his hand on his heart before walking out the door.

The good feeling in the damaged heart, thought Hewitt. How much is it worth? He pumped up the sphygmomanometer. Sixty over forty. How much Aramine did he dare give? There was a temptation to remove the collar from Jeff's arm and slip it around his own. One body too much, another not enough. He placed his two hands on Jeff's head. How hot? How hot? Time for another sponging. If only the excess blood pressure could be poured from one body to the next, helping both at the same time. Was he more concerned for himself or his son? Would I die so that you could live? Hewitt wondered. Would Betsy? Would anybody? Are there people so filled with love that they would sacrifice their lives for another? Is it love? Or do they just want to die and get it all the hell over with. Mrs. Markham was ready to get it the hell over with. Her daughter was down there now giving her the news of the day—war, high prices, the new television shows—all the things you lost along with your life. What would Jeff want to know about right now?

"Jeff," he said, leaning over almost into the boy's ear, "can you hear me? It's Dad." Dad. Jeff called him Dad. Jojo called him Daddy. What did Bobbi use? When she was Jojo's age, she called him Daddy. But what did she say now when she talked to him? Did she call him anything? He couldn't remember her addressing him directly, looking at him directly, for . . . . how long had it been since she last talked to him except for answers to direct questions? Looks. All that girl gave him now was looks. Black, brooding, hateful looks. Jeff too. Except his looks were more of fear than anything. Why the Christ should. . . .

"Jeff," he said a little louder, "it's Dad. Wake up, Jeff. You've got to wake up, Jeff. Can you hear me? Everything's going to be all right. We're going to do a lot of skiing together this winter, you and I." He thought back on last winter with Jeff on the ground and good old dad yelling that he'd never learn to ski if he didn't keep his goddamned. . . . "And maybe we'll get a snowmobile and go camping in the woods. Or if we get tired of the snow, we can all go, all of us, down to Grandpa Prentiss' "—had he ever said Grandpa Prentiss before? Had he ever referred to Prentiss except—"and we'll swim in the pool and maybe go out for some deep sea fishing . . . there are all kinds of things we can do, Jeff, all kinds of things. You're only eleven, and there are all kinds of things for you to do yet."

The boy's chest was heaving in and out with the face burning before him, and Hewitt wanted to rip out all the tubes delivering their drip, drip, drip, and hold the boy in his arms until he came to and told him that he wanted to go skiing with his father, that he wanted to ride the snowmobile and visit Grandpa and they'd do all sorts of things together, like. . . .

"Doctor! Doctor!"

Hewitt turned toward the door but couldn't really see the form that went with the female voice because his eyes, his eyes, were blinded by tears, tears that filled his eyes so that he couldn't see clearly, and he was afraid to talk, afraid that. . . .

"Doctor!" She was coming toward him, and he could see from the white that it was the nurse, he recognized the voice of the charge nurse, and. . . .

"Yes," he got out, "yes, what is it?"

"They just called from the third floor. Your patient down there has had another shock and they wanted to know if—"

"Stay with the boy," he said, as anxious to get out before she saw his eyes clearly as he was to check Mrs. Markham, "and call me if there's any change."

He ran quickly down the stairs and into the third-floor corridor, where a nurse was talking on the phone at the desk. She pointed into Mrs. Markham's room, and Hewitt went in quickly to join the two nurses at the bed, one of whom handed him a stethoscope as the other pumped up the blood pressure again. Thready . . . not there . . . thready . . . not there . . . thready.

"Let's get some oxygen into her," he said, and one of the nurses went quickly into the hall.

"Nasal tubes?" asked the other, and he nodded.

The first nurse returned with the oxygen canister on the dolly, and Hewitt helped them rig up the apparatus, bending the tubes so they fit the passages exactly.

"OK," he said, "let's go."

The first hiss caused the back to arch, and Hewitt mistook it for a death throe before he realized what was happening. He could feel his own heart racing as he checked the reflexes of the other arm. This had been a big one. He could find no reactions to nerve stimulation. Once more he bent over the chest with the stethoscope. The regular beat had returned—slow, ponderous, heavy—but regular.

"Is her tongue all right?" he asked without looking up.

"There's control there, Doctor," said one of the nurses. "The saliva's going down all right."

"We'll have to watch that closely for a while," he said. "Can you people monitor in here by yourselves?"

"It's a slow night," said the other one. "We won't have any problem."

"Is her daughter still here?" he asked.

"She went home about five minutes ago. But she left her number and asked us to call if there was any change. Should we call her?"

"Yes. Tell her what happened." He looked down at Mrs. Markham and moved out of the room, the nurses following. "Tell her that this can go on for some time but that it isn't likely."

"Yes, Doctor. How's your boy?"

"He's . . . coming along. I'll be upstairs if you need me again."

He looked at the door leading to the stairs for a moment and then walked down to the elevator and pushed the button. He was going to lose somebody that night. Bardwell. Casey. And somebody else. Would he be satisfied with the old lady? Would the old lady be enough? Or did the boy have to go, too? Why not me? he asked. Why not me? *I*

*never took much pleasure out of life, and now there is
none. I came out of a cold womb and have been looking for
warmth ever since. There is none.*

The elevator door was standing open before him, and he
entered and pressed five. When the door opened again on
the fifth, he saw that the hall was deserted with no one at
the charge desk. He hurried down to Jeff's room, expecting
to find all the nurses there, but it, too, was empty. He and
the boy were alone in the world, fighting their battle, while
all others went their own way. Mrs. Markham was down
there fighting hers. All strangers wandering the earth for a
little while and then returning to the dirt. There had to be
something more. There had to be something more than
that. There had to be some warmth somewhere, something
that. . . .

He thought he saw the boy stir through the haze in his
eyes—tears again, for Christ's sake—and he brought both
hands up and rubbed, the action hurting with the roughness of the cornea, and it took him a few moments to regain
clarity, his head moving up and down and up and . . .
YELLOW! There was yellow there in the urinometer and
he fell to his knees at the foot of the bed to check the cc's
that had passed through the system and out the tube, and
he jumped to his feet to the catheter in the subclavian
where he watched his hands, steady as rocks, make the necessary adjustments and . . . EIGHT . . . the reading was
eight, and he grabbed a stethoscope and pumped up the
blood pressure, watching in rapture as the systolic registered one hundred and the diastolic sixty, and he pulled the
earpieces down around his neck and looked at the boy, his
son, who would soon flutter his eyes and come out of his
coma with a vagueness and a burbling and a movement of
his head from side to side as . . . Hewitt couldn't stand a
moment longer and moved to the chair, where he sat down
heavily, his arms on his lap. How many vows had he made
that night? he thought ironically. Could he remember them

all? Would he keep any of them? He wouldn't yell at Jeff about the sloppiness of his Christies. He'd take him for a picnic on a snowmobile. He'd talk to him. He wouldn't drink. He wouldn't drink. The thought of an ice-cold vodka sliding down his throat brought a smile to his face, and that was how the nurse found him when she walked into the room.

"Oh, Doctor," she said, "I didn't see you come back. We had a scare in Five O Seven. Is there anything you want done?"

"No," he said, "things are fine. We've got some good signs," and his hand waved in the direction of the bright-yellow urine that was dripping steadily into the plastic bag.

"Well," she said, smiling in return, "there was never any question that we wouldn't with you on the case. You never lose any."

He thought of the old lady dying just below and Casey all alone in the funeral home and Bardwell encased in dirt. No more drinking. He had promised there would be no more drinking.

"I'm going to call my wife now," he said. "Would you stay here until I come back?"

xxii

HER head was so full of Jeff that when she drove up the driveway into the garage, she couldn't really remember the trip from the hospital. His face had been before her all the way home, so thin and pale after the hot fever of the night, the eyes seeming to drift around without any steady focus and the lips with pieces of dried flesh hanging off them. Alex had rubbed them carefully with Vaseline when she had called the condition to his attention, explaining that the fever had cracked and peeled them, but that they would soon respond to treatment.

The needles in his arms had frightened her terribly, even though she knew it was established procedure. It was one thing to wheel the book cart around and see IV's in other people, but this was flesh of her flesh, blood of her blood. Alex had been terribly careful to explain what each bottle contained and what it was doing to help Jeff regain his strength and combat the infection. Alex had been terribly careful about everything when she arrived, and it was only after he had left to make the rounds of his other patients before going home to get some sleep that she stopped to consider exactly how careful he had been.

It had been possible to do only so much fussing over Jeff, and he seemed only semiconsciously aware of her and his surroundings. She could have sworn that he had smiled at her when she first came in and called his name, but then he dozed and nodded the rest of the time, moving his head once or twice, but otherwise quiet under the covers.

"It will take awhile for the strength to return," Alex told her. "We'll keep pumping the penicillin into him until the infection is cleared up, but his body just wants to lie there and recoup right now. All the vital signs are normal, and he's running only a couple of points of fever. He's a good, tough kid."

It had been a different Alex talking, a gaunt, blond-whiskered Alex who was taking pride in his son's beating out the biggest competitor of them all. There was no mention of how the infection started, which had loomed so importantly in all her thinking since the night before. She kept waiting for the outburst that would describe her stupidity as a person and negligence as a mother. But it never came. It was Alex, and it wasn't Alex. He put his arm around her shoulders when he introduced her to the nurses who came in, all of whom seemed to find some errand or another while she was in the room.

"This is my wife, Betsy," he would say, and they would all gurgle over how pleased they were to meet her and how fine Jeff was doing.

This is my wife, Betsy.

Coming home in the car, she had said it aloud to herself, not even conscious she was saying it while she was aware she was listening to it.

This is my wife, Betsy.

There had been something in the way he had said it, some quality that wasn't there before. It stirred memories of when they were going together, before they were married, those few short weeks, but she was unable to pull any solid incident out of the past that would relieve the tension

crowding in on her. There had been no sleep the night before, but she had never felt so wide awake in her life, so full
of energy that was seeking an outlet for release. Jeff was
going to be all right. She could tell this the instant she saw
him even though he looked so frail and pained in the midst
of his tubes and bottles.

God, she was hungry. As she came through the door, she
was already planning for eggs, fried eggs, two of them, and
toast, rye toast, three slices, and bacon, she was sure there
was some bacon left in the refrigerator, as many slices as
were in the damn package, and without taking her coat off,
she went to the stove and prepared the coffeepot. As she
turned to the sink for water, she almost dropped the whole
thing on the floor at the sight of Bobbi, in her purple dressing gown, standing there watching her.

"My goodness," said Betsy, "what are you doing here?"

"I decided to take the day off."

"Is Jojo home, too?"

"No. I gave her breakfast and packed her off."

"Where's your father?"

"Sleeping, I guess. He said he was going right to bed, and
I haven't heard anything. How's Jeff?"

"He's fine. I mean, he's coming along fine. There's quite
a way to go yet. But Dr. Stanton came in while I was there
and checked him over, and he said he was fine. And then
Dr. Stern came in and checked him over and said he was
fine. And then a Dr. Hall came in, he's a resident, and he
checked him over and said he was fine. And your father had
already checked him over and said he was fine."

"Sounds like the doctors are more dangerous than the infection."

They both laughed, and Betsy went over and hugged her
daughter out of sheer joy, grateful that Jeff was going to be
fine and that she had a beautiful daughter and that she was
going to be eating some eggs and toast and drink hot, strong
coffee.

"Will you see if there is any bacon in the refrigerator?" she asked, as she dropped her coat on a chair. "And did you have any breakfast?"

"No," said Bobbi, opening the refrigerator and rummaging around until she came up with a half-full package of bacon, "but I think I'll have some with you."

They set to work without any talking, Bobbi setting the table while Betsy pulled out eggs and butter and toaster and bread and gathered all together by the stove.

"Did your father eat anything?" she asked as she cracked four eggs and skillfully dropped them into the pan.

"No. Didn't drink anything either."

"Why do you say that?" asked Betsy, turning away from the eggs and looking sharply at her daughter. The brightness was gone as instantly as a cloud across the sun. It would come back in the natural course if she let it alone, but she couldn't under the circumstances. There was too much at stake.

"Why do you say that?" she repeated as she saw the dark look come over her daughter's face that indicated she was about to sink into her teen-age shell.

"I don't know. It's just that that's all he seems to do around here. Yell at somebody and drink."

"Did he yell at you this morning?"

"No, he just said that Jeff was OK and he was going to bed for a few hours."

"You mustn't say things like that about your father."

"Why not? They're true. I don't know why you stay married to him."

The smell of burning penetrated Betsy's mind and she turned quickly to the stove to see the eggs all brown around the edges and the margarine black on the sides. She lifted the pan off the burner, all appetite gone, burned out, and turned off the stove. The coffeepot was bubbling brown, and she flicked that switch, too, before pulling down a cup from the shelf and pouring it full. Lifting the cup to her lips, she let the hot liquid flow down her throat, scalding her, but didn't stop until the heat hit her stomach.

"I stay married to him because I love him," she said evenly, pushing at the loose flesh on the roof of her mouth with the tip of her tongue. "He is my husband, the father of my children, and I love him. That is why I stay married to him."

"How could you love him? He doesn't love us. He doesn't love you. He doesn't care about any of us."

"What about Jeff?" said Betsy turning. "He spent all night saving Jeff's life. Doesn't that mean something?"

"That was because Jeff was a patient. He cares more about his patients than he does about us. They're the only ones who get to see him. Jeff had to almost die in order to get his father to pay some attention to him."

"Bobbi, why are you talking like this? You know your father cares about us, all of us."

"He doesn't care. We'd be better off without him."

This is Betsy, my wife. No, that wasn't how he had said it. That had been the night before when he had been so drunk and he had told her about Vietnam and the colonel. She had decided she was going to leave him while she was going for her coat to go to Frank's wake—oh, my God, is today the funeral? no, tomorrow—and she had stopped to check Jeff and. . . .

This is my wife, Betsy. That's what he had said to the nurses.

Was there going to be something different? Once Jeff was back home and everything returned to normal. *Normal.* My God, we can't live like that anymore. Better divorce. She's right, the child is right. Better divorce than existing like that again.

"Why did you marry him?" asked Bobbi. "Why did you marry him in the first place?"

Betsy took another drink of the coffee. Because of the condition of her mouth, she could taste nothing, only feel the warmth, but that was enough for the moment. Her sixteen-year-old daughter wanted to know why her mother had married her father. In the first place. She was entitled to an answer.

Cradling the cup in her two hands, she thought about the first place. "He was visiting a college friend in our town," she said softly, hearing the drawl slip in as she thought back to that time, to that place, "and he was in the finals of the guest-member tennis tourney, and he had just finished his internship and was taking a few weeks off before going into residency, and the sun was behind his head when I first saw him, shining on those sweaty golden curls, and I knew right then I was going to marry him."

The heat of the coffee cup brought her back to the kitchen, and she could tell by the look on Bobbi's face that the words had pierced through the shell of cynicism that her daughter protected herself with and reached the soft inner core that fed itself upon pictures taped to bedroom walls and hackneyed poetry by soulful homosexuals.

"Did you think it was always going to be beautiful?" asked Bobbi.

Betsy shrugged. "I knew it was always going to be beautiful. And I still believe that. I feel that two people can have a satisfactory relationship right through their lives. My parents have."

"How do you know?"

"What?"

"How do you know that your parents are happy? I know that my parents are not happy. Am I wrong about that?"

"When I say happy, Bobbi, I don't mean running around giggling all the time. Your father and I have accomplished a lot together. We've established a practice here, are bringing up three fine children, have a place in the community. That's what life is. You do your thing until the next generation takes over."

"There's got to be more than that."

"What do you mean?"

"Like love. Where does love come in among all this?"

"It's there. There's love in this family. We love you, and we hope you all love us."

"Daddy doesn't love us!" The vehemence with which this came out made the sound clash off the walls, and they both looked up in apprehension, suddenly aware that he was up there, maybe sleeping, maybe not, but up there and capable of coming down among them in his wrath and fury and. . . .

"He loves us," said Betsy in a strained voice, bringing the cup up to her lips and drinking. "It's just that he has a lot of pressure on him, demands on his time and his mind, and he's sort of lost sight of us in the rush."

"If he really loved us, cared about us, he would make room for us, would make some time for us. There are plenty of fathers as busy as he is who still have time for their families."

"It's not the same. A doctor holds life and death in his hands. He can't just drop what he's doing at any moment."

"I'm not talking about that, Mama. I'm talking about all those nights when he sits in that room and drinks vodka and watches the stupid television or when he just goes to bed without saying anything to anybody. We'd all be happier if he wasn't here at all."

"Oh, no."

"It's true!" Once more the words came out louder than before, and they both looked up quickly at the ceiling. They were afraid; they made no effort to hide this from each other. They were afraid of this man, their husband and father. They were afraid of his size and his temper and his silence; especially they feared his silence. They walked by him carefully, always aware of his physical position in relation to themselves. They spoke to him carefully, always aware of how their words might be misinterpreted to their disadvantage. His presence in the kitchen was almost as strong as if he had been there in person. He was more than a husband and father to them; he was a symbol of the unknown, of the darkness. Everything he did seemed so sure, so sudden and swift that it moved beyond their comprehension, their ability to cope.

"How can you say you love him when he acts this way toward you?" asked Bobbi, pushed as much by her fear as her desire to hurt somebody.

"What way?"

"He treats you no differently than he treats us. You might as well be me or Jeff or Jojo. You might as well be his daughter as his wife."

"Do you love your father, Bobbi?"

The girl's face broke into little pieces, each feature falling off like a cracked mirror on a wall, displaying jagged edges and black backing, one at a time until all reflection and light were gone.

"I hate him," she sobbed. "I hate him. I wish he was dead and would leave us alone."

What if he should die?

Betsy felt a sea of calm around her, secure upon her island of coffee, sipping tiny amounts of warm liquid that kept her throat and mind open.

"What if he should die?" she asked her daughter. "What would happen to us? Do you think that life would suddenly become perfect?"

Bobbi stared at her, trying to drink in the words as her mother was drinking in coffee. She had no answers to the questions.

"I'm not trying to tell you that I am happy with our present circumstances," said Betsy. "Your father and I are having problems, serious problems. They're not just something that came up overnight. It's strange. You try and think back to where it all started and you realize you're not even sure what's wrong. Part of the problem has to be me. I've come to the conclusion that I'm a perfect victim. I was raised in a house that had nothing but love in it, where people made sure that everybody else was happy. And I think, it's a crazy feeling, but I think that in the beginning of our marriage your father used to push me a little whenever I mentioned my daddy or something down home. He would push me on something or other, and I would give in to keep things peaceful. And he'd push me a little further, and I'd give in again. To keep things happy. And I think I kind of got him in the habit of pushing me on something just to see how far he could go before I fought back. And I almost never fought back. Once in a while I would flare, just for a moment, but I never really fought back. It's been a way of life with us, just as I had my way of life at my daddy's house. I'm a victim. The funny thing is that I'm the one who's always had the guilty feeling."

She turned and filled her cup again from the pot.

"Your father has always been a loner. With all the people he knows, the ones he plays golf with, and tennis, and squash, with all the people at the club, he still has no close friends. He isn't able to operate on a give-and-take basis. When we were first married, when I was so full of love that I sometimes had trouble breathing when I looked at him, I felt we did have a closeness, that we were part of each other. It was easy being a victim then. But the moment that I wasn't able to give him my full attention, when other demands were made on my time, and my love, he stepped aside, put me one pace away. It was the same with you, and Jeff, and Jojo. When you were first born, when all you could do was cry and be fed and changed and put to bed, he couldn't get enough of you. He would hold you in his arms for hours sometimes, just looking down at you, with an expression on his face that often made me jealous. But the minute you were able to make it on your own, to walk around, to talk, to make your own demands, he stepped aside again. He never wants to be in a situation where he isn't in complete control. He seems to need this; it is the only way he can live."

Betsy was listening to herself as closely as Bobbi was, hearing for the first time what she had never thought through before.

"Why is he like this?" asked Bobbi.

Betsy shrugged. "I suppose you could find some roots in his childhood. I suppose you could say he has some basic insecurity. I suppose you could say he was born with some quirk that makes him do what he does. I suppose you could say that he has a tremendous amount of pressure on him in his work and can only operate in this way. I suppose you could go on supposing dozens of things, and they could all be right and all wrong. It's so easy to pick out things in people that you know are wrong. What do you suppose your father would say about us, about you and me? Are we perfect? Are we everything he wants in a wife or a daughter? What do you think about me, Bobbi? Am I everything you want in a mother?"

"Am I everything you want in a daughter?"

"You'll do until something better comes along," she said with a wry grin. "Do you still want some breakfast?"

"Yes. I'm still hungry."

"So am I, I guess," said Betsy, turning to the stove and dumping the congealed eggs in the garbage disposal in the sink.

Bobbi came over to help her where she could, sticking a hand in to move a pan or carrying the butter from the counter to the table or hovering near in case there was something that might be needed. Both of them wanted to feel physical closeness, a sense of oneness, of being part of each other. And as they worked and as they later sat at the table eating greedily of the rich, greasy food before them, saying little, they both had their heads tilted slightly, so that one ear was cocked at the ceiling, anxious, somewhat fearful, but having to know the instant he was ready to come into their world again.

...
xxiii

HEWITT slept till twenty minutes past noon and woke with a tremendous pain just below the occipital lobe, the common area for hypertensive pressure. He could feel his brain as a separate entity in the skull, the tiniest movement causing it to bang against the bone with excruciating pain. He almost grinned with the unscientific reasoning of it. If he were a patient, he would drive his doctor crazy.

The clock in the radio clicked one of its peculiar noises, and he moved carefully to work his eyes within range of the face. Twenty-three minutes past twelve. Almost four hours. Sixteen hours without booze, four hours of sleep, and still the goddamned skull felt as if it were going to break into little pieces. Age and hypertension. Life was going to be one big barrel of laughs for whatever days were left to it. Or rather, existence. There was a difference between life and existence.

What day was this? Thursday. Office hours at one thirty. Check on Jeff. And Mrs. Markham. Anything else? God, how that head hurt. Aspirin? Or two of the green ones? Or one of the white ones? If you were careful, just the right dosage, you could go thirty years with a gentle monkey on your back. They say a lot of them are doing it. Anybody I know? Stanton? Stern? McCord? That would be something if McCord turned out to be a junkie.

He turned on his back carefully and looked up at the ceiling. Aspirin. Three aspirin and to hell with the rest of the shit. You couldn't afford to be a happy doctor. Yes, that's cancer, hee-hee-hee. Yes, you have an incurable disease, hee-hee-hee. Win or lose, the happiest horse in the race. I almost lost my son and wife last night. Hee. Hee. Hee.

He sat up, tossed the covers aside and moved his legs over the edge of the bed. It hurt, but it was bearable. Anything was bearable. Was anything bearable? Aspirin. Definitely aspirin.

As he came down the stairs, he was hit with the smell of frying grease, warm and heavy, and his mind thought of food, and his stomach rejected it. Bobbi was at the sink washing dishes and Betsy came out of the lavatory as he walked through the door. They both stared at him as if he were the ghost of Christmas future, and he stared back. There was almost a guilty heaviness to their looks, and he wondered if something was wrong with Jeff.

"Was there a call from the hospital?" he asked.

The two women—*my God, she is a woman now, with full breasts and a face that*—looked at each other for a moment in perplexity and kept their silence.

"Was there a call about Jeff?" he asked.

"No," said Betsy, "there was no call. He was fine when I left there."

"I'm not going to have a chance to check him before office hours," said Hewitt, glancing at the clock over the sink.

"He's been checked enough," said Betsy. "While I was there, there was Stanton and Dr. Stern and that resident, all of whom seemed to do the same things, and they all gave reassuring grunts."

"I'll go to the hospital after the office," said Hewitt.

"How about something to eat?"

He looked up at the clock again.

"Is there some coffee ready?"

"Right here. I can have eggs and toast in a minute."

"Just a slice of toast."

They both watched him as he stood at the counter and quickly crunched and munched and washed it down. He tried to think of something to say to Bobbi, but the words weren't there, and he finally let it go. She would wash a pan and then look at him closely as she placed it in the drainer, studying him as if for the first time.

"Thanks," he said, as he placed his cup on the saucer. "I should be home around six."

He walked over to Betsy, planted a kiss on her cheek and patted his daughter gently on the fanny. Both women turned to watch him as he went out the door, his wife with her fingertips touching the spot he had kissed and his daughter with her hand holding where he had patted. The spots felt comfortably warm to both women.

Although he was only twelve minutes late, Hewitt found the waiting room full when he arrived and Moore in a state of formal rage, which she dispensed equally between patients and doctor. Hewitt decided he couldn't put up with it for the entire afternoon, so when she brought the schedule in to him, he copped a plea.

"Sorry I'm late," he said, "but I was up all night at the hospital with Jeff."

"Jeff? Your son Jeff?"

He nodded sadly. "Septicemia. Started in the heel from a new shoe and spread like wildfire."

Mrs. Moore was of the generation that leaned toward male offspring, especially the only one of *her* doctor.

"Is he all right?"

"Yes, he seems to be coming along now, but he's in for a tough pull."

"Oh, the poor dear." There would be no problems the rest of the afternoon.

"I'm going to call the hospital now," said Hewitt, "and then we'll make up for lost time. Anything special on?"

"No. It looks like mostly flu. Mrs. Bardwell called. It was her husband had the coronary this week."

SH. SH. SH. SH. SH. SH. SH. SH. SH. SH. SH. SH.

"What did she want?"

"She wouldn't really say. Just said that she wanted to talk to you. I finally told her that I'd have you call when you were free but it was hard to know when that would be."

"OK. Send in the first one when I buzz."

"Right, Doctor." She was almost cheerful as she closed the door behind her.

The hospital switchboard put Hewitt through to the charge nurse on Jeff's floor.

"He seems fine, Doctor," said the nurse. "Dr. Hall is in with him now. Do you want to talk to him?"

"Yes, thank you."

Hall sounded bright-eyed and bushy-tailed, probably on half the sleep that Hewitt had achieved, and he rubbed the back of his neck where a slight pain persisted.

"He seems fine, Doctor," said Hall. "Still running a couple of points of fever, but that's a residual condition that should clear up in a day or two."

"How's Mrs. Markham?"

"Who?"

"Mrs. Markham. The stroke case."

"Oh." There were a few seconds of silence as Hall regrouped.

"I was just going down there, Doctor, after I finished here. But her condition must be the same, or else the nurses would have called me."

"Please see that she's kept as comfortable as possible."

"Oh, yes, they know about that, Doctor." He regrouped a little more, trying to show that he was really on top of the case. "But I don't think she's going to last too much longer."

Hewitt almost said, "It's in the hands of God, Doctor," such was his annoyance, but he, too, regrouped. He couldn't expect Hall to do all his work. It was one thing for him to put in the extra time on Jeff. Why waste some more of it on an old lady who would be better off out of her misery?

"Thank you, Doctor," said Hewitt. "I'll be there after my office hours. I appreciate what you've done."

"Any time, Doctor. Any time."

No more time, thought Hewitt, as he hung up the phone and pressed the buzzer, no more time.

The first patient was Mrs. Palestin, a classic case. She was thirty-one years old, had three children, and her husband was one of Jack Wales' hotshots, an engineer who was aggressive, articulate and gregarious, the perfect attributes for rising in the hierarchy of management. He was perpetually on the road, but when he was at home, he was either on the telephone, the golf course or his wife's back, complaining about the way she was handling the family budget, the children and their social life, based primarily on their never having been invited to one of Wales' parties. Wales had come to their house for dinner once, after turning down three previous invitations, but the return summons from the king had never come, and Palestin was beginning to have dreams about the situation.

Mrs. Palestin, a pallid blonde, was subject to headaches, menstrual periods of unremitting agony, bloat, subsequent flatulence of embarrassing proportions and crying jags that made her young children huddle in corners in fright and bewilderment. Hewitt had been harsh with her on her previous visit four months before, telling her that there was nothing wrong with her physically and that she just had to pull herself together.

Everything this time checked out the same as last time. Despite the crush in the office, Hewitt gave her the full fifteen minutes allotted, even listening carefully with his stethoscope to the gurglings in her large intestine.

Finally, her bra and blouse back on and her hair brushed into place, she sat across from him at the desk, hopefully waiting for some major sign of illness, nothing malignant, but at least a definite illness that could be treated with a capsule of some kind or a tonic, preferably one that tasted disagreeable.

"There's nothing wrong with you, Mary," said Hewitt, seeing her face start to break down into little pieces of disappointment. "And yet, at the same time, there's everything wrong with you." She looked up quickly, not yet hopeful, but at least hearing new words for a change.

"I'm an internist, not a psychiatrist," said Hewitt, "but the major part of my female practice consists of cases like yours." He then proceeded to detail the problem to her, for the first time in his professional life naming names and conditions and situations.

"All wives of men on the make go through this," he said. "My wife has to contend with the same thing!" They stared at each other in mutual wonder. My Christ, thought Hewitt, I've just added one more burden to Betsy's shoulders. This bovine will have it all over the club. "But my wife has learned to cope with it," he lied, eager to save what he could. "She has developed outside interests and tries to utilize her time to fill in the gaps. You've got to do the same thing. Your husband isn't going to change. He can't change if he is going to get where he wants to go. You have to build your life within that framework."

She was nodding eagerly, anxious that the doctor's words should prove to be an answer to her aches and pains, determined that she would do as well or better than that butter-wouldn't-melt-in-her-mouth Betsy Hewitt, but not really understanding what was being explained to her and unable to do anything about it if she did. But at least these were new words she was hearing, not the same old nothing is wrong routine. Everything was wrong, just everything, but maybe now it was going to be different and thank you, Dr. Hewitt, thank you, thank you, thank you.

He sat there a moment after she went out the door, his hand poised on the buzzer but not pressing. What did Betsy do with her time? How often did she go over to the college? Why shouldn't she teach if she was capable? His finger moved down and stopped again. There was something, something . . . Bardwell!

He pulled the phone book to him and looked up the number rather than ask Moore for it, dialed and listened to the ring.

"Hello?" That soft voice.

"This is Dr. Hewitt."

"Oh." There was a long pause. "Doctor, I've had a pain in my lower right side for two days now, and it just doesn't seem to go away. It's probably nothing, but I think I would like you to check it for me."

"Of course." He looked quickly at the list before him. The last booking was for four. "Can you come here at fo . . . at a quarter to five?"

"Yes, I can."

"All right. I'll expect you then."

He kept looking at the phone after he put it down. Why the hell had he done that? A slight shiver went through his body. Why the hell had he . . . the buzzer rang. Mrs. Moore was losing some of her good nature under the press of the mob in the office. He buzzed back, and Mrs. Philbin entered, twenty-seven years old, the mother of four children, her husband. . . .

Hewitt worked steadily from then on, concentrating carefully on each case, his mind only now and then almost pausing on Mrs. Bardwell, Sheila, before returning to the heartbeat in his ears or the red spots on the throat. And suddenly he had Mrs. Norwood before him, the name opposite 4 p.m. A blood sugar test seemed indicated, and he walked out with her to have Mrs. Moore arrange for the hospital appointment. An old man and woman were the only occupants of the chairs, and Hewitt looked inquiringly at his nurse.

"These people say they want to talk to you, Doctor, but they refuse to tell me what it is about," she said briskly, ready to fling them out of the office physically if the doctor so much as nodded permission. He gave instructions on Mrs. Norwood and told her she would be called when the results were in. "Nothing to worry about," he said reassuringly, as he walked out past the partition to where the elderly couple were sitting.

"What can I do for you?" he asked the man, who looked over at his wife without saying anything.

"You the doctor who try to help my boy," she said, not quite a question and yet not a definite statement. The accent was Italian, strong enough to indicate that English was not the language of the home.

"What boy is that?" he asked.

"The policeman, the officer, he told us what you do," the woman continued.

"The policeman?"

"That's Torchio," the old man said impatiently. "Torchio!"

Torchio. Sergeant Torchio. The boy in the car. Hewitt looked at his watch: Twenty-two minutes past four.

"Come into the office, please," he said, indicating with his hands that they should rise. Mrs. Norwood was paying Mrs. Moore in cash, which seemed to involve hunting for dollar bills in desk drawers. The old couple looked at each other again, then rose to go where Hewitt's hand pointed. As they went through the door, he paused in the threshold and turned to Mrs. Moore.

"Why don't you take off?" he said. "You've had a rough day."

"There are a million things that should be entered," she said, and he could tell by the way she said it that she did not feel like entering them.

"Tomorrow," he said. "You can get it all tomorrow. I'll see these people out. Take off."

"Tomorrow there will be a million more things," she said, standing up. "I don't know what I'm going to do around here pretty soon."

"We'll work out something," he said soothingly, and closed the door behind him.

She opened it again immediately. "Can Jeff have visitors?" she asked.

"He needs another day, I think." The door closed again.

The man and the woman were standing in front of the desk, and Hewitt motioned for them to sit down. Again, they checked each other and then sat, she on the edge of her chair and he sunken back. Hewitt could see the years of homemade wine that had traveled through the veins of the bulbous nose, the physical labor that had hardened the hands to gnarls of ironwood. Somewhere around seventy years of age but unwithered, toughening on the vine with each passing year.

Hewitt sat down in his chair and looked at them. How old could that boy have been? Eighteen? Twenty? Son? Grandson?

"That boy in the car?" he said. "That was your. . . ." The woman looked at the man.

"Carlo," she said. "That was our boy, Carlo. That was our baby, Carlo." The husband grunted, whether in assent, pain or displeasure, Hewitt couldn't tell.

"He was a wild boy," the woman continued. "He no

work steady like the other boys. He drink whiskey. He drive too fast. He no have the license for seven month now. That his brother's car he smash up. Smash up," she repeated almost to herself, and Hewitt could see tears in her eyes.

"The sergeant," she continued, "he tell us what you do to our boy." Jesus Christ, Hewitt thought, McCord's right again. They think I'm going to pay for the pasta from here on in.

"He tell us how you crawl in with him and try to save him when the car she going to blow up," said the woman. "He tell us what you try to do for our boy."

The old man grunted again.

"My husband," she continued, after looking at the old man again, "he say that you do your job, that you do what you can. He want to pay you for what you try to do for our Carlo."

Both she and Hewitt turned to the old man who had withdrawn a battered, greasy-looking wallet from his pocket and was in the process of pulling some bills from the inside.

"No!" said Hewitt, louder than he intended, causing both people to look up in surprise. "No," he said again more softly, "there is no charge for what I did. A doctor is supposed to do things like that. It's part of being a doctor. I can't take money for that."

The old man turned his head a bit to one side as he considered what Hewitt had said. Then he shoved the bills back into the compartment, folded the wallet and returned it carefully to his pocket. He nodded at Hewitt, the vestige of a smile on his face, and stood up.

"The policeman tell me you good doctor," he said. "The policeman speak true. I thank you for what you try for my son Carlo."

Hewitt stood up and walked around the desk to them. "I'm sorry it wasn't enough," he said. The woman took his hand in both hers and squeezed.

"You have son?" she asked. He nodded.

"I wish you love and joy from your son," she said. "I wish you love and joy in your life." The man nodded, and the two of them turned toward the door, followed by Hewitt.

He saw that Moore was gone, papers left on the desk where they had been dropped. Was it canasta night? Nobody said a word further as the old couple went through the door, the woman bestowing a slight smile through her tears as she turned to leave. It was twenty-two minutes before five, and Hewitt walked into his office and sat down at the desk, staring at the Buffet reprint on the wall, seeing only color and no form.

Through the blue haze he heard the outer door open and shut and the squeak of someone sitting in the ersatz leather chair. He waited a moment more and then walked out to the doorway of the reception room. There she was, pale and wan in funereal tradition, but lovelier somehow because of it.

"Come on in," he said, and she rose and walked toward him. He stepped aside and let her through, then walked across the reception room to the outer door and twisted the lock shut. As his hand touched the cold knob, he felt the sweat in his palm and looked down at both his hands for a moment, where the glint of moisture showed.

Then he walked back into his own office and sat down in his chair, across the desk from her.

"Well," he said, and the heartiness of it surprised both of them a bit, "what seems to be the trouble?"

"I . . . I have a pain down here," she said, moving her right hand to her lower abdomen, "and it just doesn't seem to go away."

"Well," he said again, "let's see what. . . ." He looked down at the desk for the folder that Moore would have. . . . "Excuse me for a moment," he said, rising and going to the outer office, where he quickly pulled the file from the case. His knees were weak and he could feel his heart pounding in his breast. For Christ's sake. He stood there a moment, drawing two deep breaths, which he let out slowly through his mouth. A day. He'd been in the ground only a day.

SH. SH. SH.

The sight of Bardwell lying on the stone table passed through his eyes, and there was the sting of formaldehyde mixed in with it. One day in the ground. Crazy. Crazycrazy-crazy. One day in the ground. Crazy.

"Tell me about the pain," he said, sitting down in his chair with the folder open in front of him.

"It's a kind of dull ache, more than a pain," she said, "and I think I've had it about three days. Things have been so mixed up that I'm a little bit confused about how long I've had it, but I think it's about three days."

"Have you been constipated?"

She looked at him in surprise. "I don't know," she said, her mind working on the question. "I can't remember whether . . . I don't know . . . I just don't know."

"Have you been able to sleep?"

"I haven't slept much, but it wasn't because of this. I knew it was there while I was lying in bed, but I slept some last night, and it didn't keep me awake. But when I woke up this morning, it was still dark, the pain was there. I wasn't thinking about it, I had forgotten it, but when I moved, I felt it was still there. So I thought I better ask you about it. I've never been sick. Neither of us. . . ." Her hand went to her mouth.

"You've been through a great deal the past few days," said Hewitt, pushing the sphygmomanometer forward and beckoning her to take the chair by the side of the desk. He put the stethoscope in his ears and pumped up on her, listened intently and then released.

"No problem there," he said, ripping the band loose from her arm and rising. "Why don't you go in the next room and take your clothes off and get up on the table and

I'll be there in a minute?" He led her down the short hallway to the examination room and saw her through, pulling
the curtain across the door behind her. As he started to
walk back toward his own office, she edged the curtain back a
bit and put her head through.

"All my clothes, Doctor?" she asked.

"You can leave your shoes and stockings on," he said.
The curtain closed again.

He sat down in his chair and looked at the digital clock
on the desk. Five-o-one. *I should be home around six*. Why
had he said that? It had been easy to say. *I should be home
around six*. And yet he'd never said anything like that before. I'll be home when I'm goddamned good and ready to
be home was the regular prescription.

He pulled the phone toward him and dialed his home
number. Betsy answered on the second ring, somewhat out
of breath.

"Oh, Alex," she said, "I just got home. Jeff seems terribly
lethargic. He slept mostly while I was there."

"His body is still exhausted. He'll be like this for a few
days yet."

"Dr. Stern came in again this afternoon. He's terribly
nice, Alex. You know, I've never really spoken to him before. He said he expected to be invited to Jeff's bar mitzvah
and I started to tell him that Protestants don't have bar
mitzvahs before I realized, and he must think I'm a real
dodo."

"Well, aren't you?"

"I guess I am." He could sense the surprise in her voice,
the wonder at his words: Is he joking? *Am I joking? Am I
joking with my wife?*

"I'm hung up here at the office for a while," he said, "and
then I'm going to the hospital. So I am going to be late."

"Alex, I don't want to go to the wake tonight. I want to
stay with Jeff for a while."

"Wake?"

"Frank's wake. This is the last night, but I'm sure Gerda will understand. Are you going with me to the funeral tomorrow?"

"What time is it going to be?"

"Eleven. So it won't interfere with anybody's office hours."

"Yes, I'll go with you."

"I'll keep dinner hot."

" 'Bye now." The wet streak on the telephone made him clench his hands together, the sweat making a suction that he ground out with friction, trying to dry them of their clamminess. He sat still a few moments longer, until the air cleared the phone of its evidence. Then he stood and started the long walk down the short corridor.

She was leaning against the edge of the examination table, the shoulders sagging but her full breasts thrust forward, the rosy nipples at a twenty-degree elevation from the mound. There was no movement to indicate she was aware of his entrance or presence, and he stood looking at her for a long moment, the incredibly smooth skin, the fine line from the nose through the jaw, the soft tuft of hair extending from the thighs. There was just the suggestion of roundness to the abdomen, and he remembered they were hikers and skiers and campers and all the other American things that engineers and their families liked to go in for. Or did they?

She turned her head slowly and looked at him, and he could feel his face flush under her neutral gaze. But she wasn't really looking at him, merely acknowledging that she had recorded his presence.

"Last time was just for a quick checkup, wasn't it?" he asked. "An insurance policy or something?"

"It was an insurance policy."

"Right. Just sit up on the edge of the table while I listen here." He checked the front and the back, moving the stethoscope around slowly, requesting deep breaths and hold it, deep breaths and hold it, deep breaths and hold it. Exhale. He palpated mightily.

"Good," he said, stepping back. "Very good. Now just lie back and stretch along the table." She complied and he looked down at her full length, staring at the womanliness until his hand involuntarily reached toward her—the breast, the cunt, the face, the belly, the thigh, the lips— until he realized in horror that the hand was out, but her eyes were closed, the eyes were completely closed. She lay there as if she were sleeping, pale and pink with her breasts rising and falling, and he saw Bardwell superimposed over her, the flesh yellow and the jaw sunken and the bones protruding sharply through the slack flesh with the sting of the embalming fluid in his eyes, and Hewitt placed his hands on the warm flesh to blot out the memory of the other one, the dead one, with Jeff lying there, too, waiting, waiting, and he pushed hard.

"Does that hurt there?" he asked, barely able to get the words out.

"Only from the pushing, not from anything inside."

"There?"

"No."

"There?"

"A little bit."

"There?"

"Yes! Right there. That's the center of it."

"But not there?"

"No. Not there."

He turned to the cabinet and removed a packet of rubber gloves, slipping them on with a double crack of sound.

"Put your legs in the stirrups, please," he said, raising her to the right height. His fingers entered into moistness, and a dizziness overcame him, not of blood pounding through constricted vessels, but a lightness of sensation, of pleasurable content.

"Good," he said, withdrawing his hand and turning

around to pull off the gloves and fling them into the basket.

"When you are dressed, come back to the office," he said, not turning around to help her and walking out without looking back. He pulled the curtain firmly across the pole, blotting out her presence and the desire that had gone through him. His hands and knees were shaking, and he could feel his heart racing in irregular strides, close to tachycardia of an alarming rate.

He sank into the chair and stared across at the painting, weak with fright at what he had almost done. There is a sickness in me, he thought, a terrible sickness. He leaned back and closed his eyes waiting for death to take him out of the mess, no more of anything. Tomorrow will be like today, kept going through his mind, tomorrow will be like today. No man pleases me. Nor woman either.

He felt so tired he could barely keep his head up. What does a doctor do when he loses his strength, when he can't answer the alarm any more? Quit and go live off old Daddy Warbucks, Mr. Southern Hospitality, the Colonel Sanders of the construction industry. *It is up to you to take care of this, not your father-in-law. I am talking about a way of life.*

And I, Mr. Jewish accountant, am talking about a way of death. I'm tired of fighting when I don't know what I'm fighting. Who is the fucking enemy?

"Doctor?"

She was standing on the other side of the desk, looking at him anxiously.

"Oh," he said, waving for her to sit down, "I'm sorry. I was up all night at the hospital, and I don't seem to bounce back the way I used to." He sat up and put his elbows on the desk.

"Yours must be a difficult life," she said, "with people calling at all hours."

"It's the name of the game. Sickness has no manners."

"Or death."

"Well! It is my belief that you have a minor infection of the urinary tract, and I am going to give you a prescription for it. You will take these tablets four times a day for a week. I think it should start to clear about the third day. I want you to call me on the fourth day and tell me how you are progressing. If the problem persists, we will take some smears to check it out, but I am fairly certain that this will do the trick, and we will hear no more of the matter."

He wrote busily on his pad and handed her the slip.

"Now," he said, "is there anything else that is bothering you?"

She looked at him closely, her legs pulled together and her purse poised, ready to rise and go her way.

"It's just that I don't know which way to turn," she said finally. "We had so many plans. Not just for now but for years to come, right through to what we would do with retirement. It's crazy, but we would lie in bed at night and talk about five years from now and ten years from now, and all of a sudden it's meaningless. There is no future for me. I look at Trish and think of my responsibility to her, but it doesn't seem important. What happens to that dear sweet girl doesn't seem important."

"I'm afraid there is a future for you," said Hewitt. "Except for a slight urinary infection, there is every indication that you have forty or fifty more years to go, enough to have grandchildren and great-grandchildren. That's a future you can't dismiss so easily."

"I know. I could see people at the wake and even at the funeral looking at me with that measured look and I could almost hear them saying, 'Well, she's still young enough to marry again.' And this morning, in the dark, while I was lying there trying not to think of the pain, it suddenly occurred to me that maybe they weren't saying that at all, maybe that was only in my mind."

"You should never feel guilty about what goes through

your mind. Everybody has thoughts that are not within the realm of polite society. Once in a while I even scare myself."

This brought a wan smile and a relaxation of the hands holding the pocketbook.

"I suppose I've got to get a good old American grip on myself," she said, "and forge ahead. I suppose the best thing would be to go back to work, but I hesitate about that because of Trish."

"Do you need the money?"

"No. Not in the foreseeable future anyway. Don was one of those overinsured people who kept worrying about what would happen to his family if something happened to him. He was almost always right about everything, and he was about this, too." The sob almost broke through her last words, but she maintained control.

"You would probably want something that would let you see Trish off to school and have you home before she got there in the afternoon."

"Yes, I suppose. Part time. But that kind of job is hard to find when you want it."

"I have that kind of job for you."

"What do you mean?"

"The paper work in this office has gotten out of control, and my nurse can't handle it anymore. We need someone part time to help us fill out the medical insurance forms, to do the billing and to keep the files straight. You could work out your own schedule."

"Oh, Doctor, you've already done enough for us. We. . . ."

He could see her mouth moving and the words coming out, but he no longer could hear any other sound than the roaring in his ears, a hollow chamber for the beat of his heart, with his eyes a film of red. *Oh, Doctor, you've already done enough for us.* Enough. Enough. Enough. More than enough. Her lips had stopped moving, and she was looking at him expectantly.

"It's something for you to think about," he said, taking a chance. "Why don't you come in and talk to Mrs. Moore on Monday to discuss what it might involve and then you can take some time to think about it if you want? We can muddle on a while longer, I suppose. But we do need someone, and you might be just the one."

She smiled, a real smile, reflecting a moment when all else was forgotten.

"I can do that," she said. "It might be good for me to plunge right in and get going, so I don't have time to sit home and brood about things. My folks wanted me to move back to the Coast, but Trish likes it here, school and skiing and all her friends. I'll call Mrs. Moore on Monday and set up a time to see her."

She stood up and he stood with her.

"Thank you, Doctor," she said, extending her hand to him, which he shook gravely, "for the prescription and for all the rest. You're more than a doctor to us."

"Call me in four days," he said, walking in front of her to the door, unlatching and opening it in one motion. "Or sooner, if there's a question."

She smiled her good-bye and was gone.

Hewitt returned to his office and stood staring at his coat on the hanger. Weak, he said to himself. "You're weak," he said aloud to the coat. You're a weak man, a weak person, he said to himself as he slipped on his coat. The phone started ringing as he was going through the outer door, and he stopped for a moment before going through and closing it. If it was the hospital, he was on the way there anyway. If it was anything else, he didn't care. For the first time in his professional career, he really didn't care.

XXIV

"OK."

Hewitt looked down at his son, whose eyes were shifted to the side, toward the wall, anywhere but at him.

"You have no trouble breathing?" he asked.

"No, it's OK."

Everything seemed to be OK. No matter what question Hewitt asked him, the answer was OK. And everything did seem to be OK, with the exception of the two degrees of fever. Hewitt looked up at the IV with the antibiotic, dripping steadily, fighting the fever, fighting the infection, fighting, fighting, fighting, drop by drop by drop. What am I fighting? he wondered. Why this sense of perpeutal unease? What have I been fighting all my life?

"Have you been eating?"

"Yup."

"What did you have for dinner?"

"Some kind of meat."

"Did you eat it?"

"I didn't like it."

"Would you like something else?"

"I'm not hungry."

"You have to eat to get your strength back."

"Mom fed me lunch."

"You have to eat by yourself, too. Your mother can't feed. . . ."

The boy's face set further into withdrawal. What the Christ difference did it make who fed him? The important thing was that he eat. Jeff. Look at me, Jeff, he silently pleaded. Look at me, son. I'll feed you. Spoon by spoon. Fork by fork. Just look at me.

"That heel's going to be sensitive for quite a while," said Hewitt. "We have to make sure your new ski boots fit exactly right."

The boy didn't answer.

"What do you think about going up to Vermont for a whole week this winter and trying some of the big trails?" asked Hewitt. "We can rent one of those chalets up there and just ski from morning to night. Do you think you'd like that?"

"I guess so."

"Would you like some ice cream? I have some pull around here, and I can get you some ice cream in a minute."

"No."

Hewitt's hand reached out and took his son's fingers in his palm, pressing slightly.

"Is there anything you want, anything at all?"

The face turned toward him, but the eyes would not look into his eyes, focused somewhere below the nose, the lips perhaps.

"When is Mom coming back? I want Mom."

There was the glisten of tears in the eyes.

"She'll be here in a little while, but I'm here now. Is there anything I can do for you? Do you want a TV in this room? We can get a TV hooked up."

"No. I just want Mom here. I just want Mom." This time the tears spilled over and wet the cheeks.

"Mom can't be here all the time. There's Bobbi and Jojo to take care of, too. You just have to be. . . ."

"I want Mom. I want Mom to be here." The sobs were heavier.

"Look, Jeff, I'll call her. I'll call her now and tell her to come over right away. Is that all right?"

The boy nodded, and Hewitt went to the phone and asked for outside. Betsy answered on the first ring.

"Hi," he said. "Jeff is pretty lonesome, and he would like you to come back and keep him company."

"Is he all right?"

"Seems fine. Homesick, I guess."

"He was fairly cheerful when I left. Did he say what's wrong?"

"He isn't saying much of anything."

"That's strange. He was babbling away all afternoon."

"Maybe it's me."

Both tried at once to bridge the silence that set in without forewarning, and it took several seconds for them to establish the correct tone again.

"I'll leave right away," she said finally. "Both girls have had dinner, and I'll leave yours in the oven."

"I can wait here till you get here."

"No, I think you had better come home. Jojo isn't quite sure about what's going on and I think she is disturbed a bit. It would probably be better if you were here when she went to bed."

"She's never needed me for. . . ."

"And you haven't talked to Bobbi today," Betsy continued, as if he had never spoken, "so why don't you come home and let them give you your dinner? Tell Jeff I'll be there shortly." And she hung up without waiting to find out any more. He looked at the phone for a moment and then placed it on the cradle.

"Your mother will be here shortly," he said, turning to Jeff. The boy didn't answer.

"I have to go see some of my other patients," he continued, "and then I'll come back. All right?"

The boy was looking at the farther wall again, and his head inclined slightly to indicate recognizance.

Hewitt walked out to the nursing station, and the charge nurse looked up at him with a smile.

"Did Dr. Stanton say anything about Jeff's temperature?" he asked.

"No, Doctor. He didn't say anything about anything."

Hewitt had three other patients to check before he went down to Mrs. Markham's room, and he almost welcomed the dimness and quiet as a sanctuary against the demands of all the others. She asked nothing of him anymore, this woman. Protection from pain. She had asked protection from pain, but her own body had provided that before his services were required.

Her eyes were closed, and only the faint hissing of the oxygen tubes going into her nose indicated that life was still going on. His eyes lifted to the IV to note the rate of drip. Oxygen and glucose. It always comes down to oxygen and glucose. Hewitt saw himself lying on the bed, the needle in his vein and the plastic tubes in his nose, oblivious to all that had seemed so important a blink before.

What had been so important a moment before? What was important right now? To make sick people well? To help old people die? To earn more money? To take vacations? To bring up the children? To watch your wife get old? To get old yourself? And helpless. And weak. And forced to abide by the decisions of others.

Who is the enemy? He remembered the old comic strip where the character had said, "We have met the enemy and they are us." Something like that. Am I my enemy? Am I the only enemy I have in the world?

He reached out and picked up the left hand that was lying so still on the cover. It was warm. Life still coursed through the body, the fever from the stroke keeping it warm and toasty on this cool fall day. Why wouldn't Jeff's fever break? Was there something going on in there, something they hadn't reached with their drip, drip, drip?

How much death was waiting around the corner? For a moment he saw life without Jeff, the house missing one, and Betsy and Bobbi and Jojo all mourning. How would his own life be different? The name dead. No more Hewitts. What difference could it make? To anybody.

"Doctor?"

He turned to see one of the floor nurses standing in the doorway.

"Yes?"

"Is everything all right?" How long had he been there?

"Yes. Has her daughter been in?"

"She was here most of the afternoon and left just before you came down. We told her we would call if there was any change."

"Make sure she's comfortable."

"Yes, Doctor."

He walked up the two flights and paused at the entrance to Jeff's room. Betsy was in there, and the two of them were talking at the same time, looking each other straight in the eyes and not noticing their husband-father just outside the doorway.

He turned and walked to the elevator and punched the button. When he arrived home, he found Jojo already asleep in her room and Bobbi washing her hair. The covered plate in the oven contained nothing that stirred his slightest interest, and he scraped it all into the garbage disposal and then carefully washed and dried the dishes.

Fatigue gripped him in every bone, and after he had undressed and brushed his teeth, he opened the closet door to scan the sample bottles sitting there so neatly. There was nothing that would benefit Alexander Hewitt. He fell asleep instantly and did not hear Betsy when she came up to check on him at nine thirty or at midnight when she finally came to bed. There were no discernible dreams during the night. He slept as if he were dead.

XXV

"In the name of the Father, and of the Son, and of the Holy Spirit. Amen."

Looking at the back of the priest, Hewitt felt his hands tighten on the rail of the pew in front of him. He had slid forward in awkward imitation of those who were truly on their knees and was balancing himself precariously on the edge of the seat, the hard wood cutting into his thigh painfully. This is my penance, he thought, mortification of the flesh.

The family were already seated at the front when the Hewitts arrived, and he had a mad urge to go down to them to let them know he was there, Hewitt was there, ready to acknowledge his responsibility for the death of their son and husband and father and colleague and friend and whoever else was in the place. It was packed, every pew solid, and a group had to shove over to make room for two Hewitts where there was really only room for one.

Heads had turned at their entrance, at first casual scanning of the new arrivals, but definite quickened interest once recognition was attained. Arms had poked bodies, whispers had turned ears, hands had pulled clothing to inform the dull, the unheeding, the ignorant, that here was Hewitt, the man responsible for the occasion, the one who had murdered young Casey in the locked confines of a brilliantly lighted cubicle in the Young Men's Christian Center. Not a Christian thing to do. Definitely not a Christian thing to do.

"May almighty God have mercy on you, forgive you your sins, and bring you to life everlasting."

How nice it must be to believe, Hewitt thought, really believe. To know that God is going to have mercy on you and forgive you your sins and bring you to life everlasting.

He looked down at his hands and saw how white the fingers were where he was gripping and released them just a bit, seeing the red come back almost instantly. Good circulation. Damn good circulation. At least the circulation was good.

"We beg you, O Lord, by the merits of your saints whose relics are here, and of all your saints, grant me forgiveness for all my sins. Amen."

What if I could go in one of those tall boxes, Hewitt mused, and tell the guy kissing the altar all of my sins? Would he have a shit fit? Or has he heard it all before? You're a small timer, Hewitt. You think you're the only man who ever cheated on his wife? You think you're the only mean son of a bitch who ever lived? Cold to your wife. Cold to your kids. Christ, guys come in here every day, right where you're sitting now, and tell me things that would make your hair curl. They want to screw around, they don't even bother going out of the family. They're cold to their wives and kids, too. They knock them cold, that's what they do. The question is, if you're so lousy at it, why do you bother with it at all? Is love such a. . . .

"Lord, have mercy."

"Lord, have mercy."

"Lord, have mercy."

Betsy leaned toward him and whispered, "What did you say?" He looked at her in surprise, for he had said nothing.

"Christ, have mercy."

"Christ, have mercy."

"Christ, have mercy."

He could feel his lips forming the words he was hearing. Had he been saying them aloud? His parents had never gone to church. Would it have made a difference? he wondered. Would I be a different person if I had something like this to fall back on, maybe not so formal, but something to fall back on when I'm scared I'm going to die, or when I've made a wrong decision on a patient, or when I find my wife's good looks as exciting as the piece of toast I have in the morning, or when I wonder what it will be like if my son should. . . .

"Cleanse my heart and my lips, almighty God, as you cleansed the lips of the prophet Isaiah with a burning coal. In your mercy so cleanse me that I may worthily proclaim your holy Gospel. Through Christ our Lord."

I want my boy to live, he thought. I've had my shot; he deserves his turn. I will cleanse my heart and lips. I will burn my cock with a hot coal. He grinned, and a woman an aisle over who had been watching him stuck her elbow in her husband's side and whispered fiercely in his ear. The man looked over at Hewitt and saw nothing but a grim visage.

"I am the resurrection and the life; he who believes in me, even if he die, shall live; and whoever lives and believes in me, shall never die. Dost thou believe this?"

I believe, thought Hewitt, and he could see Frank's body through the wood of the coffin and Bardwell lying on the stone table, pale and shriveled. I believe that death is the end of everything and the beginning of nothing. I believe there is nothing to believe in. I believe I can only help the body where the body can help itself. I believe in pain, for pain is life.

He could feel the warmth of Betsy's body pressing against him, and he moved his hand to cover hers on the back of the pew. She looked quickly in surprise, her lips opened over her even white teeth, her eyes suddenly round.

"To those who believe in his name, who were born not of blood, nor of the will of the Flesh, nor of the will of man, but of God. And the Word was made Flesh and dwelt among us."

He watched the priest standing at the foot of the coffin, giving the final absolution. Out of it. Casey was out of it. No more worries about weight or getting his dick up or seeing to it that the kids' teeth were straight and that they got in the right college and that his wife was not having a breakdown like every other goddamned wife in this community.

They were wheeling the casket down the aisle, the family following slowly, the others even more slowly. When their turn came, they edged out carefully and walked down the carpet into the brisk air, the sun shining in a brilliant blue sky, a perfect day for a funeral.

"Are you going to the office or the hospital?" asked Betsy, as they watched the family getting into the limousines and people scatter to the parking lot or the street.

"The cemetery," said Hewitt. "I'm going to the cemetery."

He knew she was staring at him, but he kept his eyes on the family, settling back in their seats, none of them talking. Their minds intent . . . intent on what? he wondered. On what life was going to be like without Frank Casey around? On what life was going to be like without Donald Bardwell around? On what life was going to be like without Eleanor Markham around? On what life was going to be like without Alexander Hewitt around?

"I'll go with you," she said. "We can leave my car here and pick it up on the way back."

"You drive me in yours," he said. "They don't need a jazzy little sports car to brighten up the procession."

She drove automatically, her mind searching for reasons behind his wanting to go to the cemetery. The Caseys were not close friends. It was only in the past month or so that Alex even mentioned Frank in passing. Twice they had been to the Caseys for dinner, and Betsy had begun to experience guilt feelings about returning the hospitality. We never entertain anymore, she realized suddenly. There had been no parties at the Hewitt house in more than a year. They went to other people's parties, they went to the affairs at the club, but there had been no occasions to warrant asking people in, no desire to share their home with others. Has it been that bleak? she wondered. Are our lives now that bleak?

"How did Jeff seem to you today?" she asked, anxious to break the silence that nourished thoughts of such desolation.

For a few moments she believed he wasn't going to answer. His body seemed shrunken within itself, and when she snatched a quick sidelong look, she thought his eyes were closed. Was he holding himself responsible for Casey's death? she wondered. He was a doctor; he knew that the time and the place were not accountable for what happened. The autopsy had revealed hardening of the arteries comparable to a man of eighty. That's what Edna Stanton had told her while she was waiting for Alex to arrive at the church.

"He's coming along," the voice beside her said, and she almost lost control of the wheel in surprise at the sound, she being back at the church and listening to what Frank Stanton had told his wife about Casey's condition.

"It's just that the damn fever won't break," he continued. "Nothing you can put your finger on, nothing to get excited about, but it just won't break."

"He seems good," she said, "except that he has no appetite."

"That's as much from the medication as anything."

"Could I bring some things he likes from home?"

"The food's not that bad there. But I suppose you could. No reason why you can't."

The procession wound around the narrow blacktop road of the cemetery and stopped by an open area where the grave stood open, the mound of dirt covered with grass-colored cloth, the green standing out from the brown of the surrounding countryside. By the time Alex and Betsy walked to the knot of people surrounding the grave the coffin had been placed on the silver-railed elevator, ready for its final plunge. The priest moved to the front of the mourners.

"*Let us pray. O God, through your mercy the souls of the faithful find rest. Bless this grave. . . .*"

Alex stepped forward through the people and stood in the forefront, his eyes glued to the coffin over which the priest was sprinkling holy water while the sounds of sobs rose in the air, gurgly noises that seemed unfit in the cold, clean air with the small warmth of the sun finding haven in the black clothes of those present, giving what help it could to the widow in her bereavement. The priest made the sign of the cross and started his last intonation. Hewitt stepped one more pace forward, putting him by himself, alone in the front of his section of the circle.

"*May his soul and the souls of all the faithful departed through the mercy of God rest in peace.*"

"Amen," said Alex, his voice alone clear through the mumbled responses of all the others.

The clatter of the rollers began, and the coffin slowly sank into the hole, all eyes riveted, nothing stirring but the disappearing rectangle of polished wood, sinking forever into the deep until called forth by the faith of those faithful present.

Everyone turned as the family was about to be led away, everyone but Alexander Hewitt, who stood there facing the grave for another moment and then turned in the opposite direction from the mass, toward the family group moving slowly to the cars.

Gerda Casey had sagged into her father's and brother's arms at the final moment, and her first stumbling steps were with head cast down, not seeing or caring where they were leading her, knowing only that her life was in the hole in the ground at the moment, about to be covered with dirt.

And then, as if she heard something, or felt something, or knew something, she stopped, her weight forcing her bearers to stop with her else they dragged her on the ground. She stopped and seemed to gather herself for a moment, shrugging off the arms that held her and looking up and ahead, straight in the face of Alexander Hewitt, standing alone, his hands by his side, legs slightly apart, braced.

Even those who had been moving off quickly stopped and looked back, caught by some break in the rhythm of the event. They saw the widow, the rosiness of her cheeks fighting the pallor of her sorrow, staring at the man who had last seen her husband alive, who had said the last words to him and heard the last words from him, the man who would forever have claim to the final second.

"Alex," cried Gerda, her voice a shrill warning of the grief and wailing that were still contained in her body. "Alex," she cried again, moving toward him at a slow run. He made no motion, his feet firm on the ground, his hands loose by his side, and the crowd tensed in anticipation of impact.

"Oh, Alex," she moaned, as she stopped within an inch of him, her tear-sodden eyes gazing up hopelessly, her arms attempting to reach around his large bulk. "What are we going to do without him?" she asked and fell against his chest as his arms went around her, holding her close to him, his head a foot above her, his eyes looking straight ahead at the gravediggers who were becoming restive at the slowness of the crowd and anxious to be about their work.

Alex turned carefully and led Gerda to her limousine, where he turned her over to the care of her father and brother again. Her head was down once more, and she wept alone to the earth.

Betsy was already in the car and behind the wheel by the time he walked down the line to where she was. They drove back to the city in silence, and before she was able to think of something to ask him in the church parking lot, he was out of the door and had slammed it behind him. She could feel the tears in her eyes as she drove to the hospital to see Jeff, but she didn't know whom they were for.

xxvi

HEWITT treated forty-seven patients between noon and ten minutes past nine P.M., and as he closed the kitchen door behind him, shoving his butt against the wood to slam it into locking position, he let his body sag against the support, air leaking out of his nose in a sigh of exhaustion.

Betsy found him in this position as she came out of the hallway, stopping quickly in alarm.

"Are you feeling all right?" she asked for the first time since she had known him. Alexander Hewitt was always all right. But there were dark circles under his eyes and tiny flecks of gray barely discernible in the blond sideburns, and the veins on the backs of his hands were starting to puff up in tiny blue knots. He's starting to show his age, she thought, a twinge of conscience not quite overriding the satisfaction she took in that realization. Even Alex. Her hand went up to her own face, the fingers reaching instinctively for the tiny wrinkles that could just be seen and not really felt. Grow old along with me, she remembered vaguely, the best is yet to be.

"Any calls?" he asked.

"None."

He pushed off from the door and slipped off his coat, which she took and hugged to her chest.

"Have you eaten?" she asked, moving off toward the closet.

"I had a sandwich and a glass of milk in Jeff's room," he said.

"He seemed hot to me and uncomfortable."

"Sound asleep when I just left him. Stanton seems to feel everything is all right."

"How do you feel about it?"

"I don't know. I keep wishing the fever would go away, and as a doctor I know that wishing has nothing to do with it. It just takes time for everything to sort itself out again. You can't pour all those specifics into the body without confusing whatever complex mechanism controls the whole thing. He's got to be on antibiotics for several days before he's cleaned out of infection. I know that. You know that. And yet we both wish that the fever would go away."

"Oh, Alex, this has been a terrible week."

"One week isn't much different from another when you get right down to it."

"But there's been this thing with Jeff and Frank Casey and my mother, and it all seems. . . ."

"Your mother?"

"Yes. I talked to them the other night and my father said she had an angina attack. . . ."

"You can go a hundred years with angina attacks."

She looked at him hopefully, not quite sure of the seriousness of his statement. Reassuring? Sarcastic?

"As long as she follows treatment and takes care of herself, it shouldn't affect her life-span one bit. Probably increase it now that she's had a warning."

Reassurance! Alex meant her well on this night.

"Are you all worn down or all wound up?" she asked.

"I don't know."

"Do you want to watch some television or go up to bed?" They looked at each other, suddenly aware that warmth and comfort and pleasurable sensations were available from one body to the other. She could feel the heat rising in her, the moisture, the fierce desire to have this man mount over her flesh and bring her to a climax of forgetfulness, away from sickness and death and worry and fear and all the other nagging little doubts that had been assailing her from all sides. Her husband, the man she loved, wanted to go to bed with her. He didn't want to shut himself in his den and drink vodka until the television screen blurred in front of him. He wanted to go to bed with her.

"Let's go up to bed," he said, and switched out the kitchen lights.

Alex accompanied her while she checked on Jojo, the almost-life-sized doll sleeping on the pillow beside her, two faces nearly perfect in their symmetry, the real and the unreal. Bobbi had fallen asleep while reading a book, the light glaring in her face, and only blinked her eyes open once as Betsy neatly removed the paperback novel and switched off the lamp. Alex put his fingers on his daughter's cheek for a moment and then followed his wife to their room.

There was a ritual awareness to their undressing, and they removed their clothes without conversation, hanging things up, discarding soiled underclothes in the basket, brushing teeth carefully, all without exchanging a direct glance.

Betsy was the first one into the bed, easing back the top sheet and sliding in between with a slight shiver. She remained propped up on one elbow, her hand ready for the light switch as Alex pulled up the covers on his side and was in with her, not touching, lying on his back, and they were in darkness.

They heard each other turning and came together awkwardly for a moment as body adjusted to body, arm to arm, leg to leg, face to face, lip to lip, tongue to tongue, and it was as if time had moved back to their first such kiss when she had decided that this man could have all she possessed, full mouth and tongue and teeth and breasts and whatever he wanted, this man would have.

She was waiting for his hands to start their slow exploration of her, all new, all different, as though never before, but he clung to her with fierceness, almost desperation, afraid to break the bond that was holding them together. She savored the taste of his toothpaste unmixed with vodka. Let anyone who maintained that vodka was odorless and tasteless come talk to Elizabeth Hewitt. She could tell you about the stink it left.

He pulled away and sank his face into her neck, his chin pressing into her breast with painful sweetness. She could feel his hardness against her leg as his hand moved down and brushed the silk of her mount, the fingers moving softly to the edges of wetness. He moved on his back, pulling her after him so that her hand was free to go down his stomach, and she rested her hand on his chest, her eyes closed in the dark, darkness on darkness, feeling the smooth silkiness of his manhood that would soon enter her in complete fulfillment.

"My," she said softly, her voice on the edge of a giggle, "your heart is sure pounding at a wild pace."

She felt his body go rigid for a moment and then relax, as if a spasm had passed through. She lifted her head and placed her lips where her ear had been, sucking tiny little kisses on the skin, the tip of her tongue tracing a sensual line to infinity. Down her head moved as she shifted her body in direct proportion to the axis needed. He softened in her grasp, the flesh shriveling in her hand so quickly that she instinctively loosened her fingers to a hollow tunnel. Quickly she moved her head down and substituted mouth for hand, moving her tongue along the tip in accustomed fashion, the saliva forming in both cheeks. Within seconds she realized that the usual reaction was not forthcoming, that there was no response no matter what she did, her tongue and teeth moving almost in desperation finally before she felt his hand come down and gently pull her away.

She slithered around and up to him again, seeking the comfort of his arms, kissing him on the lips, the face, the eyes, trying to show that it was not for lack of devotion or love or intent that she had failed. Had she failed? Who had failed? As she lay there, his hands moving up and down her back softly and slowly, stopping at the neck and then moving down again to the curve of her buttocks, she knew there was something different she did not know about, some change that had occurred in him . . . or her . . . or what? A surge of fear went through her, a premonition, a question that could not be asked because there was no known place to begin.

"I'm sorry," she said, aware as she said it that this was the worst that could have been used after seventeen years of sleeping together in more or less conjugal fashion. Sorry for what? That this last expedient no longer seemed to work? That she was unable . . . that he was unable . . . that they were unable.

"I'm sorry, too," he said, his hands still moving up and down her back in comforting fashion, the first time he had ever used those words in all their years together, and she felt a pain rip through her whole being, as when she realized her mother was in danger, and Jeff. Was this some similar danger? Alex was sorry. Alex was sorry that he could not make love to her. Was that why Alex was sorry? Or was there something else, something he wasn't telling her?

"Is Jeff all right, Alex?" she asked. "Is he really all right?"

"Yes, he's all right. Why do you ask?"

"I don't know. You seem concerned about his fever, and I was wondering if there was something you weren't telling me."

"No, there's nothing. He's all right."

"You must be very tired."

"I guess I'm more tired than I thought."

"Why don't we get some sleep? Bobbi's going to spend the morning with Jeff, and we have a lot to do before I bring her there."

She kissed him quickly and slid out of the bed to go to the bathroom. When she returned, her nightgown on, she found he had moved way over to the far side, and although she stretched her leg carefully as possible to see if she could gain warm contact with his foot, there were still enough inches to go so that the whole body would have to be moved in order for her to accomplish the goal. Better to let sleeping husbands lie, she thought, unsure whether he had dropped off as quickly as he usually did after they had union or whether the failure had him staring in the dark.

While she was pondering this, she fell asleep, somehow content despite the sexual frustration. There was something new with Alex, and it couldn't be any worse than the old, and it might be a whole lot better.

Alex was staring into the dark, the fingers of his right hand taking the pulse of the left, the tenseness going out of him with each solid, steady beat. His heart had been running away, running away from what? No more sex. Bad for you. He grinned in derision into the face of darkness. No problem if you can't get it up in the first place. No more problem for Frank, no more problem for me. Jesus. What if she had started hitting me there in the cemetery? Frank gone. Bardwell gone. Mrs. Markham going. Jeff. Is Jeff all right? I wish to God I knew. I wish to God I knew.

He could feel his eyes closing, and he let the thoughts slide, but he drifted in and out of sleep, thinking . . . dreaming . . . thinking . . . dreaming . . . until he could no longer tell which was which and they all came before him at one time or another, some together, some alone— Bardwell, Mrs. Bardwell, Stanton, Jeff, Betsy, Mrs. Markham, Mrs. Markham's daughter—and he was alone in the basement of Harney's funeral parlor, lying on the stone table with the plastic tubes plugged into him, waiting for Harney to come down and drain his blood, content that this would finish it all off and there would no longer be any worries about the pressure or erratic beats or Jeff or Betsy or people dying all the time and him dying, and he could hear the phone ringing and was wondering when Harney was going to answer it when he realized it was his phone and lifted it off the receiver.

"Dr. Hewitt," he said softly.

"Doctor, I need you," said the familiar voice. Christ, twice in one week. The old bitch must be running a fire.

"What's the problem?"

"I have pain, Doctor, pain, and I need something." She could get it up for him, no doubt about that. Or was there doubt about that? Was the condition permanent? There was only one way to find out.

"Take two aspirin and a glass of brandy," he said.

"But what if that doesn't work?"

Was Betsy asleep or was she lying there awake, listening? Suddenly he didn't care.

"Then stick two up your ass," he said softly, "and see what that does for you." He hung up and settled back in the bed. A small victory, a very small victory. But enough. Enough unto sufficient. No more pigs. No more booze. No more nothing. And he fell asleep beside his wife, his foot reaching out and touching the warmth of hers.

XXVII

THE phone rang again, and as Hewitt reached out in annoyance to shut her off, to cut the crazy bitch off once and for all, he realized that it was gray in the room, gray from early daylight. Seven thirty-five the face of the clock revealed as he lifted the receiver. Saturday. The day was Saturday, and it was seven thirty-five in the morning.

"Dr. Hewitt," he said into the mouthpiece.

"Alex, this is Frank. I'm at the hospital. Jeff's fever went up overnight, and he's running just under a hundred and two orally. The lesion is still draining and everything seems to be going all right, but I would like to give him a bolus of Isoproterenol to see if we can knock this thing out more quickly. What do you say?"

Hewitt quickly ran over everything in his mind to determine what might conflict with what. Side effects? It might do the trick. The fever was hanging in there too long.

"Yes," he said. "I think we had better try it."

"Do you want me to order it, or do you want to do it when you get here?"

"No, you do it now. Might as well get started. And I have office hours this morning."

"I'm sure there's no problem," said Stanton. "I just don't want to take any chances."

"Right. Thanks, Frank."

"Fine. See you tonight."

"Tonight?"

"Yes. At the club. Everybody's talking about the special entertainment you're bringing in from New York."

"Oh. Right. Right. See you there!"

"Who was that?" asked Betsy, getting up on her elbow.

"Frank Stanton," he said absently, thinking about the rock group that was due at the club at 8 P.M. from New York City. One year the entertainment had never shown up, and the members had practically lynched the entertainment chairman. Why had he taken on the fucking thing in the first place?

"Is anything wrong?" she asked.

"No, no. It was just about a patient."

"Did he say anything about Jeff?"

"No. But he reminded me about the club dance tonight."

"Oh, Alex, I can't go. I just don't feel like going to the dance with Jeff in the hospital and all that's happened this week. I don't have the strength, and it would be a straight ordeal."

"We have to go even if it's just for a little while. I'm in charge of the entertainment, and I have to see that it's set up right and pay the performers their guarantee. And also, we are hosting a table, if you remember. It was our turn."

"Couldn't we use Jeff as an excuse? I really don't want to go."

"You can spend the day with Jeff, and then we'll stop off to see him on the way to the club, stay a little while and stop off to see him again before we come home. That will give you more visits with him than usual."

"But I haven't even got an appointment to get my hair done."

"Wear one of those goofy wigs. The million-dollar one your mother sent you."

"Well," she sighed, "I suppose for a little while. What do you want for breakfast?"

"Bacon and eggs and toast and coffee," he said. "It's going to be a long, hard day."

The hard came early when he started to tell Mrs. Moore about the possibility of Sheila Bardwell coming to work for them.

"Is that what she was calling about?" Moore asked suspiciously.

"No. She was calling about a pain that turned out to be a urinary infection, but in the course of our discussion I discovered that she was thinking of going back to work part time, and I thought she might be just the one we are looking for."

"How do you know whether she's any good?"

"I don't. She may be terrible. She may be the worst thing we've ever encountered. But then again, she may be all right. Or even great. We won't know anything until you've talked to her and found out her experience and given me your opinion on whether or not she might do the job. All I'm trying to do is get some of the load off your back. We're three months behind in some of the insurance stuff, and I hate to see you working all the extra hours."

"Well," she said, somewhat mollified, "I suppose there's no harm in talking to her. And at least she isn't one of those young twits who would be blowing bubble gun in the office all day."

"I'm not even sure she'll take the job if we offer her one. She's still pretty confused about everything, but it won't hurt for you to feel each other out and see if you'll get along."

"I can get along with anybody."

"Well, get along with the next patient now, so we can be out of here by noon. I want to get to the hospital."

"How's Jeff?"

"He's coming along."

"I thought I might drop up after we close."

"Well, he's still running a fever and not too comfortable. Why don't you wait until tomorrow or Monday?"

"Is he all right?"

"Of course he's all right. Now bring in Mrs. Gordon and her peckerish liver."

Dr. Hall was in attendance in Jeff's room when Hewitt arrived, but he couldn't tell whether the resident was there because of the patient or the patient's sister. It was the sister who was getting an elaborate explanation about some medical marvel, and Hewitt could tell by the flush on the cheek that she was more than interested. He could remember Betsy flushing like that when he first met her, even when he first married her. The moment he said hello to her the pink would start to rise from the neck and go right up the face to the hairline. A beautiful girl, Bobbi-Betsy, beautiful girls.

When Bobbi noticed that her father was looking at her, she stood abruptly and walked over to Jeff's side, and the resident came over to report.

"The fever's back down to one hundred even," said Hall, "but he's got the Isoproterenol in him and just had an alcohol rub."

"There's some son of a bitch in there that just won't let go," said Hewitt.

"An evil spirit come to haunt us," said Hall, and Hewitt felt a shiver go through him. The sins of the fathers.

"How do you feel today, Jeff?" asked Hewitt, walking over the the bed.

"OK. Is Mom coming soon?"

"Yes. When I get Bobbi home to stay with Jojo, Mom will come along."

"I want her now," said the boy, tears welling up in his eyes.

"Look," said Hewitt sharply, "she can't be here every. . . ." His voice trailed off to silence as Bobbi moved in to take her brother's free hand, a soft croon emitting unknowingly from lips that instinctively shaped into the eternal feminine archetype.

"I just have a few patients to check," said Hewitt lamely, his hand resting on the cover near the boy's strapped arm, the fingers only a space away from contact, "and then we'll be off for home, and she'll be here."

He turned and went from the room quickly, not looking at Bobbi or Hall on the way out, and moved through his five hospitalized charges with ready speed, pausing only a moment by Mrs. Markham's bed to check her vital signs. Her eyes were closed, and she was breathing easily. Go, he told her silently, there is nothing left for you here. Go peacefully. He took his pulse as he was standing by her bed—ninety-two beats a minute. Her pulse was seventy-two beats to the minute. I am racing to get there ahead of you, he said to her again. I am racing, and I don't know where.

"The lady's daughter wanted to know if you had any message for her," said the nurse as Hewitt came out of the room.

"Tell her we are keeping her as comfortable as possible, and it is doubtful she will come out of the coma," said Hewitt.

"I've seen them come out of worse than this and be eating supper that night," said the nurse.

"I'm sure you have," said Hewitt, "but tell the lady what I told you. It will ease her mind a lot more than any miracle stories."

Jeff had his eyes closed when Hewitt returned to the room, and he motioned for Bobbi to accompany him without making a sound.

"Is that Dr. Hall married?" asked Bobbi, when they got in the car.

"Yes. To a very pretty nurse."

"Oh. Is Jeff going to be all right?"

"Of course he is."

"He doesn't look right."

"What do you mean?"

"He just doesn't look right. Like something bad is about to happen."

"He's all right. If enough people tell him he isn't right, then maybe he'll believe it, too. He's got to help himself along with the medicines. He's got to try."

"Jeff isn't like that, Daddy. Jeff isn't strong like we are."

Hewitt glanced away from the road to take a long look at his daughter. Like we are. Was she comparing herself to him? Was she proud to be like him? Like we are. Was her pulse racing to hell at ninety-two beats to the minute? And what was her blood pressure? Was the top of her skull about to come off? Like we are.

He pulled up into their driveway and braked the car, the motor still running. He could go in and watch television. Or read medical journals. Or have a long, cold vodka on the rocks, the chill burning into his stomach and cutting the pulse rate down to a normal range. Or start the drug therapy for the hypertension. Or go back to the hospital with Betsy and watch Jeff's face light up as she came in the room, as it never had lighted for him since . . . had it ever lighted for him? Jojo! Her face lighted up sometimes when he walked in the room or when she came bouncing at him from nowhere with news of this or that or nothing. He could take Jojo for a ride. Bobbi was about to slam the door shut behind her.

"Tell the answering service I'll be at the Y," he called out his window, "and tell your mother I'll be home around six." He'd get the pulse and pressure down. He'd run them right into the fucking floor.

The floor was covered with soggy towels when Hewitt arrived in the locker room, indicating that the usual Saturday slobs, the ones who were above stooping and disposing, had already been and gone. Hewitt suited up quickly but then found himself unable to decide on a course of action. Twenty sit-ups proved boring, as did a few hoists of barbells and ten pulls on the rowing machine. Opening his locker again, he took out the old handball gloves and rummaged around for the new ones until suddenly he realized where they were, and he leaned his forehead against the cool metal of the locker wall. They were with Casey's belongings somewhere, the new gym pants and T-shirt and jockstrap and sweat socks and sneakers, those bright, white sneakers. Call up Gerda and ask her if she'd mind sending over the handball gloves, he told himself. Jesus.

He stood up straight and looked at the old gloves in his hand, black from sweat and wrinkled into half their size.

"Mister."

It was no use. Steam bath. Shower. Maybe a game of bridge at the club. It was no use.

"Mister!"

It was a young man, early twenties, not too tall, not too short, with huge shoulders and thick wrists. A boy who worked with weights enough to develop but not enough to bind. Long wavy black hair that obviously had hours of attention paid to it during a week's time. Naked to the waist with the flat stomach of a man who worried about his weight as he did about his hair. A great cocksman, Hewitt could tell. Treated them rough and they loved it. When he realized that it was he who was being addressed, Hewitt couldn't quite keep the instantaneous dislike out of his voice.

"Yes," he said.

"You looking for a game?" pointing to Hewitt's hands. His eyes dropped to where the finger was aimed and saw the gloves, the old, wrinkled gloves. Was he looking for a game? What was he looking for?

"I don't know," said Hewitt, "the courts are usually booked solid on Saturday and. . . ."

"I got one," said the young man. "My buddy can't make it. We can just hit a few; no big deal."

"Sure," said Hewitt, "glad to. Glad to." No big deal. Just hit a few. The son of a bitch could probably drill the ball right through the wall. No time to think of blood pressure when you had this prick going against you. The object would be to stay alive.

The young man took his time in dressing for the court, carefully working sweat bands on his wrists and bouncing three balls judiciously on the floor before deciding on the two liveliest. His gloves were fairly new but already black with sweat. Just hit a few; no big deal.

Even before they reached there, Hewitt knew which court they would be playing on, and he hesitated a good minute before he followed his opponent inside, the man coming to the door twice from the dark to check on what was holding up the show. There was finally no more time and Hewitt walked into the blackness, standing there waiting, waiting, until the voice from the other wall said, "Jesus, shut the door, will you, Mac?"

The glare of light made Hewitt blink as the closing door pushed in the button that completed the electrical contact. He looked at the spot on the floor where Casey had dropped, and the ball came whipping off the front wall to bounce in front of him and up into his stomach. It stung and he looked over at his opponent, who was gazing back at him inquiringly. What would happen if old Hewitt dropped dead on this son of a bitch? Probably go up and see if anyone else had time for a game. Play around the body like in the old joke. What was an old joke doing in a hand-ball court with a young punk like this?

Hewitt retrieved the ball and swung, watching it arch gracefully off the wall as the boy came in and took it in the air, slashing it across the corner so that it came out at an unreachable angle. Just hit a few; no big deal. There wasn't even any give-and-take in the warm-up; this guy killed for practice.

"Ya wanna try a game?" the boy asked, after they had hit a half dozen back and forth. Hewitt nodded, the time for words all past.

"Go on and serve," said the young man.

Hewitt moved into the right-side serving box and then shifted to the left a bit until he felt he was approximately on the same spot. It was right there. Right there! And he leaned over and bounced the ball on the floor and swung his right hand, *but he kept on falling . . . falling . . . falling . . .* that huge body all draped in baggy white . . . and Hewitt was waiting for God or the gods or whoever pulled crap like that to take him off in the same manner, to blot him out the way he had old Casey, bang and done, next one please.

But he felt the sting of the ball on his hand and saw it fly out toward the wall as he moved instinctively toward the center of the court for better position as the young man came in fast and hit a high, hard one that ricocheted back down the center to where Hewitt had placed himself for his right hand to strike again and put it away in the left-hand corner.

Hewitt made four points before he lost the serve, and he was sweating heavily and breathing fiercely as he moved back into the receiver's square. I can take him, he was telling himself, I can take this son of a bitch and drive him right into the ground.

The man made five points before Hewitt knifed one by him on the left side that he missed completely. He could feel his heart pounding as he moved up to serve, but he knew that basically he was a better player than the young man in back of him, that he could win if he concentrated enough on the weak points that were being disclosed with each shot.

And so it went back and forth with each point, with Hewitt running and turning and twisting, swinging first his right arm mightily and then his left, swearing fiercely both to himself and aloud in the air to whom it might concern, smashing into the wall with soul-shocking effect, feeling his whole skeletal frame vibrate sickeningly within the fleshly pad, the sweat running down the face into the eyes with stinging cauterization, licking the salt from the lips with joyful appetite and pounding, pounding, pounding, until finally he beat the son of a bitch twenty-one points to nineteen, and he slid down the wall flat on his ass, the heart pounding so frenziedly that he feared the rib cage would not hold it, anoxia causing moments of darkness, flashing of lights, dizziness, nausea, and such exhilaration that he wanted to get up and yell it to the world, that Hewitt, old Hewitt, Captain Hewitt, Dr. Hewitt, husband-father Hewitt, could still swing in there with the best of them, could take the ass of any young punk who thought the game was in the bag. Not dead yet. Life in the old boy yet. *I've seen them worse than this and up eating supper that night.* Is that what the nurse had said to him? He was trying to shove Mrs. Markham off the way this punk thought he was going to shove him off. I'm eating supper tonight, you son of a bitch. Twenty-one to nineteen.

"You ready for another?"

He looked up to the back of the court where his opponent, body glistening with sweat, was standing there contemptuously, holding the ball in his right hand and bouncing it slowly up and down on the floor. Another? I regret I have but one game to give for my country.

"If we make it fast, we can get another one in," the young man insisted.

Why not? thought Hewitt, getting slowly to his feet. Why not finish it off one way or another?

The boy threw the ball to him, and Hewitt threw it right back.

"Loser serves," he said.

The next seven minutes were deadly agony as he went through the motions as best he could, going only for the ones within range, giving where he had to but still maintaining what control he could. Realizing the tiredness of his older opponent, the youth overreached himself with his own eagerness, spoiling his timing and playing without strategy. Consequently, when the knock came on the door, signifying that the time was up and the next group was ready to take over the court, Hewitt was leading nine points to eight. The young man looked over at the door in anger, ready to argue that there was still time left, but Hewitt was already walking over to open it, peeling his sweat-soaked gloves from his hand, moving carefully, just this side of unsteadiness.

Neither man said anything as they walked up the stairs, one behind the other. There were no trading of compliments about what a nice game it had been and how they must do it again some time.

Hewitt sank down on the stool in front of his locker and dropped the gloves on the floor. His pulse was thready, uneven, and each breath hurt in his chest. Forty-two years old. This was as close to suicide as a man could come. Crazy. Crazy! What was he trying to prove? That Casey would have died tying his shoelace? That the body was still able to take anything that was dished out to it? That he was as good as any young punk who sneered a better game than he played? You're cracking up, Hewitt. Over the edge. No wonder your blood pressure doesn't know how to behave. There's nothing wrong with you physically; it's all mental.

"Mister."

No more of this crap. Friendly games of doubles or

squash with men your own age. You can't beat youth. It was a freak. But such a satisfying freak. Such a beautiful freak. The son of a bitch.

"Mister!"

Hewitt looked up at the young man standing there, still wearing his handball gloves as if he wouldn't acknowledge that anything had been proved, that the game was over and finished and the score counted no matter what you did.

"Yes," said Hewitt.

"You can't be very lucky in love," said the young man, and turned and walked out of his life.

XXVIII

"JESUS, Alex, where the hell have you been?"

Hewitt pondered the question as he turned from closing the door to the clubhouse. Well, for one thing he had been at the hospital, where his son was running a fever of nearly one hundred and four degrees, was thrashing about on his bed so wildly that they had to strap him down to keep him from ripping the IV out of his arm, his face so mottled that he looked like a burn case. It was also where his wife had hit him on the cheek with her clenched fist, causing a red mark which was still visible.

She had struck him in anger, something he had never done to her. While Hewitt had gone out to instruct the nurses on the extra medication for the situation, she had promised her son that she would stay with him that evening and not go to the dance in her pretty green dress. When she informed Hewitt of this upon his return, he told her that it was out of the question, that they would go to the dance until he had his responsibilities squared away, and then they could return to the hospital as had been agreed the day before. She said her only responsibility was to her son, that he could go off to the dance and pick her up on the way home, or that she would take a taxi when she was satisfied that Jeff was resting comfortably.

"There is nothing you can do for him here except keep him awake," Hewitt had said.

"He wants me to stay."

"Damn it. We've got a whole table of people waiting for us. If it was going to do any good, I'd stay with you. But he's about to get some medication that is going to make him groggy, and the nurses are going to monitor him as if they were specials, and we're going to be back here in a very short time, and I tell you you're going with me."

"I am staying here."

He put his hand on her elbow to reassure her on the boy's condition again, and she, misinterpreting the gesture for an arm about to pull her from her position, struck out suddenly, her strong, thin hand clenched in frustrated anger, and caught him on the left cheekbone, the impact making both of them flinch backward.

They looked at each other, the child, the dance, forgotten, as they regarded this new factor in their relationship. How many times had she braced herself in the past few years as she waited for his hand to come out cracking and blot everything from her mind in the pain of physical impact? But he had never made that move. Now she had.

Two nurses came into the room and busied themselves with Jeff, one with the hypodermic, the other with the piggyback IV. Betsy moved over to the chair and retrieved her coat, slipping it on while Alex wrote the telephone number of the club on a slip of paper for the head nurse and instructed her that he be called if there were any change.

Betsy walked out of the room first, straight to the elevator, where she stood until Alex overtook her and punched the button. They rode to the country club in silence, each considering at what point conversation might be resumed but getting no further than vague feelings that when the right moment came, it would happen.

"I was unavoidably delayed," said Alex to the chairman of the house committee. "What's the problem?"

"No rock band from New York, that's the problem," said the chairman, who held the Ford franchise and acted accordingly. "They were supposed to be here early so that everyone would be greeted by a blast of music as they came in the door. We've had stark, raving silence until the dinner trio got here. Now everybody's starting on his main course, and they're still not here. We're getting thirty bucks a couple for this thing, Alex, and nothing had better go wrong."

"They'll be here," said Alex, more out of bedside reaction than conviction. "They won't pass up this much money." Since they had already received half in advance, Alex wasn't positive they would bother about the rest. Four hundred bucks isn't bad for not doing a night's work.

"Can you call somebody?" asked the chairman.

"It's Saturday night in New York City just like anywhere else," said Alex. "Who the hell could I reach?" He had dealt with a man named Philip Miles of the Shanahan Talent Agency. How many Miles were there in the New York phone book? Miles and Miles and Miles. A bad joke, thought Hewitt, a bad joke all around.

"Go eat your dinner," he told the chairman. "They'll be here by dessert."

The Hewitts deposited their coats and walked into the big ballroom, which was circled with tables full of noisy people. There had obviously been private cocktail parties before the official cocktail party, and Hewitt could tell by the whoops of laughter that most of the women were as high as the men. It was going to be one of those famous nights, a benchmark that would be recalled by many in years to come as one of the happiest or one of the most dreadful events of their lives. There would be few in between.

Jack Wales was in the midst of telling a dirty joke to the Hewitt table where there were six people—the Waleses, the Stantons, and the Athertons—and four empty chairs.

"I'm telling a Japanese joke," Wales explained to the Hewitts as the men rose graciously for their hostess, "and I don't want any interruptions until I finish."

The Hewitts and the men sat down quietly as they were told, and the women exchanged silent smiles of greeting.

"So the little Japanese girl said to the American who had just been given the hot bath treatment, 'You all numbah one kreen now except faw wax job.' "

Wales' Japanese accent was far from polished, but he was good enough to hold everyone's eyes solidly on him.

" 'You want a wax job?' "

Hewitt was wondering about the two empty chairs at the other end of the table. Who was late? He couldn't remember Betsy mentioning anyone else.

"And just as she had him hard as a rock on that teakwood block," said Wales, "she brings this big wooden mallet out from behind her back and smashed it down as hard as she could right on the tip of it, and the wax flew out of both his ears," roared Wales, convulsed with laughter, spit flying from his mouth, trying to pour his drink into him while watching the reaction of the others. Stanton and Atherton smiled politely. Mrs. Stanton looked puzzled, and Mrs. Atherton looked pained. Betsy had not heard a word of it, her mind at the hospital.

"What are these extra chairs for?" Hewitt asked the captain, who was bringing a bucket of champagne to the table. The man reached into his pocket and pulled out a card, checking the names on it against those he knew to be present.

"Dr. and Mrs. Frank Casey," he said.

Betsy's hand flew to her mouth. "I forgot," she said. "I forgot. Gerda called me on Monday, and I made the extra reservation, and I forgot. I just forgot."

"Get the chairs out," Hewitt told the captain.

"But, Doctor, I have to collect stubs for every reservation," protested the captain.

"I'll pay," said Hewitt. "Now get them out."

The man looked undecided for a moment, but he was a professional, and he realized from Hewitt's tone and look that the chairs had to go.

"Where's Casey?" asked Wales.

They all looked at him, and he returned the gaze equably, half drunk and content, happy to be away from the shop for a few hours and eat and drink and dance too closely with other men's wives.

"My God," said Atherton, "you've been in Japan. Casey died on Wednesday."

Wales, his glass halfway to his mouth, turned ashen. They could all see the liquid trembling in the glass, just as they could feel the trembling inside this man, who never trembled, who only made other people tremble.

"Heart attack?" he asked.

"Cerebral hemorrhage," said Hewitt, wanting to hurt as he was hurting, to frighten as he was frightened.

"Jesus," said Wales, bringing the glass up to his mouth and downing the contents in straight swallows. "Live for today. Waiter!" He looked around wildly, seeking help, the only kind he knew.

Two waiters appeared with plates of filet, deep fried potato balls and fat white stalks of asparagus. Wales told them loudly he wanted another round for everybody and to keep their eyes open for future needs. Hewitt quietly ordered a glass of soda water with a slice of lemon in it.

"Where's your rock-and-roll band, Alex?" Frank Stanton called across the table. "I was told to bring earmuffs tonight."

"They're coming in from New York," said Hewitt. "Running a little late."

"I was drinking hot sake yesterday," said Wales, "and

having my back massaged by the toes of a little yellow cutie, and here I am tonight drinking good old American scotch and wondering what kind of a massage I'm going to get."

"I'll massage you all right, old bucko," Marian Wales told him, "right in your brain where you need it most."

"As usual," he sighed, "you've picked the wrong spot."

The captain came over and leaned close to Hewitt.

"There is a call from the hospital, Doctor," he said, "and they say it is an emergency." Although he tried to keep his voice low, the music forced him to enunciate distinctly, and the whole table heard him. Betsy dropped her knife and fork on top of the food she had been toying with and stood up quickly, looking down the table at her husband. Frank Stanton rose next to her.

"Is it Jeff" he asked. "He seemed fine this morning. Is there something with Jeff, Alex?"

"I'll find out," he said, heading for the telephone in the bar, hearing Wales call out, "What the hell's wrong with Jeff?" and Betsy close behind him. Convulsion? Shock? White cells gone crazy? Had he killed his son for a lousy rock-and-roll band that didn't even show up in the first place? What has priority? Social or family responsibility? Have I killed my son by neglect? Did I kill Casey? Am I killing myself? He could feel the blood pounding in him, the tenseness ripping through his shoulders like a strait-jacket of fear. Am I going to live with fear the rest of my life? he wondered. There had been a taste of it in Nam, but it had been mixed with excitement. Now there was just the fear, a craw full of it, more than he could swallow. Nausea gripped him in spasms, and the coldness in his belly made him put his hand there as though he could bring warmth.

The bar was a bedlam with both men and women bellied up to it, shouting at each other in gleeful abandon.

"Alex! Alex!" he heard from all sides. "Where's the rock-and-roll band? Where's the rock-and-roll band, Alex?"

He looked neither left nor right but worked his way to the phone on the wall, feeling Betsy squirming along behind him.

"Dr. Hewitt here," he said into the phone.

"Doctor? Dr. Hewitt?"

"Yes, it's Dr. Hewitt." He was forced to shout at the same level as the rest of them.

"Doctor, this is Mrs. Tarbell."

Tarbell? Tarbell? He didn't know any Tarbell.

"Yes."

"I'm calling about Mrs. Markham, who is your patient."

Markham. Mrs. Markham. The air whooshed out of him, and he leaned against the wall, feeling for the first time Betsy's hand digging into his arm. He nodded at her, signifying that everything was all right. Was it all right? What about Jeff?

"Yes," he said.

"She expired five minutes ago," said Mrs. Tarbell, who would be charge nurse for the night.

"Yes," he said.

"When I went in on the regular check, she was gone," said Mrs. Tarbell. "Her condition had been stable fifteen minutes before."

"Yes," said Hewitt.

"Do you have any instructions, Doctor?"

"Do you have her daughter's phone number there?" He felt Betsy's hand loosen from his arm and then disappear.

"Yes, Doctor. It was on the instruction sheet."

"Please call her and tell her. I'll be coming by in a little while, but if she wants me before that, she can call me at this number."

"Thank you, Doctor."

"Nurse, did you. . . ."

"Yes, Doctor?"

"Never mind. I'll be along soon."

He hung up the receiver and stared at the phone on the wall.

"Was it anything about Jeff?" asked Betsy, forced to shout almost into his ear.

"What?"

"Was it about Jeff?"

"No. It was one of my patients."

"Did they say anything about Jeff?"

"No. Nothing about Jeff."

"I'm going back to the hospital," she said, turning and starting to walk back toward the hallway.

He reached out and caught her arm, noticing as he did the small blue imprints in a circle just above where he held her. His fingerprints. His fingerprints on his wife. The black marks of a marriage gone wrong. The women in his examining room, some embarrassed, some defiant, angry— *and then he squeezed me here . . . and then he punched me here . . . and then he slapped me here . . . and then he pinched me here . . . he's a sick man, Doctor, sick, sick, sick.*

"Let me get this music straightened out, and we'll both go," he almost pleaded, loosening his hold a bit.

"I'm going now," she said, not really looking at him, the body tense and ready to leap to freedom.

"It will take just a few minutes," he said.

"I'm going now; my son needs me."

The smell of booze was in the air all around him, slopped over on the polished mahogany of the bar, exhaled from ninety mouths that were babbling away in happy bliss, unheedful of systolic pressures or tachycardia or death hovering on the horizon, booze, booze, beautiful booze, that made the cold feeling go away and the hands stop trembling, the hands, the hands, the hands.

"I need you," he yelled, loud enough so that those in the immediate vicinity turned in surprise.

"You don't need anything but yourself," she said, facing him, placing her hand on his wrist and pushing evenly to remove his grasp.

"We'll go together," he said, tightening his hold. She had won. To hell with the booze and the rock music and the rest of the crap. They should be with their son.

"You don't know how to go together," she yelled, trying to twist away from him, thinking he was insisting she wait as usual until he was ready.

Surprised, Hewitt held firm, unable to understand what was occurring, afraid to let go. He sensed the people around him, felt the weight of their eyes, more and more each second.

Tears were spurting from Betsy's eyes as she tried to break loose, twisting this way and that.

"You bastard," she yelled, "you dirty bastard! You leave us alone! Leave us alone! Just leave us alone."

Hewitt felt a hand come out of the crowd and fall gently on his arm. There was no pressure; merely an indication that the public was present at a private situation. He loosened his fingers and looked at his wife, who stood there with one strap off her shoulder, her face blotched and covered with tears, the small blue marks on both her arms for all to see. Betsy Prentiss Hewitt stripped naked in the bar of the country club.

The hand on Hewitt's arm now pulled gently, and he turned to face a man with whom he sometimes played golf. Not a friend; a golfing companion.

"Hey, Alex," said the man, pausing a moment as he sought a subject, "where are the rock-and-rollers?"

"Coming," he said, forcing the word up from his stomach.

"Well, let me buy you a drink anyway. What'll you have?"

The hand was still on his arm, and Hewitt turned his head to check on Betsy, but she was gone. He leaned to move toward the door, but the hand still held him, and the smell hit him hard again, the happy voices breathing life into the air.

"Vodka," he said. "On the rocks. And make it a double if you're serious."

It appeared quickly, and he drank it right down. Two more people bought him drinks before he left the bar. Shit, he kept saying to himself. Shit, shit, shit.

When he returned to the table, only Frank Stanton was sitting there among eight tubes of melting parfait and full glasses of bubbling champagne.

"Jeff all right?" asked Stanton as Hewitt sank into a chair beside him. He was tired, terribly tired. Young punks have their vengeance one way or another.

"Yes," he said, "Jeff's fine. It was about another patient."

"I had a peculiar one this morning," said Stanton. "I was doing a vasectomy and the guy went out on me, just like that. Died. Forty-three years old. His heart blew into a million pieces."

"Did he have a history?"

"I don't know. Didn't really know anything about him. Don't even know who his regular doctor was. He came in by himself last week and we set it up."

"Does that bother you?" asked Hewitt, drinking the champagne in the glass in front of him.

"What?"

"Having a patient go on you? Not just suddenly. Any patient."

"Isn't that Cindy Huber over there?" asked Stanton, peering across the room. "I thought Sam . . ."

Hewitt looked where Stanton was pointing and saw Cindy talking to a man and a woman. She was dressed in a pale blue gown and she looked lovely, the dark circles under her eyes accenting the paleness of the face in an intriguing manner. She stood stiffly, her eyes roaming the room while her lips moved mechanically, and she caught Hewitt straight on, locked in on him and held.

Is he dead? he wondered. The picture of Sam Huber lying in his deathbed flashed before him, the IV, like the one beside Jeff's bed and the one beside Mrs. Markham's bed, dripping its life-giving solution into veins that would no longer receive. And Cinderella came to the ball. No, he wasn't dead. He was lying there still, and she was starting to make the break into widowhood, unconsciously hoping to get things in the right, the inevitable direction. Should he ask her for a dance?

Jack Wales came back to the table alone and planked down beside Hewitt, who was drinking his second glass of champagne.

"What kind of a week did you have, Alex?" he asked.

Hewitt seriously considered the question.

"When you get right down to it, when you think about it," he said finally, "it was just like any other goddamned week. Like they all get to be after a while."

Wales had not listened to the answer. He had been busy signaling a waiter to come over.

"We can't drink this piss," he told the captain, who never let his eyes get very far from Mr. Wales at any time. "Bring me a double scotch on the rocks and my friend will have . . . do you want another soda water, Alex?" Nothing ever got by Jack Wales.

"I'll have a double vodka on the rocks," said Alex.

Alex drank another lukewarm champagne while waiting for his drink. He wanted to call the hospital to check on Jeff, but he had left specific orders, and the nurses would think it peculiar. What the hell did he care whether or not they thought it peculiar? It was his son, wasn't it? Just as he stood up, the waiter brought the drinks and he took three huge gulps, the last one almost choking him.

"Be back," he mumbled at Wales and Stanton, noticing that they were looking at him peculiarly. "Phone," he said, and moved toward the bar again. But before he was halfway around the room, the house chairman moved quickly to his side and grabbed him by the arm. Jesus, thought Hewitt, I need an extra arm just to be pulled on. He wanted to shake the man off, as his dog did a stick, but there was no strength there, and he was forced to halt his progress.

"Alex," the man hissed, "you've got to come into the grill room."

"I've got to make a phone call."

"No. You've got to come with me. Right now. This is an emergency."

A night of emergencies. Mrs. Markham had been an emergency. And she was dead. Jeff was having an emergency. Was he dead? And now here was another emergency. Who was dead in the grill room? He followed, as much out of curiosity as anything. His head was light, and his knees were weak, and his feet were heavy as lead. I am going to fall down, he was thinking, and if I do, I am just going to lie there and rest.

"Alex." He felt his arm taken, and he turned obediently. It was McCord, good old McCord, accompanied by a very dark man in a very peculiar tuxedo. Hewitt tried to remember if there had been any kind of color breakthrough in the thin white line at the club, but no recent uproar came to mind, nothing since that do-gooder Mrs. Kempton had brought a black to lunch and someone had written the board complaining that they smelled like cabbages. If he had to describe this one in such terms, Hewitt thought, he would categorize him as rancid oil. The man looked like rancid oil.

"I don't think you've met our Dr. Shrinar," said McCord, "who joined us last week as a resident in internal medicine. This is Dr. Alexander Hewitt, one of our noted internists."

"Ah, yiss," hissed the swarthy man, "I have heard of Dr. Hewitt."

His speech was peculiarly precise but at the same time insecure, as though he were translating it from more than one tongue at a time.

"Dr. Shrinar is from India," said McCord, "and he has already spent one year at a hospital in Idaho."

"Idaho," said Alex. "That sounds as though it might. . . ." He felt a pull on his arm and saw the house chairman, his face red as a two hundred on the systolic, looking at him pleadingly. This man was in pain. Without saying good-bye to either doctor, Alex followed his chairman into the grill room.

There, in the semidarkness of the side lights, he saw a sight to confound the eyes and account for the emergency description of the situation. There were eight of them. One was a naked woman. While Hewitt was looking at her, she reached into a small suitcase on the floor beside her and pulled out a pair of bikini pants with long tassels attached, and stepped into it neatly, pulling it up snugly over her ample hips. A thin bra was next retrieved from the bag and slipped around her pendulous breasts, heavy dugs with giant nipples that shimmered purple in the soft light. None of the five men or other two women paid the slightest attention to her, each one intent in adjusting his own costume, all of which looked like gypsy attire with a mod twist.

"Who are these people?" the chairman whispered in Hewitt's ear. "They say they were sent from New York to be our entertainment, but they do not look like a rock-and-roll band. Alex, you've got to do something."

Hewitt walked over to the group and stood there trying to sort them out, waiting for some indication of a leader, a spokesman, or even someone who would acknowledge his presence.

The men seemed to range in age from the late thirties to the early sixties. They were all swarthy in complexion, and three of them had flowing mustaches that curled in the air to sharp points. The woman he had watched costume herself looked to be in her late thirties, while one of the others seemed even older, and the third one, the only one with any semblance of prettiness, couldn't have been much more than eighteen or nineteen.

The one thing these people had in common, men and women, were large hooked noses, even the pretty one. On her it looked rather Cleopatra, on the other women ugly, and on the men forbidding, as though they might be fierce warriors or, at the least, eaters of spitted baby goats.

"I am Dr. Hewitt," he announced.

The young girl looked up at the sound of his voice, but the others continued their individual pursuits, the women adjusting their costumes and the men withdrawing strange-looking musical instruments from cloth bags. Fingers began plucking strings, lips wrapped around long pipes and a tambourine banged against a knee with jingling urgency.

"Who is in charge here?" asked Hewitt.

The tambourine man looked at him appraisingly for a moment, brought his free hand up to twirl the end of his mustache and then walked over.

"*Salaam,*" he said, bowing slightly and moving his hand rapidly from his forehead to his chin to his chest. "*Salaam aleikim.*" And shifting the tambourine, he twirled the other end of his mustache.

"I think there's been some sort of mistake," said Hewitt.

"Mistake?" The eyebrows arched, and the nose looked fierce.

"Yes. I arranged with the Shanahan Talent Agency of New York to have the Speedy McAlistar band play for us tonight. Where are you people from?"

"We are from New York," the man said proudly. "We are from Shanahan. Mr. Miles send us."

"You are not Speedy McAlistar," Hewitt stated.

"I do not know from him," said the tambourine man. "I am Kaleem Ferris and these are my family. We play music, and the women dance."

"Well you're not supposed to play here. You've got the wrong place."

The man scowled mightily before turning to his troupe and breaking forth in high-pitched gibberish. One of the older women screamed back at him in a torrent of sound, and his neck suddenly began to expand as though air were being pumped into it under enormous pressure. The tambourine banged against his thigh with a crash and stilled the woman instantly. He turned back to Hewitt.

"This is the right place," he said. "I have sheet." He dug into the flowing scarf that held up his pantaloons and pulled out a folded piece of paper which he thrust defiantly in Hewitt's face. It was a memorandum from Philip Miles to Kaleem Ferris and on the paper were the instructions on where to go and when to get there. Hewitt instantly recognized the travel directions he had given Miles over the phone, hearing his own voice repeating them as he read the words over twice. The son of a bitch. The New York son of a bitch. The dirty kike New York son of a bitch.

"Pack up your stuff," he said. "You're not playing here."

"We have contract," the man shouted. "You must pay us our money. We have contract."

"I have a contract with Speedy McAlistar," said Hewitt, "and that's the only guy who's going to get any money around here."

"I know nothing about this man. We have contract."

The circle closed in on Hewitt, men and women both, and he could smell the stale sweat that exuded from the soiled costumes and the heavy odor of the women, a mixture of perfume and frying grease, and he could feel his heart pounding in his chest with his own perspiration pouring down his forehead and clouding his eyes with mist. What was he doing here with a bunch of crazy, stinking tambourine players in the grill room of the goddamned country club? Was this some kind of purgatory? For letting people die? For making people die? Jeff! And Bardwell. *SH, SH.* Who was trying to tell him what?

"Alex. Alex."

A figure burst through the circle, white shirtfront on black tuxedo. Friend. The nausea was in his throat from the stink and the noise and the vodka in his belly fighting the champagne.

"Alex." It was Picard, the chest man. Picard. Chairman of the whole goddamned dinner dance. The guy who had talked him into being head of the entertainment committee.

"Alex. The crowd is getting restless out there. Bring on the entertainment."

"There is no entertainment."

Picard slowly turned around the circle of faces, all staring at him intently, dislike and contempt etched under every nose.

"Who are these then?"

"The talent agency sent the wrong crew. They were supposed to send a rock-and-roll band and what we got is . . . is . . . I don't know what."

"We are musicians," said Kaleem loudly, "and dancers. We play the *drbekee* and the *oujd* and the *zamoor*, and my sister, Khraman, she dances like all the furies together. We have contract."

"For Christ's sake, Alex," said Picard between gritted teeth, "we've got to put something on out there or this will be the biggest screwup the club has ever had. This is the most money we've ever charged for any affair, and everybody and his brother bitched about it. If you don't put these people on out there in five minutes, there's going to be hell to pay."

Hewitt felt the tiredness sinking over him in deep waves. When had he last had a good night's sleep? When had he last had a minute to himself? When had he last not been scared? What the hell was there to be scared of? What the hell did he give a shit if these gooks went out there or didn't go out there or if everybody was in an uproar because good old Alex screwed up the entertainment? Was this what the hell his life had come down to, furnishing Saturday night entertainment for the town's top pricks and prickesses? He turned to the tambourine man.

"OK," he said, "you go on."

"First you give me money," said the man. "Mr. Miles say four hundred dollars."

"I've got a check in my pocket," said Alex, reaching inside his jacket.

"No check. Cash. This our money. We get cash."

"Where the hell am I going to get four hundred dollars in cash?" said Alex.

"No cash. No play."

"Alex," said Picard, "give me the check. I'll get cash from the steward."

"No cash. No play."

"I'll be back in two minutes," said Picard. "Get them ready."

Knowing they had won their point and their cash, the troupe returned to their instruments and their costumes, and in five minutes Picard had returned with a bundle of tens and fives, which the leader carefully counted before dividing it up among the whole group.

"Go out there and introduce them, Alex," said Picard, "and for God sakes let's get this thing going."

"What do you call yourselves?" asked Alex.

"Kaleem Ferris and his singers and dancers," answered the tambourine man, banging his instrument across his thigh and twirling the right point of his mustache.

Alex turned and walked out to the ballroom, sensing the whole group following close after. A thin figure stood in the doorway, a woman, and he smelled the cinnamon perfume of Cindy Huber even before his mind sorted her out. Unconsciously, he inhaled deeply through his nostrils and filtered it out softly through his teeth in a long sigh.

"Alex," she said, turning to block enough of the doorway to stop him. The feral heat from behind was pushing on his back, but there was no moving her except by physical force, and he knew there must be eyes already on them, wondering whether poor Sam's wife was asking their doctor if there was any hope.

"I must talk to you," she said.

"Has there been any change?"

"No. He's the same. It's about us. I must talk to you about us."

"There is no us, Cindy. There's you. And me. And all these goddamned people out here waiting for me to introduce the entertainment." His left hand moved out in a semicircle.

"I told the woman I would be home at eleven," she said quickly. "Come by after that. We have to talk."

Emile Picard worked his way through the throng and pressed against Hewitt's back.

"Come on, Alex," he said. "It's twenty minutes to eleven."

Cindy turned and walked away, leaving cinnamon in the air, and Alex thought of when he burrowed into her secret parts, his nose and tongue combined into one sensual vacuum, sucking up the ions of spiciness until they exploded in an electric shock of desire. He shook his head briskly and walked across the dance floor to the little stage where the dance trio were about to pick up their instruments again. The ballroom was only a little more than half full, with people chatting desultorily over their cold coffees or sipping on fresh drinks. Many were in the bar and some in the various hallways and side rooms. A few had even gone home, some from an excess of drink, others from boredom.

Hewitt made the one step up to the platform and turned to the microphone.

"Ladies and gentlemen," he said into it, but no sound came forth. As the saxophone player rose to flick the little switch controlling the power, the drummer, wanting to do his bit and half-smashed from free drinks dispensed by a bartender buddy, gave a mighty roll on the drums that seemed to go on and on with the tenacity of a summer thunderstorm. People crowded in from the bar and the other rooms and hallways, anxious for any kind of action that would break up the monotony of what had turned out to be just another Saturday night at the club. There were shouts and whistles and banging of silverware against glasses.

"Ladies and gentlemen," said Hewitt, surprised for a moment by his amplified voice reverberating off the walls, "this is not the moment you have been waiting for. One of the worst-kept secrets of the war was that we were going to have a rock-and-roll band here tonight to blast you right out of your seats. Unfortunately, the bandleader, Speedy McAlistar, had to have an emergency vasectomy"—*died right on the table; heart blew into a million pieces*—"and could not be with us. However, at great expense we have brought you a different extravaganza, direct from New York City"—(*that son of a bitch; that dirty son of a bitch*)—"Kaleem Ferris and his singers and dancers."

As Hewitt finished, there was a clash of the tambourine across the room, and as all eyes turned to the sound, Kaleem leaped from the doorway and started banging his skin plate on every jut of his body, moving quickly toward the stage in cadence with the jingles and jangles and solid thumps.

And just as he reached Hewitt, who was starting to move off to the side, there came the wail of the flutelike instrument, high, piercing sounds that made the skin tighten all over the body, and two of the men, gliding as one across the floor, back and forth and sideways, but always gaining ground, finally came up to the tambourine man, who started peppering his body again as they pointed their instruments straight at the ceiling and wailed as though they would never see their camels again.

The drummer and the plucker of the stringed instrument then came bursting through the door and played their way across the floor, the hands and fingers of the drummer beating so quickly on his two skin-covered tubes that they were little more than a blur in the dim lights of the dance floor.

The wild rhythms and shrill voicings of the pipes, the insistent demands of the drums caught the crowd immediately, and loud laughs of delight came from all sides of the room as people quickly sought their own tables or sat down with friends where they were, intent on not missing a thing of this strange Scheherazade that had suddenly entered their lives.

"Where are they from?" everyone was asking everybody else. "What country are they? Did you ever in your life . . . have you ever . . . where are they from?"

Hewitt moved around to his table, where the Stantons, the Athertons and Jack Wales were sitting. As he slid into his chair, Mrs. Stanton arched an eyebrow at him and mouthed, "Where's Betsy?" He moved his right hand vaguely in the direction of the bar, and she nodded just as the music came to the crashing close. There was one flick of silence before the applause rose up from all over, accompanied by shouts and whistles and banging of empty glasses on tables. Alex picked up one of the dozen full drinks on the table and drank it in two gulps, his throat so parched he could scarcely breathe.

"Jesus, Alex," yelled Gus Atherton, pounding him on the back, "you sure picked a good one. They're fantastic."

"Have a drink, impresario," said Jack Wales, handing him another full glass. "You've earned it."

The music rose again, and ten seconds later there was a collective "AH!" from the crowd as the first of the dancers glided through the door, the woman Hewitt had seen naked, her arms straight out, her large feet bare and not much else covered as she whirled her way across the floor, the tassels spreading in a wide circle, her arms and legs moving wildly until she was directly in front of the musicians, where she and the music stopped dead. No one breathed.

There came a thin wail from one of the flutes to break the silence, and the drummer started a slow beat with only two fingers as another flute joined in and then the *zamoor,* faster and faster and faster as the woman moved in cadence, her body rippling in every pore, and then, as though a spring had been released, her stomach started moving in a circle, faster and faster and faster, the navel flashing by like the red light on a police car in hot pursuit, the flesh seeming to extend three feet beyond the radius of her hips.

"A belly dancer," Wales breathed reverently, looking at Hewitt with a new respect. "A fucking belly dancer," he repeated to himself, just as the other two girls came whirling out of the doorway, surprising the audience, a few women screaming, and then they were all three moving in cadence, the music so wild and bizarre that people were shaking in response, a few of the younger girls jumping forward and trying to imitate the motions of the entertainers.

The three dancers split up, whirling around the room in different directions, widening their circles until they reached the audience, where they continued their gyrations. The pretty one came straight across to their table and stopped next to Jack Wales, her body shining with sweat as her belly moved around and around in dizzying motion. Without missing a beat, she reached down with her right hand and pulled her bikini pants a good six inches away from her body, her huge brown eyes focused directly on the man as she inched almost close enough to touch him.

"What is she doing?" Bertha Atherton was screaming. "What does she want?"

Hewitt looked around the room and saw that the other two dancers were doing exactly the same things as the girl at their table. He was dizzy from the drink, so close to vomiting that he had to keep swallowing in huge gulps, fighting off the inevitable for only a short time. Christ! Christ! Christ!

Jack Wales leaped over and peeked inside the bikini and

then turned to look at the people at the table, his eyes round with wonder. Once more he looked inside, and then he hopped three inches off the floor.

"I got it," he cried. "By Christ, I got it." And reaching into his pocket he pulled out a clip of money, ripped a bill from the pile and stuffed it into the bikini. There was a gasp around the entire ballroom as all eyes had been caught by Wales' leaping to his feet and had then followed the subsequent action. Two other men jumped up and pulled their wallets from their pockets, but one of the wives moved in and shoved the dancer away, hard enough to make her fall on the floor. Scores of people then stood up, and there was enough shouting and yells to almost equal the wild shrieks of the musicians, who did not seem at all disturbed by the event but kept right on playing.

The dancer regained her feet and walked over to the wife, who had turned her back to berate her husband. It came as a complete surprise to her, therefore, when she received two large hands on her back that shoved her right across the table, bringing cloth and dishes and drinks with her as she landed on another woman and the two of them went down and were lost.

As people moved onto the floor, obscuring the view of what was happening, Hewitt felt his arm grabbed again, and there was Dr. McCord, with his little dark friend beside him. McCord's face was red, bright red, and he was shouting as if he were in pain.

"What kind of person are you to bring this filth into our club?" he yelled. "Have you no decency? Have you no regard for people?"

Hewitt stood up, towering over the little white man and the little dark man. Have I no decency? he wondered. Have I no regard for people? He was going to throw up.

Turning quickly, he ran into the hall and out the side door to the parking lot, where a fine snow had covered everything with white, barely enough to cover, but white, all white. The cold air hit him like a punch to the stomach, and he ran over to the back of a car and vomited mightily, feeling the splash come back in his own face from the wind that was blanketing his cheeks with wet. The sweat was congealing on his body like heavy oil, and the effort of throwing up was so great that he could feel new sweat, warm sweat, forming under the old.

It stopped, it finally stopped, and as he stood there, his head lifted to the sky, gulping as much air into him as he could hold, he felt the tears of frustration and rage and sorrow running out of his eyes.

Doors began slamming behind him and people started coming out, their voices rising in indignation as they chattered away to each other, sounding unreal in the whirling snow. Hewitt moved quickly down the line until he found his car and slipped inside, starting to shiver in the cold. His head joined his hands on the wheel as he tried to sort things out.

Jeff! He had to check on Jeff. Why the hell didn't Betsy come so they could get going? She always . . . Betsy had gone. Christ! Betsy had gone.

He pumped the accelerator and turned the key. As the motor warmed, he turned on the windshield wipers and the lights. People were pouring out of the doors now, and he drove quickly through the lot to the road, held up only once as a car cut in front of him.

Mrs. Markham. As he stopped to look both ways before entering the main highway, he suddenly remembered Mrs. Markham, and his foot faltered on the gas, and he almost stalled out. Mrs. Markham dead. And Jeff. There was an ice-cold feeling in the pit of his stomach, and as he drove carefully to the hospital, both his legs trembled, at one time so much that he almost pulled over to the side of the road. But he was a doctor, and there was a sick patient to be checked. He couldn't stop now. He couldn't stop ever.

XXIX

THE light snow stopped falling while Hewitt was driving to the hospital, but his shivering was uncontrollable even though the heater and fan were on full blast. He couldn't remember whether he had worn a coat, and it suddenly became very important to him that he should remember. They had come in the door of the club, and Fussy Freddy had rushed up to them and started babbling about there being no band and while they were hanging up their . . . he had worn a coat. It was still back at the club. For a moment he tried to visualize what had happened after he had run out, but before any concrete images could be set, he arrived at the hospital and circled right around the driveway to the main door, where he parked.

There were only a few people in the reception area, but Hewitt felt conspicuous in his tuxedo and headed for the stairwell to climb his way to Jeff. Holding the rail, he went one step at a time, and as he ascended, he sensed a hollow in his stomach, a gnaw of hunger. When had he last eaten? There had not even been an attempt to touch the food on his plate at the club. He would have a sandwich when he got home. Or maybe here. The nurse would get him one. If Jeff were awake, if Jeff couldn't sleep, he would sit in the room with him and eat his sandwich, stay with him until he fell asleep. *Jeff. Jeff.* Guilt lay on him with a dead man's weight. That soldier he had carried from the helicopter to the tent. You could tell he was dead from the weight. The weight was different.

He stood outside the door marked 5 for a moment, holding the handle but without the strength to pull. They would have called if the boy hadn't been all right, wouldn't they? Suppose it hadn't been Mrs. Markham? Suppose it had been Jeff? And he had been screwing around with a bunch of crazy gypsies while his son. . . . A doctor couldn't stand there every minute with every patient. But a father could. Slowly he pulled the door open and entered the corridor.

There was only one nurse at the station, busily filling out a chart, and Hewitt let his heel click to apprize her of visitors. As she turned her head in response, a smile lit up her face. Sophie Driscoll. Hewitt felt his whole body relax as he realized that this old pro was looking after his son again. Jeff was all right. Jeff had to be all right if Sophie Driscoll held the floor.

"Well," she said, standing up and looking him over, "have you come to take me to the ball?"

"How's my son?" he asked, his voice husky.

"Sleeping like a lamb," she said. "The fever broke about 9 P.M., and he went subnormal for an hour, but at ten he was right on the button, and I gave him a rub and tucked him in for the night. Dr. Stern came in while your wife was still here and checked him through. He said there shouldn't be any problems from here on in."

"She's gone?"

"What?"

"My wife left?"

"Oh, yes. Dr. Stern told her to go home so the boy would

go to sleep. He told her all her troubles were over, and she started to cry, and he told her she wasn't going to do the boy any good with that kind of face. I guess it's been quite a strain on you people the last few days."

Hewitt walked over to the doorway and looked in. Jeff was in deep sleep, and even in the dim light Hewitt could see that the color gradations on his face were normal. No fire burned within. Medical science had triumphed again. There was no strength in his legs, and he walked into the room and sat down on the leather chair, never taking his eyes off his son. The blanket on his chest rose evenly, steadily, normally.

I have a son and two daughters, Hewitt told himself. Two daughters and a son. They give me obedience. What do I give them? I have a wife. She gives me obedience. And love. Does she give me love? She says she gives me love. What do I give her?

He stood up and approached the bed, looking down at the sleeping boy. His hand went out, then stopped an inch away from the boy's arm, then moved forward and took it lightly by the wrist, the fingers curving around the solid steady beat that was going at a nice eighty-five per minute. He shifted the fingers to his own wrist for two beats and then dropped his hands by his sides. What the hell difference did it make?

Nurse Driscoll was still alone when Hewitt returned to the hall, and she offered him Jeff's chart. He checked it over and noted a medication change for the morning.

"What have you got on your beautiful jacket?" asked Driscoll, standing to peer closely. "It looks like dried. . . ." She sniffed delicately. "You wait right here, Doctor," she said, and trotted off to the medicine closet from which she returned with a bottle and a soft pad. Tipping the bottle over the pad, she wet the cloth and then started to rub briskly at Hewitt's lapels. The stink of ether engulfed him, and for one horrible moment he thought he

was going to be sick all over again. But there was no deny-
ing the indomitable Driscoll, and she finally finished to her
satisfaction without getting an unjust reward for her efforts.

"There," she said, "now you can go home to your pretty
wife in respectable condition."

"I have to go down to third first and sign a death certificate," he said.

"My, you're having a rough week. That poor man with
the coronary on . . . was it Monday? . . . and now. . . ."

Bardwell! She had been there for Bardwell.

"How come I wasn't called when Mr. Bardwell had his
attack?" he asked. "Or Dr. Stanton? We've been trying to
track down what happened all week. I can't understand
why. . . ."

"But Dr. Shrinar said he would call," she said. "When it
was over, when we'd done the whole routine and he was
gone, I said that we should call Dr. Stanton, and he said he
would take care of it. Didn't he call?"

"No, he didn't."

"Well, you know, Doctor, that some of these foreign people aren't used to our customs. He just came here from
somewhere, and he doesn't speak very good English, but I
was sure he understood about calling. He definitely told me
he was going to call."

"All these gooks are a pain in the ass," said Hewitt.

"Well," said Driscoll, "I will admit that usually they are
more trouble than they're worth. But he did the drill pretty
well with that Mr. . . ."

"Bardwell."

"That Mr. Bardwell. If he could have been saved, Dr.
Shrinar would have pulled him out of it. He didn't miss
one trick right down the line."

"Well, I better get down there and do my trick. Thanks
for looking out for my son so well."

"You have a nice boy there, Doctor. And a pretty wife.
You're a lucky man."

Lucky, lucky, lucky, lucky, lucky, he said to himself, as he went down each step. A lucky man.

There were all kinds of nurses and aides running around in the third-floor corridor, and the sight of Hewitt in a tuxedo sent them off into gales of giggles, each one trying to outdo the other in saying something that would attract the handsome doctor's attention. The alcohol was now sitting sourly in Hewitt's system, and he had no appetite, for food or games. His first words to the head nurse scattered the covey down the corridor, most of them to disappear in rooms or hiding places accessible only to the tiniest of mice.

"You have a death certificate for me," he said, and she handed him the metal folder to which the paper was attached.

"Has the body been removed?" he asked.

"No, Doctor. The funeral home called and said they were having trouble with their hearse and they would be delayed."

"Has the daughter been here?"

"Yes. She got here shortly after the patient expired. She asked if she should wait for you, but I told her it was impossible to say when you would get here since there was nothing further you could do."

Nothing further you could do.

Hewitt turned and walked down the hall to the door of Mrs. Markham's room. While he stood there, one of the young nurses came out of the next room and walked by him, carefully looking straight ahead. He opened the door and went in, closing it behind him.

The floor lamp in the corner furnished the only light, its single sixty-watt bulb dimly revealing the still figure on the bed. The nurses had prepared her for removal, and the bandages on her head looked like a nun's coif.

My, you're having a rough week.

I am tired of death, thought Hewitt. I can no longer take it. Or am I tired of life? he wondered. That article in the

Journal by the psychiatrist, "America's Preoccupation with Death," with all those passages from the writers—Hemingway, Mark Twain—all that bullshit about fear and the unknown. But I feared the unknown *SH*, he acknowledged, two letters that scared the living shit out of me. And they turn out to belong to a gook doctor named Shrinar who doesn't speak good English. A black shadow of the McCords of the world. *SH*. *SH*. Shrinar. Shrinar. Are all my fears like this? My fear of fear? My fear of death? It isn't just the writers; it's everybody. It's just that a writer uses words to exorcise his fears. And I practice medicine. I do God's work.

Do I do God's work? he asked the still figure before him. Do I do good work? You suffered no pain. I promised you there would be no pain, and there was no pain. But were you afraid? Inside there where I couldn't reach, were you afraid? We can take away the pain, but can we take away the fear?

"I am afraid," he said softly. "I am as afraid to live as I am to die." And I am afraid to be loved, he suddenly realized, looking up in wonder, as though the woman in the bed might have said it to him, a voice from the grave making him see himself for the first time. I am afraid to be loved, he repeated, rolling it over in his mind so that he could taste all its implications. Just as he asked, demanded, that his patients put themselves completely into his hands, so he had always been afraid to commit himself to anybody —his wife, his daughters, his son. He had been in his parents' hands, and he had vowed never again, never would anybody control his body, his mind, his hands. If there are no commitments, there can be no expectations.

Betsy would be running his life as his mother had. Bobbi and Jeff and Jojo, all running, running, running. He would belong to them and not himself. All that he had achieved would . . . what had he achieved?

"What have I achieved?" he asked the woman before him. Like him, she had known fear. He had been closer to this woman in this week than he had ever been to anybody. And now she was dead, and he was alone again.

Fear is lonely, he realized, and loneliness is fear. He could hear the nurses in the hall, laughing over something, and he wondered if they were afraid. Is everyone afraid? Is everyone lonely? He had always been lonely, always. But the fear, had the fear been there, too? Hiding under the rocks of the mind to be turned over by the pressure of the blood, the beats of the heart?

SH. SH. A little dark man who forgot to call the attending physician.

Hewitt laughed, a short, hard laugh of self-contempt, of self-analysis, of self-containment. No more *SH.* Explain to the little bastard that you had to call the attending physician in cases like this and there would be no more *SH*, no more fears of the unknown avenger who had stolen a patient in the night.

My, you're having a rough week.

But the week was almost over. At the midnight witching hour the new Hewitt would rise from his own ashes, a Hewitt frightening to behold in his strength and purity. That these dead shall not have died in vain. Bardwell. Casey. Markham. And Jeff, almost Jeff. And my marriage, almost my marriage. And my wife, almost my wife. And my daughters, almost my daughters.

He turned and went out the door, closing it gently behind him. The head nurse was sipping a cup of black coffee at her desk, warming her hands on the cup. Hewitt wrote quickly on the sheets attached to the board, signed his name and handed it over to her.

"Were you at some special celebration, Doctor?" she asked.

Uncertain, he looked at her for a long moment before he remembered the tuxedo.

"No," he said, "nothing like that. Just another Saturday night at the country club."

"Well, it's too bad it had to be interrupted."

"Not really. It was a good time for me to leave. As a matter of fact, I may never go back."

He felt warm and steady as he walked out the door to his car, and as he slid behind the wheel, he held his hands out before him to note their steadiness. There were pills for blood pressure; there were pills for everything. You just had to live within your limitations. He would tell Betsy. Tell her about what? Tell her he'd been fucking other women? Tell her what a shit he was? Tell her about the fear? Tell her about death? Tell her what? What the hell would any of that solve?

He would tell her about *SH*. Once he told her about *SH* and the fear, that would be a start, a place to go from. Betsy would understand. She would help him. Once he started telling her, she would help him with the rest of the telling, make it easy for them to go on from one thing to the next.

You have to take care of your own, Slotnick had said. That's my only own, he thought, my wife, my son, my two daughters, my two daughters and my son. They have to have their chance too.

I will tell her about *SH*, he concluded, as he started the car. That will be a beginning, a good beginning. His hands were steady as he drove to his home and family, and he turned on the radio and listened to soft music coming from somewhere out in the dark.

XXX

BETSY lay back on the foam rubber pillow and carefully folded the sheet and blanket so that they fit exactly under her armpits. Every joint of her body ached as though she had been beaten with sticks and the slightest movement seemed to grate bone upon bone.

Rig for silent crying, she kept saying to herself, puzzled as to its origin until she finally remembered the submarine movie she had been watching on television with Jeff the week before. She smiled as she recalled how cool he had felt when she placed her hands on his cheeks, how different from the hotness of the days before. That nice Dr. Stern explaining it all so patiently, the blood pressure and the temperature and the heart rate, and showing how the wound was drying up, no need for the drain. How upset he had become when she started crying. *All your troubles are over. All your troubles are over.*

She could feel the pains start to ease in her bones, and it felt so warm and comfortable in the bed that she tried to think of things to keep her awake, to hold the sensation as long as possible. Alex. Think of Alex. He would keep her

awake all right. Or put her to sleep. Rig for silent crying.
When she had stopped in the doorway of the bar to see if he
was coming with her to the hospital, was that the moment?
When Jimmy Slater had grabbed him by the arm and offered him a drink? Was that the moment? When the glass
had touched his lips?

Suddenly she wanted a cigarette, to feel the hot smoke
going down her throat into her lungs, but she couldn't
move in all that warmth and comfort, the sheet soft against
her arms, the fresh smell of clean sheets, every day in
Daddy's house, no more, no more, and the pillow seeming
to hold her head right in the air. Rig for silent crying.

He had to have his vodka. When she had come in from
the hospital, standing alone in the kitchen, her skin all
bumps from the cold, that was what had stuck in her mind,
him standing there at the bar with that glass raised to his
lips, unaware of her or Jeff or any of the people around
him, just waiting for that booze to hit his stomach. And
she'd taken a glass and put ice cubes in it, just the way he
did, and poured it half full of vodka, just the way he did,
and swirled it around a few times, just the way he did, and
took a big swallow, just the way he did. Her lips curved in
the tiniest of smiles. And almost threw up from the raw
taste, gagging all over the kitchen, the tears running out of
her eyes . . . *rig for silent crying* . . . her chest aching
from the effort, not at all the way he did.

What did you want from me, Hewitt? she wondered.
What did you want that I couldn't give? Could anybody
give it to you? I licked your prick, and I took your shit, and
it wasn't enough. I gave you my devotion and all my time,
all the time I had. I gave you three beautiful children. She
could feel the tears working out through her closed eyelids
. . . *rig for silent crying* . . . three beautiful children. I
gave you love.

But I am tired, she thought. I am too tired to give anything more. The warmth was all through her body now,

and there was no ache, no ache at all. And she realized how much ache there had been in her the past weeks, months, years, how tired and aching she had been. No place to turn. Mama's gonna die. Daddy's gonna die. Only Hewitt goes on forever. No mercy in golf. No mercy in tennis. No mercy in marriage.

A good doctor. Maybe a great doctor. Wind or rain, snow or sleet, day or night. Saved my son. Couldn't save me. How could a man be such a good doctor and such a bad husband? Father? Which is more important? Am I a better wife or mother? Or neither? Is there anything that Betsy Hewitt does well? Except look pretty. And that's all done now. Gray at the roots. Wrinkles at the corners. Aches in the bones. Empty in the mind. *Rig for silent crying.*

Oh, you bastard, Hewitt, she moaned, trying to raise her head from the pillow, but the tired was too great, the effort too much. You've made me less than a woman, she thought, less than a wife, less than a mother. And you never let me know why. Doesn't there always have to be a reason for everything? Doesn't there always have to be a reason? No mercy in tennis. No mercy in golf. No mercy in marriage. No mercy in life. I can't beat you. You win again.

She wanted to smile. She wanted to actually form her lips into the curve that would signify a smile, but she was too tired, too done, too gone. You win again, she thought. But you lose.

XXXI

THE air pocket between the kitchen and the storm doors forced Hewitt to use the full push of his body to attain the click of the latch sliding into its metallic groove. He turned the lock and walked into the kitchen where the glow of the pink fluorescent tube over the sink cast a soft haze over everything. Ten minutes past midnight; a new day had begun.

And a new Hewitt. New Year's Eve in November, time for resolutions. I shall not kill, he resolved. I shall not commit adultery. I shall not covet my neighbor's wife, who is a fat pig on the north side and an old witch on the south. I shall not covet my neighbor's wife's ass. His mouth tasted like an Ethiopian's crotch at high noon in August. Who used to say that? he wondered. Someone in college? In Nam? The war that would never end. Can a man change? If a war can end, a man can change.

He looked around the kitchen in the warm glow, everything in its place and ready to be of service. Wife and children snug in their beds. No, not Jeff. But he was snug. Tonight he was snug. She had said there was a sore on his heel. The cobbler's child. The cobbler's wife.

Was she up there angry? She'd never run out before. All those drunken occasions when her nose had been dragged in the shit while people watched or turned their heads in disgust, she'd never run out. But tonight, or rather last night, she picked up her doll and left.

Has she left? he pondered, as he turned off the light over the sink and stood in the darkness, his hands resting on the cool enamel. Has she packed up the kids and taken off for dear old Mammy and Pappy? Angina. His right hand went up to the left side of his chest and pressed in hard. She wouldn't leave Jeff. No matter how pissed off she was, she wouldn't leave Jeff. She's up there waiting, and I will tell her I am sorry, and I will tell her about *SH*. I will tell her about my blood pressure. I will make love to her. I will lick her till my prick gets hard. Putting his hand out before him, he felt his way to the stairs and mounted slowly.

At the top he turned and saw the bright white flare that came from the night light in Jojo's room, which he and Betsy had argued over so fiercely. Betsy could not understand anyone being afraid of the dark. You're always telling them they have to be tough, she had yelled, and yet you let her become dependent on a light. How do you explain the dark to someone who had never been afraid of it? Jojo and he knew. Betsy and Bobbi and Jeff never would.

There was a dim light in his own room, reflecting out of the partially closed bathroom door. She was in bed; she had not run away. He could see the profile of her face as she lay on her back, and he moved over to the chair by his bureau to remove the sodden tuxedo, peeling the layers off slowly and folding them across the cane seat. He rubbed his hands across his thighs and felt the dried sweat on his skin, oily to the touch, and a vision of the belly dancer, the young one, came before his eyes, holding her skirt away from her body so that Jack Wales could thrust his green bill into her bush. Christ, what a mess. And Cindy Huber. Was she standing in her hallway looking out the window? He looked over at the phone by the side of the bed. Was it about to ring? No more. No more. She lay there sleeping quietly. A quiet woman. Would she wake when he crawled in? Maybe he should take a shower, let the noise of the water let her know he was home. He didn't feel like a shower. Dirty as he was, he was just too goddamned tired to take a shower. But he had to brush his teeth, his Ethiopian crotch. No woman could forgive a man who had a mouth tasting like that.

Naked, he entered the bathroom and hitched his little brush to the electric motor. There was no toothpaste. Not even an empty tube to squeeze blood from. Putting down the brush, he opened the cabinet door and saw three small boxes of Colgate resting on the top shelf. He slipped one from its carton and leaned down to place the cardboard in the wastebasket. A flash of yellow caught his eye. As he straightened up again and started to unscrew the top from the tube, his heart gave a heavy beat. Extra systoles. Yellow. He reached down and pulled the wastebasket out. There it was. The yellow sample packet. Sodium Secobarbital U.S.P. Two tablets per packet. Physician's sample. Quickly he dumped the wastebasket over and scrambled through the papers. Two. Three. Four. Five. All empty. Two per packet. Ten capsules of Sodium Secobarbital.

He whirled around and tore into the bedroom, switching on the light on her bedside table. She lay there, somewhat waxen-looking in the glare. His hand slipped around her wrist, the two fingers moving into position. Slow. Slow. He went quickly to his bureau and retrieved his watch, then took up the pulse again. Thirty-eight. Thirty-eight goddamned beats. Ten tablets. Was that all she took? Through his mind flashed that moment at Mrs. Markham's house, her daughter's house, when the tube with the red top had only three tablets in it. Had she been stashing them against this night? Doriden. Had she taken any Doriden? He ran back to the bathroom and scrabbled through the papers. Just the five. The closet. He ran to the closet and jerked open the door, his eyes scanning the shelves. There were tiny bottles of the drug on the top shelf, but they did not seem to be disturbed. How many had she taken? And of what?

Going back to the bed, he lifted her eyelid. Constricted. Two hours. It couldn't be much more than two hours. When had she left the hospital? Had the nurse said? Two hours. It must be around two hours.

Ripping back the cover from the bed, he exposed her body completely. You bitch, he thought, you bitch. Do you want to die? Do you want out so badly that you want to die? Leave your kids and just go away? Leave it all to old Hewitt to take care of? Is this your revenge? Do you want to die? Do you want me to just leave you here to die?

He picked up her left leg, squeezing the Achilles' tendon as hard as he could, and was rewarded with a slight moan. Dropping the foot, he went to the bureau and found a long metal shoehorn, which he used to pry open her mouth. As he touched the back of her throat, she gagged slightly, and he withdrew the shoehorn.

Not too deep. Two hours. Couldn't be any more than two hours. Get her to the hospital and pumped out and . . . and . . . and then everybody knows that Mrs. Dr. Hewitt tried for the deep six. Did you hear about Hewitt's wife? Betsy? Not Betsy. Yes. Betsy. But why should. . . .

"Daddy?"

Bobbi was standing in the doorway, her hair in her eyes, her hands half raised as though to ward off a blow.

"Daddy, is something wrong?"

She suddenly started as though touched by a live wire, her right hand going up to her mouth and her eyes bulging at him. He looked down and saw he was naked, his penis turgid with blood, and he turned quickly to the chair and pulled on his tuxedo pants, slipping the suspenders over his shoulders.

"Daddy, what's wrong?"

"Your mother's taken too many sleeping tablets. Run down to my car and bring me my bag."

"But, Daddy, how—"

"Go quickly," he barked. "Time is important." She disappeared from the door.

"Lavage," he said aloud, closing his eyes for a moment and trying to visualize what might be used. "Lavage." He went into the bathroom again and pulled open the top panel of the built-in medicine cabinet. Ice bag. Hot-water bag. Enema. Thin tube for the enema. Quickly he unrolled the coil of rubber. A good five feet. Taking the old pair of surgical scissors from the second shelf, he snipped off the attachments at both ends.

Bobbi was standing by the bed near her mother, holding his bag in her hand.

"Run down and get me a pan of cold water," he told her, taking the bag from her.

"Is Mom going to . . ." she started to say and then stopped, turned and was gone again.

He snapped open the bag and removed the top trays, rummaging in the depths until his hand felt the rubber cylinder. Thank God for Mrs. Moore, that old pro, who insisted that the doctor carry the kitchen sink in his bag in case he ran into a situation where a kitchen sink was required. He pulled the fifty cc syringe from the case and removed the plastic tube from it, squeezing the bulb to test its resiliency. Never been used. Rubber still strong.

Bobbi came into the room with a large pan of water, spilling it over the sides onto the rug as she came over beside him. Hewitt brushed his clothes off the chair and brought it over beside Betsy, taking the pan and placing it on the cane bottom. He scrunched the pillow under her neck so that her chin was tilted in the air and pried her mouth open. Holding the tube in his right hand, he started to thread it into her mouth, and just as he reached the edge of the throat, he stopped. There was something else. Something else. He closed his eyes again and tried to visualize the procedure. Thread it in and pump in the water and then pump it out . . . pump it out . . . pump it out. The end of the tube. That was it. Might stick to the stomach wall. The scissors. No. He stood up withdrawing the tube, and looked around wildly. Sharp and pointed.

He turned and left the room as Bobbi called after him, but he was already down the stairs and into the kitchen. Switching on the cellar light, he ran down to the basement and over to the workbench. There was a whole jar of thin nails right in front of him, and he grabbed a hammer and one of the nails and started pounding holes in one end of the tube, four, five, six times, until he could see clearly through them.

Bobbi was shaking her mother by the shoulders when he entered the bedroom, sobbing terribly, and saying, "Mama, Mama," over and over again. He shoved her aside and adjusted the pillow before pushing the tube into Betsy's mouth. Carefully he started to thread it down her throat. Laryngospasm, he kept thinking. Laryngospasm. Betsy coughed, and he breathed a sigh of relief. It was in the trachea, and she was able to cough.

"Daddy, what are you doing?"

"I'm going to put about three feet of this tube into her stomach," he explained, his voice and hands suddenly steady, Dr. Hewitt talking to a young female on the edge of hysteria and detailing the medical procedure so as to allay fears. "And then I'm going to pump the water into her with the syringe, and then I'm going to pump the water out again until we have as much of the sleeping tablets as we can get. If she has only taken water-soluble tablets, which I think is the case, she should be fine." But what if she has taken Doriden? he wondered. What if she is loaded with those, too?

"Get my stethoscope out of the bag," he told Bobbi, as there were only about two feet of tube remaining. She pulled the instrument from the case and handed it to him. He inserted the pieces into his ears and then forced the end of the syringe bulb into the resilient tube. It was by no means perfect, but it fit snugly enough. Placing the end piece of the stethoscope below Betsy's sternum, he pumped the syringe and heard the air gurgle into her stomach. Just right. Just about right.

"Run down and get me another basin," he said, and as she left the room, he dipped the syringe into the pan of water and filled it as much as possible. He then threaded the end into the tube and squeezed the water out with steady pressure. It flowed into the stomach area with a sound like a rushing stream in the earpieces of the stethoscope. As Bobbi returned with a flat pan, she saw him placing another full syringe into the tube and pushing it out with his right hand.

"Put the pan on the bed," he told her, and then started to pump out. Gagging mightily, Betsy suddenly clamped her teeth on the tube and Hewitt stopped, watching her closely. She relaxed, and the lines went out of her face, her whole body sagging. Was she going under all the way? He was out of his mind doing this. Get her to the hospital before it was too late. He pumped vigorously and felt fluid in the syringe. Slipping it out of the tube, he squeezed the contents into the empty pan. He dropped to his knees and put his eyes within close range of the viscous fluid. There they were! Flecks of red. Flecks of red.

He filled the syringe with clear water and pumped it in. And again. Then he pumped out. More flecks of red. It was working. He lost count of how many times he repeated the procedure. Bobbi refilled the water basin four times in the bathroom and emptied the refuse pan twice. Finally, the liquid coming from the stomach was relatively clear and Hewitt could discern no more red spots. Betsy was beginning to gag more frequently, and one time she almost bit through the thin rubber tube. Her heart had picked up a few beats, and he carefully pulled out the tube, millimeters at a time, until it was clear and her teeth came together with a click.

"Is she all right?" asked Bobbi.

"I think so," said Hewitt, placing his arm under her left leg and raising it in the air so that it dangled from the knee down. With the edge of his other hand he tapped under the knee, and there was a slight jerk in response. Carefully he replaced the leg on the bed and bent over his wife's face.

"Betsy," he said, slapping her cheek lightly with his stiffened fingers. "Betsy."

She moaned slightly, her eyes fluttering several times.

"She moved her foot," said Bobbi excitedly. "I saw her foot move."

The pulse was up to forty-six and Hewitt pulled the covers to his wife's shoulders, placing her arms on the outside.

"Should we walk her," asked Bobbi, "and give her black coffee?"

"No," said Hewitt wearily, "we just try to keep waking her up until she comes round by herself. Why don't you see if you can get her to respond?"

Bobbi moved hesitantly to the head of the bed and leaned over her mother.

"Mom," she said softly, barely audible.

"You'll have to practically shout," said Hewitt. "She's still in pretty deep."

"Mom!" Bobbi yelled. "Mom! Mom! Mom!"

Betsy's eyes fluttered several times and remained open for a long moment, looking up at her daughter. A soft moan escaped her, and the eyes closed tight again.

Hewitt sank into the easy chair across the room, barely

able to hold his head up. I am getting old, he thought. These night calls beat the hell out of me.

Bobbi moved away from the bed and sat down on the little chair in front of her mother's dressing table.

"Will she be different?" she asked.

"What?"

"Will she be different when she wakes up?"

"What do you mean different?"

"Well, she's been the same as dead. Will things seem different to her now?"

He could hear the lecturer as though it were yesterday, the tall, austere man with the silver-gray hair and the voice that had several generations of Boston behind it. *Suicide is a hostile act.* A hostile act. Did she hate him that much? Underneath it all, was the hatred that strong that she would take her life to show her contempt for him and their marriage? It was no grandstand play for sympathy. No note. The packets discarded where they would not easily be found. Suppose he had just slipped into bed and gone to sleep, to wake up in the morning beside a corpse? Get my breakfast, Betsy. No answer. Get your own. Take care of the kids, Betsy. No answer. Take care of them yourself. Just do what I say, Betsy. No answer. Lick my prick, Betsy. No answer. Lick it yourself.

"Yes," he said, "things will seem different. To all of us."

"Why did she do it?" asked Bobbi. "Why did she try to kill herself?"

"I don't really know," said Hewitt. "You can only guess. I presume it was mostly to do with me. Whatever it was, she could no longer cope with it. Or put up with it. I guess it was because of the things I do, the way I act."

"Why are you this way?"

"What?"

"Why do you do the things you do? Why do you act the way you do?"

Why? Why indeed. Because of my genes? Because of my

parents? Because of my grandparents? Because I was an only
child? Because I was in the war? Because I am a doctor? Because I am afraid? Because I am afraid and don't know what
I am afraid of? Because of all those reasons? And because of
none of those reasons.

"Are you unhappy with the things I do?" he asked. "The
way I act?"

She tilted her head a bit, uncertain of what she wanted to
say and how she wanted to say it.

"Unhappy is not a good word for it," she finally managed. "You're my father and I love you; I really love you.
But you have never let us love you, and that makes us unhappy. And we don't know if you love us. Do you love us?"

Love, thought Hewitt. It always comes down to love.
They all use the word as though they know what it means. I
don't know what it means. I don't know how to love. I have
to start at the beginning, learn what it means to love.

"Yes, I will love you," he told his daughter.

A moan came from the bed, and they looked over at
Betsy, whose eyelids were fluttering. The fingers of her
right hand twitched several times as she sighed and relaxed
into sleep again.

Hewitt stood and walked over to the bed.

"Betsy," he said sharply, "Betsy," and he shook her by
the shoulders. Her eyes opened, and she moaned again,
looking straight up at Hewitt. He moved his head to the
side, and her pupils followed before the lids closed again.
The pulse was sixty-two, strong and steady.

"Hey," said a small voice. "What's all the noise?"

Jojo was standing in the doorway, digging her right fist
into her right eye, the pajama bottoms low on the hips and
the top on backward. Hewitt's heart gave a great leap as he
saw his tiny daughter standing there, and he held out his
arms to her without saying a word.

"Is Jeff all right?" she asked as she came toward him.

"He's fine," he said as he lifted her in his arms and

walked over and sat down in the armchair. Bobbi sank into the chair across the room, and they all sat there and looked at Betsy on the bed. Jojo snuggled down in Hewitt's lap, warming his groin, wriggling until her back was joined exactly to the contours of his stomach.

Hewitt looked at his wife breathing easily on the bed, his elder daughter sitting quietly across from him and his younger flesh to flesh with his body. They are of my body and of Betsy's, he realized. Her love is in them, and I will add mine to it.

Will there be a happy ending? he asked himself.

There is no happy ending, he answered, nor any kind of ending. There is only ending.

Then what makes it worth the try?

It has to be love. For I have experienced all the others, and they are not worth it. It has to be love.

Will tomorrow be different? he wondered.

No. There will be flu bugs and housewives' complaints and cancer and kidney stones in the office. There will be Sheila Bardwell and the temptation of the flesh. There will be Sam Huber and Cindy standing there like a tiger about to pounce. There will be all those battles of vodka waiting to ease the cold in the pit of the stomach. There will be the blood pressure pounding through the weakening vessels. There will be Gerda Casey suddenly realizing that this was the man who took her husband into the court. There will be McCord and some other *SH* to make you afraid to put one foot in front of the other. There will be the same things over and over and over again until the end.

But there will be Betsy. And Bobbi. And Jojo. And Jeff. And there will be me trying to find out about love. Old Come-to-Jesus Hewitt, trying to find out about love. Right to the end. All the way. Not here today and gone tomorrow. Forever. Scientific project, grant in perpetuity. On love. Love. Love. Love.

And he squeezed his youngest daughter just a bit to feel

the warm flesh push back into his own flesh. And he looked over at his elder daughter, who was trying to keep from falling asleep in her chair. And they all sat there, father and daughters, waiting for their wife and mother to sleep her way back to life. To their lives. And Hewitt was afraid. But for the moment, at least, he had no fear.